THE IRISH YANKEE

Book One in The Dawn of America Series

REGAN WALKER

This is a work of fiction. Names, characters, places and incidents either are the product of the author's imagination or are used fictitiously. Any resemblance to actual events, locales, business establishments or persons, living or dead, is coincidental.

THE IRISH YANKEE

Copyright © 2025 Regan Walker

Paperback ISBN: 978-1-7354381-8-4

PRAISE FOR REGAN WALKER

"Regan Walker is a master of her craft. Her novels instantly draw you in, keep you reading and leave you with a smile on your face."

—*Good Friends, Good Books*

"Walker's detailed historical research enhances the time and place of the story without losing sight of what is essential to a romance: chemistry between the leads and hope for the future."

—*Publisher's Weekly*

"Ms. Walker has the rare ability to make you forget you are reading a book. The characters become real, the modern world fades away, and all that is left is the intrigue, drama, and romance."

—*Straight from the Library*

"Spellbinding and Expertly Crafted...Walker's characters are complex and well-rounded and, in her hands, real historical figures merge seamlessly with those from her imagination."

—*A Reader's Review*

ACKNOWLEDGEMENTS

I am grateful to Patrick O'Brien, the award-winning maritime artist, who graciously gave his permission to me to use his painting of the *Margaretta* on the cover of *The Irish Yankee*. Also pictured are the *Unity* (in the center) and the *Falmouth Packet* (on the left). He donated the original painting to the Hannah Weston Chapter of the Daughters of the American Revolution in Machias, Maine, where it hangs in a place of honor in Burnham Tavern, still in existence today.

My beta readers provide invaluable assistance, including Dr. Chari Wessel, expert in all things nautical; Liette Bougie, my French-speaking Canadian reader, and my critique partners, Jackie and Mary. Many thanks!

THE COLONIES IN 1775

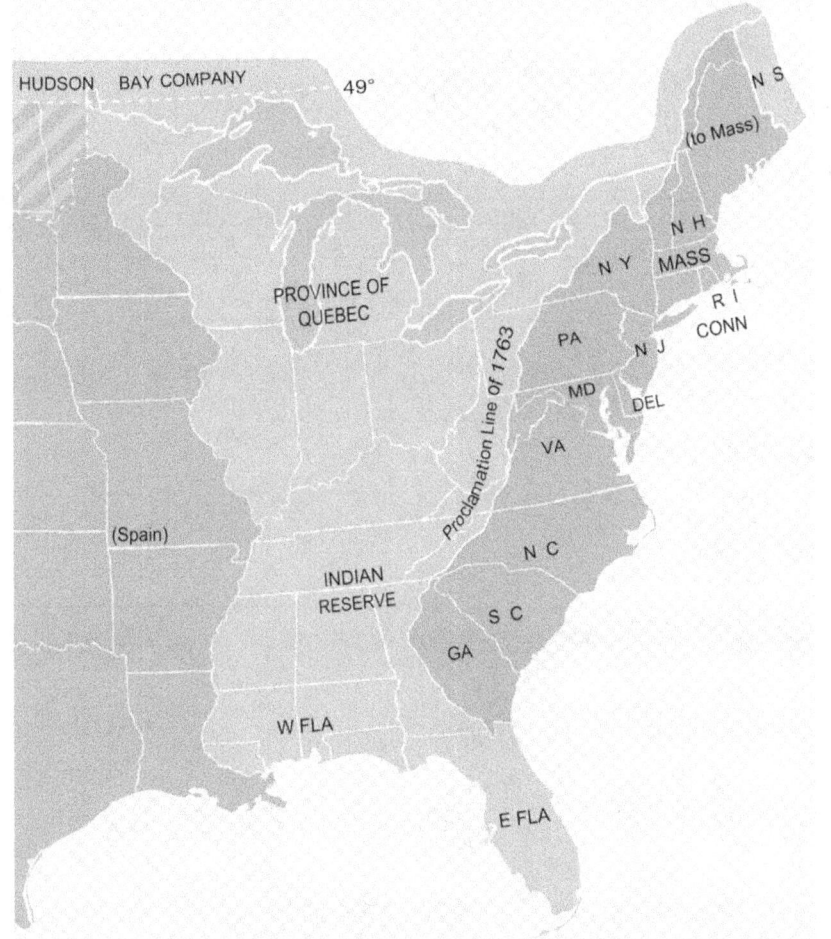

From the National Atlas of the United States.
Note: Maine is a part of Massachusetts.

CHARACTERS OF NOTE

JEREMIAH ("Jere") O'BRIEN
ELIZABETH ("Lizzy") FITZPATRICK
ANNIE FITZPATRICK, Lizzy's younger sister
THOMAS FITZPATRICK, Lizzy's father
SEAN FITZPATRICK, Lizzy's younger brother
MORRIS and MARY O'BRIEN, Jeremiah's parents

Jeremiah's brothers:

> CAPTAIN GIDEON O'BRIEN
> CAPTAIN JOHN O'BRIEN
> LIEUTENANT WILLIAM O'BRIEN
> DENNIS O'BRIEN
> CAPTAIN JOSEPH O'BRIEN

MARY O'BRIEN BURNHAM, Jeremiah's sister, wife of Job Burnham
JOB BURNHAM, owner of Burnham Tavern in Machias
REVEREND JAMES LYON, congregational minister and leader of the Machias Committee of Safety, and his wife Martha
LONDON ATUS, servant to Reverend James Lyon
COLONEL BENJAMIN FOSTER, and his wife Elizabeth ("Beth")
EZEKIEL FOSTER, Ben's brother

WOODEN FOSTER, Ben's brother and Machias blacksmith

RICHARD ("DICK") EARLE, servant to Jeremiah

ICHABOD JONES, shipowner and Boston merchant, a Loyalist

STEPHEN JONES, Ichabod's nephew and Machias merchant

GENERAL THOMAS GAGE, Commander of British Forces in America

VICE ADMIRAL SAMUEL GRAVES, British Commander of the North American Station

WILLIAM CHALONER, Machias surgeon from Annapolis, Nova Scotia

ISAAC TAFT, Machias fisherman who joins Jeremiah's crew

CAPTAIN JAMES MOORE, British captain of the *Margaretta*

DONALD MCDONALD, surgeon on the *Machias Liberty*

GENERAL GEORGE WASHINGTON, Commander in Chief of the Continental Army

BRIGADIER GENERAL HORATIO GATES

MAJOR GENERAL ISRAEL PUTNAM

MAJOR GENERAL CHARLES LEE

COLONEL JOSEPH REED, Washington's secretary

THOMAS MIFFLIN, Washington aide-de-camp and eventually his quartermaster general

JOHN TRUMBULL, Washington aide-de-camp and artist

JAMES WARREN, President of the Provincial Congress

JOHN LAMBERT, captain of the *Diligent*

STEPHEN SMITH, privateer captain, who captured the *Loyal Briton*

THE PRIVATEERS

They were the daring American seamen who seized British merchant ships during the Revolutionary War. Initially operating in the shadows as a pirate militia of the sea, they successfully disrupted British supply lines to aid the Continental Army. General George Washington encouraged them and American Patriots embraced them. Eventually they were armed with letters of marque, transforming them from outlaws to official heroes, allowing them to seize enemy vessels as prizes of war. Individual colonies (states after 1776) commissioned privateers, and in March 1776 the Continental Congress began issuing commissions. America's fledgling navy never had enough ships to do all they did without the help of the Patriot privateers. While the ports of Boston, New York and others were blockaded by squadrons of British warships, the privateers managed to slip to sea and spread destruction. Their success was so profound it led the British merchants to protest the continuation of "the American war."

THE IRISH YANKEE

In June 1775, amid the Revolutionary War's early stirrings, Irish Yankee Jeremiah O'Brien, seizes a British-armed schooner off the Maine coast to thwart the cargo of lumber she was escorting from reaching British forces in Boston. Inspired by this daring victory, Jeremiah leaves his lumber business to command privateer vessels, relentlessly pursuing British merchant ships across dangerous waters. Defying the British navy's tightening grip on the Massachusetts coast, he risks his life and his ships to capture many prizes. Yet his greatest battle may lay onshore: winning the heart of Elizabeth Fitzpatrick, a fiercely independent woman who loves the freedom he fights for. Only a man worthy of the title "the hero of the Lexington of the Sea" could earn her love and prove himself worthy of her strength.

"Sink or swim, live or die, survive or perish, I am with my country from this day on. You may depend on it."
– John Adams (1774)

CHAPTER 1

Burnham Tavern, Township of Machias, Maine, Colony of Massachusetts, early May 1775

FLICKERING CANDLES CAST shadows on the faces of the men sitting around the table in Job Burnham's tavern. The air was redolent with the warm, earthy aroma of pipe smoke mingled with the scent of burning pine. The table was crowded, for Jeremiah had urged many to come. These were troublesome times and much that was at stake needed to be discussed.

The weight of the choices they would make pressed heavily on him. The thought of bloodshed and loss coming to their town added a heaviness to his mood. But excitement, too, flooded his veins, for their cause was independence and freedom. Their cause was liberty.

Except for Jeremiah's father and the Boston merchant, Ichabod Jones, the men who had taken their places with Jeremiah were, like him at thirty, young and fit in the way lumbermen were who made their living felling huge trees for the sawmills his family owned. Among them were his five younger brothers who looked to him as their leader. Even Reverend James Lyon, the congregational minister in Machias, who had come at Jeremiah's request, was only forty.

It being a cold, rainy night, the fire burned steadily in the large hearth, its crackling flames familiar and comforting. As children, Jeremiah, his brothers and their older sisters had gathered around the family's hearth listening to their father's stories of life in Dublin under British rule, a life that sent Morris O'Brien fleeing to America where he married and his children were born.

In his parents' home in Machias hung the O'Brien coat of arms and a portrait of Brian Boru, the High King of Ireland from whom they were descended. Jeremiah's family was close with a proud heritage.

His sister, Mary, wife of Job Burnham, set a tankard of ale before each man, beginning with him. "Evening, Jere. Are you responsible for so many here tonight?"

He looked up at her with fondness. Like all the O'Brien children, she had blue eyes and a shade of brown hair that was all her own. "I do believe I am."

"There's venison stew and biscuits if you're interested," she offered.

Jeremiah nodded and several of the men murmured their interest, for Mary's stew was always tasty.

One man was missing, one who needed to be here. Jeremiah had been waiting for him. Moments later, just as the stew was delivered, with a gust of wind that sent candles sputtering, Colonel Benjamin Foster entered the tavern. "Sorry to be late," he said, doffing his cocked hat and cloak before taking the seat next to Jeremiah.

"No matter," replied Jeremiah, "you're here now."

"Any stew left?" Ben asked Mary as he set aside his ivory pipe and accepted a tankard of ale. "I didn't have time to dine with Beth and the children."

"I'll bring you a bowl," she replied.

Letting out a breath, Jeremiah opened the conversation. "We must discuss the word that has reached us from Boston."

"What word?" asked Ben, his dark brows drawing together. In his forties and the leader of their local militia, Ben would be the first to want to know any news of significance.

"The first shots have been fired," said Jeremiah, gazing into the faces of his brothers and friends eager to hear more. "American blood has been spilled by the redcoats at Lexington and Concord in an attempt to seize the militia's weapons."

"With what result?" asked the colonel. "Did the militia fire back?"

"Indeed, they did," said Jeremiah. "Dr. Warren in Boston had notice of the British intentions to seize weapons and arrest Samuel Adams and John Hancock in Concord. He sent Paul Revere and William Dawes as riders to spread the alarm. In every town from Boston to Lexington the call to arms was sounded. Seventy militia met the British on the Lexington Common. The redcoats fired, killing several Patriots. But by the time the redcoats reached Concord an hour later, four hundred militia were waiting for them. The British were attacked from all sides." With a smile, he added, "It turned into a rout."

Setting down his tankard, Ben sat back in his chair and crossed his arms, as Mary delivered his stew and biscuits. "So, the war has finally begun."

Jeremiah glanced at his brothers, gauging their reactions. The two younger ones clinked their tankards together. Gideon, the closest in age to Jeremiah, who ran their second sawmill, nodded. John, whose personality was much like Jeremiah's, had the strongest reaction. "The revolution is here!"

"God grant it may be true!" exclaimed Jeremiah's father, who had longed for the colonies' independence.

"In light of this," said Jeremiah, "I move that tomorrow we raise a liberty pole in front of the town's meeting house." All knew the significance of the pole being raised around the colonies, a symbol of America's defiance of British rule. "We are Sons of Liberty, now is the time to show our allegiance for all to see."

"Agreed!" came the shouted reply from around the table.

Pleased with their reaction, Jeremiah said, "We should also appoint a Committee of Safety to supervise the town's affairs while we ready for war as called for by the Provincial Congress." Since 1774, the Patriots had been organizing and training militias at the urging of the Provincial Congress. Turning to Reverend Lyon, the town's minister, who Jeremiah knew to be a Whig and an avid Patriot, he said, "I nominate you to lead the committee."

The good reverend nodded. "Aye, I'll do it, and gladly."

Ichabod Jones cleared his throat, and began to speak, his voice as smooth as polished oak. "Pardon me for interrupting, but shouldn't this be decided at a town meeting to give weight to what you propose? We don't want to rush into rebellion over tavern talk."

Murmurs rippled through the room, eyes darting uneasily. Jeremiah clenched his jaw, watching the merchant closely, wondering where his true loyalties lay. Jones had homes in both Boston and Machias and two sloops that carried the town's lumber to Boston for sale. In exchange, he brought needed provisions to the townspeople, who were more concerned with timber, fishing, and trade than farming in what was rocky soil.

Jones shifted in his seat, avoiding Jeremiah's gaze. He had long suspected Jones' sympathies lay with the British with whom he did business. However, Jeremiah would not resist a town meeting, for he doubted not the result. "Since we are a people who love law and order, I think that is a reasonable suggestion."

Heads nodded.

An hour later, Jeremiah left the tavern for his home on the river, a two-story house he had built the year before. Like many in Machias, it was painted red. He was happy to see the rain had stopped. As he walked along the riverbank, thoughts of the British storming Machias, of his brothers' blood staining the sawmill yard swirled in his head. Yet the fire of independence burned in his heart, a wild heat he'd first felt listening to his father's tales of the O'Briens' past glories defying the British Crown. But this was no longer just his father's fight. "This is our time, our generation, our fight," he murmured to himself. "We must not shrink from the task before us."

THE NEXT MORNING, the sun rose in a clear blue sky. Jeremiah's step was light with new purpose as he and his Negro servant, Dick Earle, walked along the bank of the Machias River running full with the spring rains. They were headed to the meeting house. Dick's gaze was sharp, his eyes focused straight ahead, as if he too felt the importance of what they were about.

Many families were there as they arrived, their children running about outside, for families were large in Machias. Their parents, waving to Jeremiah, told him they had heard the news discussed in the tavern and were eager to hear more.

The scent of new pine wood permeated the air as Jeremiah and Dick entered the meeting house. The furnishings had yet to be completed so that the seating was only planks of raw wood. Men mingled about, discussing the recent events, while the women, dressed in their simple homespun with white aprons, spoke together in small groups.

When Reverend Lyon brought the meeting to order, Jeremiah explained the attempt by the British to seize weapons on their way to Concord to arrest Samuel Adams and John Hancock. He didn't have to remind them of the Provincial Congress' proclamation urging the colony to be ready for conflict with the British. Like other Massachusetts towns, Machias had formed a militia years before, so that many had muskets, rifles or pistols. A few had hunting rifles. Others had no weapons save pitchforks and axes.

Wooden Foster, Ben's brother and the Machias blacksmith, asked about weapons that might still be needed. That fueled a discussion of what they had and what could be purchased.

One man said, "We have weapons but we need ammunition."

Wooden was quick to reply. "I can cast balls faster than the British can march."

That brought a smile to many faces, even the women.

In the end, the people agreed to take the necessary steps to be ready for conflict with the British should it come. A Committee of Safety was appointed with the good reverend to lead it.

Ichabod Jones stood next to his merchant nephew, Stephen Jones. Neither had spoken. While Jeremiah had questions about Ichabod's loyalty, he was confident Stephen was a Patriot whether he admitted it to his uncle or not.

Reverend Lyon told them that John Hancock, President of the Massachusetts Provincial Congress, had called for a day of prayer and fasting to be held on the 11th of May. Reading from the document he'd received, he said, "The day is to be set apart with no labor or recreation so that the people of the colony can humble themselves before God." Looking up from the paper, Reverend Lyon added, "We should gather on that day for communal prayer."

The families nodded their agreement.

"It is fitting we do so," said Jeremiah's mother, Mary.

Before the meeting was concluded, Ben Foster gave a stirring oratory urging the raising of a liberty pole as Jeremiah had suggested the night before. "As it has in other towns," said Ben, "the pole will be a symbol of our commitment to America's liberty and independence, one we'll defend with our lives if the British dare challenge us!"

Murmurs of assent rippled through the crowd.

"A liberty pole it is!" shouted one man.

"One that will be seen by all on the river!" insisted another.

Thus it was agreed a liberty pole should be erected outside the meeting house where it could be seen from the Machias River that ran through the town.

When the meeting adjourned, Jeremiah, his brothers and several men who considered themselves Sons of Liberty, headed into the forest to select a tall pine tree. Cutting it down, they stripped it of its branches, leaving only a tuft of greenery at the top in keeping with tradition. They floated the liberty pole down river and then carried it to the deep hole in front of the meeting house that others had prepared.

With a loud thud, the pole dropped into the hole, its tuft of green swaying high above. Once it was secured with rocks and soil, Jeremiah and the men gathered around it while their families and the townspeople watched. Each man pledged himself to resist the mother country and to shed his own blood in defense of the colony should it be required.

As they stood united, a mix of fear and determination gripped Jeremiah's heart. He could see in the men's expressions the concern for their families, their dreams, and the blood that might soon stain their hands. A visible demonstration of their unity was needed. With a firm commitment to the cause, Jeremiah lifted his musket into the air and fired, the loud report a proper finish to the solemn ceremony.

One by one, his brothers and every armed man joined him, muskets blazing in unison. The echoes of the shots faded into the spring air, leaving only the scent of gunpowder and the shadow of the liberty pole against the sky.

ELIZABETH FITZPATRICK STOOD to one side, watching the raising of the liberty pole. The people stared up at the tuft of greenery high above them, on every face an enraptured look. A scene that never could have happened in their home in Onslow, Nova Scotia where the British governed. It was why Reverend Lyon had convinced her father to move his family to Machias just a short time ago.

Her father stood nearby, arms crossed. She could see his sawmill master's eye judging the pole's grain even as he nodded at the men's cheers, for Thomas Fitzpatrick was glad to have left Onslow.

Her younger sister Annie's cheeks flushed with joy as she gripped Elizabeth's arm. "Lizzy, look—they're not afraid to speak of liberty!"

Their younger brother, Sean, chose that moment to dart forward. Picking up a stick and mimicking the Patriots gathered around the pole, he shouted. "I'll fight the British too!"

Elizabeth grabbed his collar. "Back here, you little fool. At ten, you're too young to join the men!"

"Aw, Lizzy," he said, reluctantly turning to her.

Elizabeth stood tall, the sun's heat warming her red hair, her callused hands, rough from years of Onslow chores, tightening on Sean's collar. "One day," she told him, pride mixed with fear. "Just not today." As she spoke the words, her eyes met those of the Patriot leader, a tall, bold man with light brown hair queued at his neck. Beneath his cocked hat his eyes were a brilliant blue, and he had a ready smile.

"Let the lad join us, Miss," he said, his eyes glinting with a challenge. "He's got the right spirit for the fight ahead."

"He's got spirit, aye, but I'll not lose him to your grand cause just yet," she snapped, her cheeks burning with defiance more than fluster.

Her father uncrossed his arms, a faint nod suggesting he approved of his son's spirit, though his gaze lingered on Jeremiah.

Seeing her father's expression and Sean's pleading expression, she grudgingly released him to join the Patriot leader who the other men were calling Jeremiah. Growing up in this town, Sean would become a Patriot, too. Would he one day die for the cause of liberty as many would?

Elizabeth's thoughts shifted to Onslow. It had been difficult to say goodbye to her friends and begin a new life in a new land, but she had done it willingly knowing what it meant to her father. In Onslow, British rule smothered defiance, and the redcoats took liberties. The day her father came home to find an officer pressing his unwanted attentions on her, he'd snarled, "They've taken our liberty; they won't take my children." That day, he vowed to join Reverend Lyon in Machias.

"Would there be work for you there?" she had asked him.

"The town has several sawmills, and one is in need of help."

Her eyes filling with tears, she told him, "Whatever you say, Papa." When he lost his wife to sickness, Lizzy and her siblings lost their mother. Only sixteen, she assumed the role of surrogate mother. All these years later, her father still mourned though he tried to hide it. What he needed was to start over in a new place. Reverend Lyon had given them the chance, and yesterday they arrived in what would be their new home.

As the men began to disperse, Martha Lyon approached, her smile warm as she adjusted her shawl. "Lizzy, my husband and I want to introduce you to the O'Briens. They are anxious to meet you and have invited all of us to dine with them. They're leaders here and own the two largest sawmills." She glanced at Sean, still waving his stick. "Six strapping sons in the family, good models for Sean."

Good models? Lizzy asked herself. Maybe, if they could teach him to survive, not just fight. In Onslow, she had seen too many boys fall to British guns to trust anyone fully with her brother.

Martha Lyon continued, "The O'Briens have three daughters, too, all married. The youngest, Mary, is wed to Job Burnham, our tavern owner."

Elizabeth nodded, her stomach tightening at the thought of Sean caught up in the O'Briens' world—six strapping sons who'd shape his dreams, for better or worse, as their sawmills would shape her father's hopes.

THOMAS FITZPATRICK WAS pleased with what he had witnessed in Machias. The people were welcoming, patriotism ran high, and the large piles of logs and stacks of lumber lining the riverbank told him the mills were prosperous. Here he could build a life for his family where they would know freedom. Here perhaps he could look to the future and finally let go of the past.

Arriving the day before, Reverend Lyon had settled them into his own house where they would be guests until Thomas could build a house of their own. Last evening, with the women speaking to one side, his friend, James Lyon, drew him to the fireplace. "A year ago, Morris O'Brien sold his second mill to his son, Gideon. It's that mill where your skill and management ability are needed."

"What about his other sons? You say he has six."

"Aye, his eldest, Jeremiah, works the first mill with his father, the one they call the Dublin after Morris' home in Ireland. The others help and some cut timber as well."

When he didn't respond, Reverend Lyon continued. "They came to Machias ten years ago from Scarboro south of here and have done very well. They are respected in the community and active members of the church." With a knowing smile, he added, "You might consider them for your daughters, Thomas. None are yet married."

James' wife, Martha joined them then, bringing with her Lizzy, Annie and Sean. With them were the two Lyon children, a boy and a girl Thomas recognized from Onslow. Lizzy was carrying a baby she held close.

"You will remember our two oldest, John and Phebe, from Onslow," said James. "They are now six and five."

"You two have grown," said Thomas to the two smiling children. "Do you recognize us?"

The boy, John, nodded and said, "Sean's grown, too."

"He's but four years older than you," said Thomas.

"We have two more children who were born here," said Reverend Lyon. "Our three-year-old named James, after me, and the baby, Jeremiah, born this January, named after the eldest O'Brien son, who has done much for our family, a leader we are proud to honor."

Lizzy gazed contentedly into the babe's eyes, his little fingers grasping hers. Time had slipped away from Thomas as he realized his eldest daughter at twenty was past the age many girls married and old enough to be a mother.

"Our children will stay here while we go to the O'Briens' home," said Martha. "We have a girl who helps. Hannah will see them fed and put to bed." Then turning to the young Negro servant in blue, she said to Thomas, "You will remember our servant, London Atus, who was with us in Onslow."

The young man, who had been standing to one side, stepped forward. "Mr. Fitzpatrick," he said, dipping his head, "it is good to see you here."

Thomas offered the young man his hand. "It is good to be here, London, thank you."

At Martha's urging, Lizzy handed the baby to Hannah and they left for Morris O'Brien's house where a warm welcome awaited them. The house was a prominent one, two stories with a gambrel roof and a central front door. Paned windows on both stories welcomed the light. A perfect model for the home Thomas would build for his family.

It was clear to him that Morris was proud of his six sons, who lined up to greet them as they entered the house. Tall, handsome, clean-shaven and well-spoken, they had firm handshakes. Gideon's steady gaze spoke of his work with the sawmill, while John flashed a grin that mirrored Jeremiah's boldness. All six paid Lizzy and Annie much attention, the girls' red hair drawing the eye of their Irish hosts. Thomas detected a spark between Jeremiah and Lizzy, perhaps from their afternoon encounter.

Lizzy stood stiffly, her red hair glowing in the candle-light, her gaze flickering warily to the O'Brien sons, while Annie's eyes sparkled with shy delight at their compliments. Lizzy, his serious daughter who had taken on much responsibility with the death his wife, would be reluctant to join in any frivolity, but Annie, sheltered by her sister's care, would freely enjoy the company of so many handsome young men.

As Thomas scanned the room, he noted the home was simple in decoration but large and comfortable. Pride in their Irish heritage hung on the walls with the O'Brien coat of arms and a portrait Thomas recognized as the Irish king, Brian Boru. There had been many Irish families in

Onslow, and Reverend Lyon told him there were many in Machias.

The O'Brien house soon buzzed with laughter, the scent of roast chicken and fresh bread mingling with the smell of pine logs burning in the hearth, the flames casting shadows on the rough-hewn walls.

Morris O'Brien gestured to the table where his wife, Mary, and a servant were setting out many dishes. "Let us take our places," he said.

Once they were seated, they bowed their heads and Reverend Lyon said grace. He thanked God for the freedoms they had in Machias, for the blessing of friends and family and for the dinner of roast chicken they were about to eat.

As the O'Brien sons heaped food onto their pewter plates, Morris explained how they came to Machias. "I was a tailor in Dublin, and it remained my occupation when I first came to the colony. Which may explain the fine cut of my sons' clothing," he added with a smile.

Thomas nodded as he glanced at the well-dressed young men. "You made a bold change," he replied, his own shift from Onslow's mills to Machias fresh in his mind. "I admire your courage to make the leap."

"Here, I found a new trade my sons and I love," Morris continued. "The Province of Massachusetts granted Machias township status five years ago, giving each man two hundred and fifty acres, and requiring the town to build eighty homes, cultivate five acres and build a meeting house for the worship of God. My sons and I did this willingly, using skills from Scarboro. There, I taught Jeremiah and the boys to read the Bible, spell and cypher, to handle the plough, the pitchfork and the rifle, to raft lumber and to sail a boat. Jeremiah and his brothers have used their sailing skills here when schooners need help navigating the river."

Thomas paused as he sipped his cider, marveling at O'Brien's resourcefulness, and wondering how it shaped his eldest son into the confident man now eyeing Lizzy.

Gideon, who resembled his brothers, leaned in. "It is the mill Father sold to me that needs help. Reverend Lyon says you bring experience."

"That's true," said Thomas.

Reverend Lyon agreed. "You'll find no better mill-man."

Thomas accepted the compliment and said to Gideon, "I would love to see your mill. I have already admired the wood waiting for shipment."

GIDEON'S VOICE, STEADY as he spoke of the mill with her father, faded into the background as Lizzy felt the weight of Jeremiah O'Brien's gaze across the table. The eldest son, with his light brown hair and blue eyes glinting in the candlelight, had a boldness that unnerved her. She'd observed it earlier at the liberty pole, his easy smile, the way he'd welcomed Sean to join the men, as if war were a game for boys. Now, he leaned toward her, his voice low but warm, stirring the air between them.

"Your brother Sean has a fire in him, like you," he said, his grin teasing. "Machias will shape him well with the mills to work and trees to fell, and a revolution to prepare for."

Lizzy's stomach tightened, her fingers gripping the

edge of her plate. *Fire's fine, but it burns out fast,* she thought, memories of the abuses of Onslow's redcoats flashing through her mind—the officer's leer, her father's fury.

She met Jeremiah's gaze, her tone sharp despite the flush creeping up her cheeks. "Fire's fine, Mr. O'Brien, but I'd rather he learned survival than soldiering. Revolutions demand more than boys of ten have to give."

His eyes didn't waver, the glint in them sharpening. "Not mere soldiering, Miss. 'Tis freedom we fight for. And I'd wager at twenty you've fought harder battles than most."

The words struck her like a spark, too close to the truth. She had fought—every day since her mother's death, to keep Annie and Sean fed and clothed, shielding them from grief while her own heart ached. But freedom? It was a word she'd heard too often in Onslow, whispered by men who'd died for it. "Aye, I have," she said, her voice steady despite her racing pulse. "So keep your freedom talk light. Teach him if you must, but teach him to live, not just fight."

Jeremiah leaned closer, his tone earnest. "Maybe I will. And maybe you'll show me how to hold a family together—you've done well by your siblings."

Her breath caught, his words unraveling her guard. He saw *her*, not just the fiery redhead whose guard was always up, but the weight she carried. It stirred something dangerous in her, a warmth she didn't know she could feel. She lowered her gaze to her plate, hiding the faint smile tugging at her lips as she moved bits of chicken around with her knife. *Flattery won't win me,* she told herself, though her cheeks burned hotter.

Beside her, Annie nudged her under the table, whispering, "Can we go see the mill?" Her voice held a spark of the girl she'd been before Onslow's shadows. "And the river?"

Jeremiah sat back, his grin widening as if he knew he'd struck a chord, then spoke again, his voice lighter. "You're new to Machias. Let me show you around the village tomorrow. The Dublin mill, too, where I work with my father. Annie and Sean are welcome to join us. They'd enjoy the river and the falls. I'd wager, too, that Sean would fancy watching the mill wheel at work. It's a fine sight on the river."

Lizzy's heart skipped, caught off guard by the offer. The mill, the village. It would be a chance to see Machias through his eyes, to learn more of the place where her father hoped to build their future. Sean, who was sitting too far down the table to have heard the offer, would leap at the chance, eager to follow this leader of the Patriots, and that worried her more than her own racing heart. But with Annie and Sean along? It was a proper gesture, one her father would approve, though it didn't quiet the flutter in her chest. She glanced at her sister, whose eyes lit up at the idea, then back at Jeremiah, his gaze steady, waiting. "Perhaps," she said, her tone cautious but not unkind. "If my father agrees."

His smile softened, a promise in it. "I'll ask him myself, Miss."

Lizzy nodded, her mind racing as she stole another glance at him. He was trouble, this millman with a sailor's skill, but trouble she couldn't quite turn away from.

"The cause of America is in a great measure the cause of all mankind."

– Thomas Paine (1776)

CHAPTER 2

ELIZABETH STOOD WITH Annie and Sean in front of Reverend Lyon's house, her gaze stretching to the river where the sun glistened on the water, promising a warm day. The breeze caressed her skin as she adjusted her straw hat. She'd made sure Annie wore one, too. Sean wore a cocked hat like the heroes he emulated.

Their father, who had left earlier with Gideon O'Brien to look at possible sites for their new home before going to Gideon's sawmill, had told her Jeremiah would pick them up at ten that morning.

It was a quarter past now, per the Lyons' shelf clock, and Lizzy's impatience flared.

"There he is!" shouted Sean, as Jeremiah came into view, his long strides eating the distance.

He arrived in front of her, a sheepish smile on his face.

"You're late, Mr. O'Brien" she said, her arms crossing as she fixed him with a stare. But her heart skipped at the sight of him, for he was truly handsome.

"I am," he admitted, his smile widening, his charm softening her edges. "Had to save a rope at the Dublin mill. I thought to impress you with my heroism."

He winked, and Lizzy's lips twitched despite herself. "Impress me by being on time next," she teased, her tone lighter than intended.

His laugh warmed the air between them.

Softening, she asked, "Nothing serious, I trust?"

"No, just a frayed rope," he said, grinning, "but an important one." He glanced downriver. "It's a good day for our tour. Fishing boats are returning, hopefully with cod, haddock, flounder. And once the lumber's loaded on Ichabod Jones' sloops, they will sail for Boston. What would you like to see first?"

"The mill!" shouted Sean.

Annie smiled, nodding her agreement.

Jeremiah gave Lizzy an inquiring look. When she nodded, he said, "Why not? The mill it is."

They took the path west along the river leading to the Dublin mill. Jeremiah said, "The Machias River flows over seventy miles from the lakes above to reach the village. The name Machias, in the language of the Passamaquoddy, means Bad Little Falls, a reference to the steep stretch here." To Sean, he said, "I assume you know from your father's work in Onslow it's the falls that supply power for the wheel and saws."

Sean nodded, keeping his eyes on the mill ahead, the

sound of the falls growing louder. "He explained that but I want to see yours."

Jeremiah laughed, telling her he was likely a good older brother.

As they walked on, Jeremiah explained, "The falls power our mill, and the river gives us life. Above the falls, the water's fresh, home to salmon and alewives this time of year, coming up to spawn in the lakes and streams. The Passamaquoddy taught us to harvest the alewives in spring, smoking them to last through winter." He paused, pointing downstream where the river widened toward the bay. "But below the falls, the tide brings in saltwater from Machias Bay, mixing with the river's flow. It turns brackish down there, and you'll find striped bass and smelt feeding in the shallows. The river's a lifeline for us, providing fish, timber and trade."

Sean, his eyes wide with curiosity, turned to Jeremiah. "Do the salmon jump the falls?"

Jeremiah chuckled, ruffling the boy's hair. "They try, lad. Some make it, some don't."

Lizzy lingered at the edge of the falls, the mist cool against her skin, the faint scent of salt on the breeze hinting at the bay to the east. She glanced at Jeremiah, his tall form silhouetted against the river, and felt a quiet admiration for the man who knew this land so well.

"We harvest the wood in winter," he went on, speaking in a louder voice as they neared the falls. "Not just pine, but birch, cedar and fir. The snow cushions the felled trees and the cold prevents spoilage. In spring, we float the logs down to the mills that work all spring and summer to cut timber."

Standing before the falls, the river's roar filled Lizzy's ears, as it rushed wildly over the rocks. At the mill, the pounding sound drowned out all else. The wheel groaned under the flume's torrent, its buckets spilling with a steady splash.

Jeremiah offered her his hand to help her up to the mill's floor, his callused palm warm against hers as he steadied her up the incline. His gaze lingered on her face, a flicker of something, admiration perhaps, before he released her, leaving her skin tingling where his touch had been.

He had the hands of a working man who knew what it was to hoist logs and cut timber, though she imagined with workers to help, he did less of it these days.

Annie and Sean climbed easily. Lizzy could have done so, too, but she was glad Jeremiah had offered his hand.

Once inside the mill that overhung the river, Jeremiah pointed to the waterwheel and shouting over the din, said, "This is the heart of the mill. The river's drop powers the saws. My father and I built it with our own hands." After explaining the wheel, Jeremiah leaned closer. "What do you think, Miss Fitzpatrick? Could you manage a mill like this?"

Lizzy met his gaze, a spark igniting. "With the right teacher, perhaps," she replied, surprising herself with her boldness. The gears clanked and the sash saw bit into a log with a rhythmic thud. The plank floor vibrated beneath her feet.

"Our father's mill had a wheel much like this," said Annie speaking over the noise of the falls.

Lizzy watched the water flow over the top of the large

wheel, filling the buckets that turned it.

Jeremiah stood beside her, close enough for his jacket to brush against her arm. Leaning in, his breath warm against her ear, he said, "Since the river makes a good drop here, the overshot wheel works best."

Sean stared, on his face a look of fascination with the system of gears and axles that enabled the saw blade to rotate up and down, cutting wood. Pointing to two men feeding a large log into the blade, he said, "Look how fast it saws!"

Morris O'Brien, who had been speaking with the two men, came to greet them. "Welcome to the Dublin!"

"Thank you for letting us see it," said Lizzy.

Her brother had questions, and Jeremiah's father patiently answered them. Then he asked Sean, "Is this like the Onslow mill your father worked?"

Sean drew his brows together as he cast a gaze at the gears. "Yours is faster, I think."

"Aye, could be," said Mr. O'Brien, nodding. "We've worked hard to make it so."

Several minutes passed before a long board emerged, the men finishing the last inches by hand.

"Have you seen enough?" Jeremiah asked.

"Yes," she said. "Sean could watch all day but we should move on so as not to disrupt the work."

Jeremiah told his father, "I'll be back after I show the Fitzpatricks around the village and the river."

Mr. O'Brien nodded and bid them a good day.

As they stepped down from the mill, Jeremiah again offered his hand. "Careful now," he murmured.

Lizzy felt her pulse quicken, caught off guard by the

warmth in his blue eyes.

She was glad when they had walked some distance away so she could once again hear their conversation more easily. Sean had run ahead, and Annie walked on Jeremiah's other side.

"Is Gideon's mill like the Dublin?" she asked Jeremiah.

"For the most part. We made a few improvements when we built that one. My brother is grateful to have an experienced man like your father joining him. There will be wood aplenty and men to help when he is ready to build your home."

"Thank you," she said. "That means much to all of us."

JEREMIAH HEARD THE gulls shrieking before he saw the fishing schooner tied at the landing. "They must have a good take," he said to Elizabeth, stealing a glance at her as they approached the ship. The sun caught her red hair beneath the straw hat framing her face. He found himself admiring the determined set of her jaw and her quiet strength. Her attention on Sean, she didn't notice his gaze, but the sight stirred something in him, a longing he hadn't expected.

Sean, already at the fishing boat, turned. "A huge haul!" The lad's enthusiasm reminded Jeremiah of his youngest brother, Joseph.

"'Lo, Jere," said Isaac Taft from the deck of his small schooner, his blond hair blowing free of his cap. "Showing the newcomers around?"

"Just so." Jeremiah introduced the Fitzpatricks, and

then asked, "Success today?"

"Yes. Salted most at sea, but fresh fish remains for the village. At least for now," Isaac added, his tone darkening.

"What do you mean?" asked Jeremiah, concern furrowing his brow.

"Word's come the British Parliament has passed a new law, the Fisheries Act, banning us from Newfoundland waters and the Atlantic coast without their leave."

"But that will end the colony's fishing!" Jeremiah protested, his voice rising with frustration.

"Not just Massachusetts, Jere. All the colonies. They intend to enforce it with a naval blockade and worse, I expect."

Jeremiah exhaled sharply, shaking his head.

Beside him, Elizabeth's hands clenched, her face tightening as if a memory gripped her, perhaps of the British in Onslow. Jeremiah felt a surge of protectiveness, wishing he could shield her from the coming storm.

"How will we survive?" Isaac asked, "My crew has young ones to feed. Machias isn't known for its crops."

"For the time being, we can help with the sale of lumber," Jeremiah said, glancing upriver where Jones' sloops, the *Unity* and the *Polly* readied their sails. "But there will be little lumber being sold to the British."

Turning to Elizabeth and Annie, Jeremiah explained, "A severe drought last fall prevented us from laying in sufficient stores, so we are low on food and provisions. The Fisheries Act will only make the situation worse."

"Aye," said Isaac. "The town will soon be in dire need. We'll be existing on clams, fish from the lakes and blueberries."

"To where do those sloops sail?" asked Elizabeth, her eyes sharp.

Jeremiah had spoken with Ichabod Jones that morning, so he could answer with assurance. "Jones in the sloop *Unity* and Nathaniel Horton, in the *Polly*, are heading to Salem. It's an active seaport, but if they find no market there, they'll try Connecticut. The British control Boston."

Biding Isaac and his crew a good day, Jeremiah turned to walk back to the Lyon house with Elizabeth. Sean darted ahead, losing his hat in the dust. Jeremiah scooped it up and brushed it off. "With many children in Machias, stray hats abound."

"Sean's always losing his," said Annie.

Elizabeth watched her brother, running ahead, his red hair confined only by the queue at his neck. "Sean is happy here."

"And you, Miss Fitzpatrick? Are you glad you came despite our situation?"

"More than you know," she replied, meeting his gaze. For a moment, the world narrowed to the two of them, the air charged with unspoken possibility.

As they reached the reverend's house, Jeremiah paused, his hand brushing hers as he handed her Sean's forgotten hat. "I hope I've not disappointed, Miss Fitzpatrick—despite my tardiness."

She smiled, her lips curving in a way that made Jeremiah's heart speed. "Not entirely," she said, her voice teasing, "but I'll be watching you."

"I am counting on it, Miss" he said with a grin, as he turned toward the mill.

ICHABOD JONES STRAIGHTENED his cocked hat as he stepped off the *Unity* onto Boston's bustling Long Wharf, the tang of salt and tar sharp in the air. The harbor teemed with British sloops-of-war, their red ensigns snapping in the wind, a stark reminder of the Crown's grip on the city.

Ichabod was behind schedule, for he had not intended to come here. Per his original plans, he had sailed to Salem where he discovered the town in turmoil due to the outbreak of fighting in Lexington and Concord. Those he spoke with told him Boston was also in distress. He had wanted to remove his household goods still in Boston as well as the families of two relatives but had remained away knowing that would not be easily accomplished.

Massachusetts militias had blocked land access to Boston, and because the British had retaliated for the Boston Tea Party incident by enacting the Port Act the year before, Boston Harbor was essentially closed to all ships except those allowed by the British. As a merchant, he could enter Boston Harbor, but he could not leave without their permission.

As he considered his options, a plan took form in his mind. He would sell lumber to the British, load his household goods and the provisions for Machias and then seek a meeting with General Gage.

While he was accomplishing this, he encountered Nathaniel Horton on the docks. Horton commanded the *Polly* for him. "Why are you here?" he asked surprised to see him.

"I could ask you the same question. You will recall my family is here, and I want to get them out. General Gage has yet to declare martial law, but the British are shooting suspected rebels on sight. It's not safe."

Ichabod nodded, understanding all too well. He had removed his wife to Machias earlier, but unfinished business drew him back. "Have you sold the lumber?"

"Aye and the British were glad of it. They are expecting reinforcements and need more barracks for their soldiers."

"This can work to our advantage, Nate. Gage is the royal governor of Massachusetts and, by all accounts, he is a fair man. He has a need we can fill and perchance he'll strike a bargain."

"It's worth a try," said Horton. "Though the Sons of Liberty in Machias will not be pleased to learn we have sold their lumber to the British and intend to sell them more."

THE NEXT MORNING, Ichabod entered the grand hall of Province House to find the air thick with tobacco smoke and murmuring redcoats. Stating his purpose, he was shown into General Thomas Gage's office.

The general stood by a map of the colonies, his stern face lined with the weight of command. He turned, his blue eyes fixed on Ichabod, sharp as a hawk's. "Mr. Jones," he said, his voice clipped, "your sloops carried Machias lumber, I'm told."

"Aye, they do."

"We need it for barracks for new troops arriving in July, and repairs for our ships. The Crown will pay well." Taking a seat behind his desk, General Gage wrote out a note and sealed it with wax. "Here," he said, thrusting it into Ichabod's hand. "I am sending you to Vice Admiral Graves. He and I are not the best of friends, but he has charge over enforcing the Port Act. Only he can allow you to leave."

Ichabod thanked the governor and a short time later stood before Admiral Graves. The older man's white wig had been carefully styled, his gold-trimmed dark blue jacket elegant over his white silk waistcoat. It made for a polished, if severe appearance added to by the stern expression in his brown eyes. Accepting the note from Gage that Jones handed him, the admiral read it slowly, then fixed Ichabod with a cool stare. "You propose to return to Machias and bring us more loads of lumber?"

"I do, fine pine cut by the town's mills. In exchange, I will bring much-needed food and provisions for the hundred families that now live in the area. It has been my trade for the last ten years. But Machias grows restless and the Patriots there speak of freedom."

Graves paced with his hands clasped at his back, his expression unreadable. "Very well. I will send an escort, the HMS *Margaretta*, to see your ships back. Captain Moore, one of my best midshipmen, will ensure compliance. We'll not have rebellion in the lumber trade, not when His Majesty's army needs it."

He slid a purse of coin across the desk, heavy with promise. "Deliver the lumber, and there's more where that came from."

Ichabod took the purse, its weight a cold comfort. He thought of Gideon O'Brien's new millman, Thomas Fitzpatrick, a steady sort, and Reverend Lyon, a calm Patriot. But Colonel Benjamin Foster and Jeremiah

O'Brien had the fire of rebellion in their eyes and the men of Machias followed their lead. "I'll deliver," he said, his voice steady despite the unease curling in his gut. "But I'll need protection. The river's full of whispers."

"You'll have it," Graves replied. "Moore's orders will be clear. Any resistance, and he'll burn Machias to the ground."

Ichabod nodded, but as he left the admiral, the purse heavy in his coat, a chill ran through him. He'd secured his trade, but at what cost? He pictured his wife in Machias, her laughter fading under British guns. The *Unity* and *Polly* would sail back with British protection, and he feared Machias would see him not as a merchant, but as a traitor. Jeremiah O'Brien's face flashed in his mind, those blue eyes burning with defiance. This was no longer about lumber. It was about war, and those living on the river awaited his return.

Machias, Maine, Massachusetts, 2 June 1775

JEREMIAH LEFT HIS house on the river, heading to the Dublin mill, the words he had penned a week ago to the Provincial Congress repeating in his mind. Words written in desperation, for their food stocks were nearly depleted and the settlers located in more isolated areas faced famine. Ichabod Jones was long overdue.

> *We must now inform your honors that the inhabit-*
> *ants of this place exceed one hundred families, some of*
> *which are very numerous, and that divine Providence*
> *has cut off all our usual resources. A very severe drought*

*last fall prevented our laying in sufficient stores; and
had no vessels visited us in the winter, we must have
suffered; nor have we this spring been able to procure
provisions sufficient for carrying on our business...we
must add, we have no country behind us to lean upon,
nor can we make an escape by flight; the wilderness is
impervious, and vessels we have none.*

*To you, therefore, honored gentlemen, we humbly
apply for relief. You are our last, our only resource...we
cannot take a denial, for, under God, you are all our
dependence, and if you neglect us, we are ruined.*

Jeremiah's gut churned with worry. They had yet to
hear from the Provincial Congress. Their food stores had
dwindled to provisions for only a few weeks, and Ichabod
Jones' sloops had not arrived as expected. Speculation was
rampant as to what could have happened to them. The
pork and flour they would bring were needed to see
Machias through the next several months.

He had not yet reached the mill when Elizabeth Fitzpatrick stepped into his path. Jarred from his musings, he
looked up. "Miss Fitzpatrick. What can I do for you?"

"Morning, Mr. O'Brien," she replied with a smile. "I
was hoping you might have heard from the Provincial
Congress."

Had she grown lovelier in the last week? Her blue eyes
more radiant? He had been so busy at the mill and
concerned with the families in outlying areas, he'd not
seen her since last Sunday's services, and now it was
Friday. He shook his head. "Alas, no."

At a shout sounded from behind him, Jeremiah
turned. Slowly making their way upriver were the *Unity*

and the *Polly*. "Thank God," he said as relief flooded him. "Jones' sloops have returned."

Elizabeth tilted her head with a puzzled look. "What ship is that following them?"

Casting his gaze farther, he glimpsed a red ensign flying above a schooner. "God in Heaven, it's a British man-of-war!"

"What could that mean?" Elizabeth asked, a look of trepidation on her face.

"It means that Jones has shown his true colors. He's an agent of the British government."

That evening, Stephen Jones, Ichabod's nephew, called a town meeting for the next morning at the request of his uncle. "He has a proposal to submit to a vote," Stephen told Jeremiah. "Admiral Graves allowed his departure from Boston on the condition he return with cargoes of lumber."

Jeremiah flashed him a pointed look of disbelief. "Boston! He told me he was sailing to Salem. And lumber for the British?" He shook his head. "We cannot do that."

"I am sorry, Jere. It wasn't my idea," said Stephen. "You know where my sympathies lie." Stephen was a merchant, a respected member of the community and a Patriot, but in this instance, he was acting on instructions from his uncle.

"The warship that accompanies your uncle…the *Margaretta* with her crew of twenty men, her four four-pounders and a dozen swivel guns mounted on the railing…whose idea was that?"

Stephen averted his gaze. "General Gage sent the schooner to ensure the execution of the condition."

"I see." Jeremiah frowned. "And what condition is that?"

"I will have it tomorrow morning for all to see."

The next morning, at the town meeting, a paper was handed around for the people to sign, agreeing that Ichabod Jones' sloops could carry lumber to Boston and promising to protect him and his property. Dissent rippled through the gathered families. Their concern was clear: This would mean aiding the British and defying the Provincial Congress.

"Why else would Jones need a British warship to secure our signatures?" asked Colonel Foster, his voice a low growl.

"I will not sign," said Jeremiah. "Nor will I be a tool of the British or protect Ichabod Jones, who acts as the king's agent." Across the room, he saw Elizabeth Fitzpatrick watching, nodding. The fire in her eyes matched the fire in his heart.

His temper surged that afternoon when, stepping from the meeting house to the riverbank, he watched the *Margaretta* glide closer, her guns trained on the shore, the creak of her rigging a grim promise.

His brother, John, arrived, breathless. "Jere, I saw Ichabod Jones board the *Margaretta* to speak with the captain—Midshipman James Moore. It was after this she began sailing closer to the town."

"So," said Jeremiah, "Ichabod would use the threat of British guns to coerce the people."

John nodded. "So it would seem."

The next day, in the meeting house, the Sons of Liberty, including Jeremiah, his father, his brothers, the Fosters and Reverend Lyon, denounced the paper and its implications. But many in Machias were frightened.

"We are but prisoners of war," said one man.

"We need food for our children," pleaded a woman, her voice breaking as she clutched a toddler. Her gaze darted out the window to where the *Margaretta*'s guns threatened.

Despite Jeremiah's protests, many signed the paper. With the signatures in hand, Jones ordered his vessels moored to the village wharf, allowing the barrels of pork and flour and other provisions to be distributed, but only to those who had not opposed the contract. This so angered the Patriots that they came to Jeremiah and Ben, demanding they capture Jones and stop his supplying the king's troops with lumber.

Before this could be discussed, the *Margaretta*'s captain, whose ship was by now moored before the meeting house, expressed his displeasure in seeing the liberty pole rising prominently. Moore stepped ashore, his navy blue jacket adorned with brass buttons that gleamed in the sunlight, the white lace on his cuffs marking him an officer. His black cocked hat sat firmly on his head, and a smallsword hung at his hip, clinking softly with each step. Despite the salt-stained edges of his coat, his uniform was in perfect order, a stark contrast to the rugged Patriots gathered on the riverbank.

"Take that pole down!" he demanded of the people spilling out of the meeting house. His voice cracked with the authority of a young midshipman. Jeremiah believed Moore to be several years his junior. "My orders are preemptory and must be obeyed, or it will be my painful duty to fire upon the town!"

John, standing with Jeremiah and Stephen Jones, retorted, "That pole, sir, was erected by the unanimous approval of the people of Machias!"

Moore's astonishment showed as he reared back his head. "I repeat, my orders must be obeyed. That pole must come down, or I'll fire!"

"Must come down?" John asked, incredulous. "Those words are very easily spoken, my friend, but you will find it will be difficult to enforce them."

"What!" exclaimed Moore. "Am I to understand that resistance will be made? Will the people of Machias dare to disregard an order, not originating with me, gentlemen, but with the government whose officer I am?"

"The people of Machias," replied Jeremiah, "will *dare* do anything in maintenance of their principles and rights."

At this point, Stephen Jones intervened, urging calm. "It will not serve your purpose, Captain Moore, to set fire to our town." He continued to cajole, convincing the young midshipman to allow another meeting of the town. "It might be better attended and with a different result."

Moore agreed, fixing the day a week from now by which the people must take down the pole or he would fire on the town. Jeremiah thought the midshipman's prestige in the eyes of his crew, who were watching, was seemingly at stake.

At a meeting the next day, Jeremiah and his five brothers pleaded with the people, rousing even the passive to a desire for action. "The liberty pole represents all we believe in," said Jeremiah, "all our country fights for. We made oaths…"

Heads nodded at the reminder.

Colonel Benjamin Foster stepped forward, his broad shoulders filling the meeting house doorway behind him, his weathered face alight with righteous fury. He raised a hand, silencing the murmurs, then slammed his fist on the table, his voice booming. "Hear me, good people of Machias! We stand at a crossroads, where fear bids us bow and honor bids us rise! That liberty pole," he pointed toward the riverbank, "is no mere timber. 'Tis the banner of our cause, raised by our hands. And, as Jeremiah has reminded us, sealed by our oaths, proclaiming we will not be slaves to a distant king! We've bled for this land, through drought, through famine, and soon through the Fisheries Act that starves our nets. Now, they send a warship to bend us? To burn our homes if we dare stand tall? I say, let their guns roar! Let their fire fall! For we'll not strike our colors, nor bow to a tyrant who knows not the grit of Machias' heart! We'll not give our lumber to enrich their army and repair their ships. Who among you will stand with us to keep that pole aloft, as a beacon for liberty, for our children, for the fight that burns in every free man's soul?"

The crowd erupted in cheers, even the most timid roused to indignation, their voices a defiant chorus. Jeremiah smiled at the heart of the people so valiantly displayed. The vote, when taken, was not surprisingly in favor of keeping the pole.

Afterwards, Elizabeth approached him, her hand on his arm. "I fear you have stirred the pot, Mr. O'Brien." Her smile was warm yet wary. His pulse quickened. Her touch lingered long after she let go.

"Aye, the pot boils. What does your father say?"

She looked to where Thomas Fitzpatrick stood with Reverend Lyon. "He is with you and the Patriots. Reverend Lyon, our host, is one of you. After all, my father brought us here to get away from the British."

"Has he selected a site for your home?"

"Yes, next to your brother, Gideon's house."

"'Tis a good spot. Meanwhile," lowering his voice to a whisper, "my mother plans to cast balls for our muskets."

"I know," she said, her grin wide. "Annie and I will be helping her."

Jeremiah couldn't resist a chuckle at the daring of the Machias women.

As the crowd dispersed, Reverend Lyon suggested the Committee of Safety meet at Burnham Tavern on Saturday, the 10th of June. Jeremiah agreed.

The secret meeting turned into a planning session.

John Lambert, his dark eyes intense, began the meeting by noting Captain Moore had stated his intent to attend the next day's service, a fact Jeremiah believed Lambert raised with a purpose in mind.

"We have until Monday before Moore will fire on the town," said Ben Foster. "If the British captain intends to attend services tomorrow, 'tis an opportune time to capture both the *Margaretta*'s captain and Ichabod Jones. Capture," he emphasized, "not kill."

"But who will be the one to seize the captain?" asked Lambert.

"I claim that privilege," said Jeremiah's brother, John. "You, gentlemen, can aid me."

"We'll need to assure the people are ready to act with

us," said Lambert.

"I propose," said John Wheaton, "that we ascertain the powder and balls we have. Several of us should carry concealed arms and, once the captain is seized, we can then capture his vessel."

"A bold move," said Ben Foster, "one I fully agree with."

"An act of open rebellion," added Jeremiah's father.

"We are aware of that, Father," said Jeremiah, "but while the king may call it rebellion, we who are engaged in it know it by another name—revolution."

To Jeremiah's surprise, his father shook his head. "I worry over the scarcity of provisions and the difficulty of obtaining additional supplies. Have you considered how vulnerable we are?"

"Aye, I am aware," said Jeremiah. "You may not yet know, but we've sent messengers to the people of Mispecka, Pleasant River and Chandlers Mills, inviting them to join us and requesting reinforcements. Many have come and are waiting in the woods, and more are on the way. The people are united."

"I hope they come with arms and ammunition," said Ben Foster.

"I'm afraid not," said Jeremiah. "I'm told there is a scarcity of powder at Pleasant River. But those who have no muskets or only scant ammunition will be armed with pitchforks and scythes. And the women of Machias are spending this whole afternoon melting lead to cast balls. Your brother Wooden assists them. My own mother, in her zeal, melted up an old pewter teapot for that purpose in spite of our remonstrances, for it was a sort of heirloom. The women, if possible, are more crazy about keeping the pole erect than are the men." Into Jeremiah's mind came the face of Elizabeth Fitzpatrick and her words telling him she would be helping his mother.

"Very well," said Ben Foster. "Tomorrow, we will make Jones and the British officers our prisoners."

Reverend Lyon nodded gravely. "Guns will be permitted in tomorrow's service to assure our plan holds."

"There is nothing so likely to produce peace as to be well prepared to meet an enemy."
– George Washington (1780)

CHAPTER 3

Congregational Church, Machias, Maine, Massachusetts, Sunday, 11 June 1775

JEREMIAH, HIS FAMILY, and his servant, Dick Earle, took their places on the rough boards that served as seats in the meeting house. The air was thick with tension as they stowed their weapons around the building, beneath seats, behind beams.

The day was warm and sultry, the windows open to allow in what breeze there might be. The falls, a quarter-mile away, could be faintly heard, along with birdsong outside the meeting house.

Just offshore lay the *Margaretta*, her guns glinting in the sun. Jones' two sloops were anchored in the river, one at the falls, above the *Margaretta*, the other in the river a half-mile below the British warship.

Somewhere coming through the woods Jeremiah knew Ben Foster would be leading his men from East Machias along with those they had summoned from other villages.

Machias residents filed into the meeting house. Women arrived with their men, including the Fitzpatricks, who sat near the back. Among the parishioners was London Atus, the reverend's Negro servant, who took a seat by the rear window.

Captain Moore arrived with his second in command, Midshipman Stillingfleet. They took their seats next to Ichabod Jones, who had just entered. All three sat in the front. Jeremiah's brother, John, who'd been waiting outside, slipped inside and sat behind them, stowing his pistol under his seat.

From where the English captain sat, the windows allowed him an extensive view of the river and his ship.

Reverend Lyon in black robe and white wig took his stance behind the pulpit at the front of the room. After opening with prayer for the service, he spoke a hymn aloud, likely one he'd written himself for he was a talented hymn writer.

> *O Lord, to my relief draw near,*
> *For never was more pressing need;*
> *For my deliv'rance, Lord, appear,*
> *And add to that deliv'rance speed.*

The singing followed and once that ended, the sermon commenced, speaking of their God-given freedoms. Midway through the sermon, London Atus, the reverend's servant, gazed out the window where Ben Foster's group of armed men were crossing a footbridge that connected two islands in the river. Jeremiah, too, had been watching them, hoping they would remain unseen.

It was not to be.

London, who apparently had not been taken into the reverend's confidence, must have feared the armed men meant harm. With a great cry of "Lord a-mercy!" he jumped out of the window and fled into the woods.

Captain Moore and Midshipman Stillingfleet shot up from their seats and seeing the approaching Patriots, fled. Confusion erupted, sending those gathered into an uproar. In the rushing around, Ichabod Jones escaped to the woods.

Moore and his officer reached the shore where a boat awaited to row them to their ship.

By the time the Machias Patriots had secured their guns and gone in pursuit, Moore and his officer had boarded their ship and commenced firing on the town.

From the shore, Jeremiah shouted over the explosion of gunfire, "Strike your colors to the Sons of Liberty!"

Moore answered, "Fire and be damned!"

Jeremiah's jaw tightened, and he raised his musket, signaling the Machias men who had taken cover on the shore, whereupon, a volley of musket fire raked the hull of the British schooner. The sharp crack of gunfire continued as a haze of gunpowder smoke rose above the river and shouts of defiance filled the air.

The *Margaretta* replied with swivel guns blazing, their loud booms shaking the water, followed by the snap of musket fire from the British crew. The acrid stench of the gunpowder burned Jeremiah's nostrils.

For an hour the two sides fired away, after which the *Margaretta*, her hull pierced with musket shot, weighed anchor, set sail and dropped down the river out of reach.

A few of Machias' men had been wounded, though not seriously, and the women hurried to tend their wounds.

During that day and evening, parties of men from neighboring towns continued to arrive in the village, some with muskets, some armed with pitchforks, and some with scythes fastened on poles. By the end of the day, one hundred Patriots stood together.

On Monday morning, Machias was a scene of great excitement. Jeremiah had slept little, expecting another battle. Men paraded the village with their various weapons, while the women searched every nook and cranny for powder and lead.

Elizabeth found Jeremiah on the riverbank discussing plans with Ben Foster and John Lambert.

"The women of Machias have more ammunition to offer you," she said, handing Jeremiah a pail of lead balls. "And two young women, Hannah and Rebecca Weston, walked all night through the woods from Chandlers Mills to bring powder and balls they found after their men left for Machias."

Elizabeth's eyes held his, a quiet strength in them. "Come back to us, Mr. O'Brien," she said. Glancing at Ben and John, she added, "You, too."

"You see?" Jeremiah said to the two men as he accepted the pail. "The women of Machias are brave Patriots."

Ben smiled at Elizabeth. "I stand amazed at their

pluck. My wife, Beth, has our children gathering metal for my brother Wooden to fashion into balls."

Elizabeth nodded and said to Ben, "Your wife, Mr. Foster, is a leader in our effort."

Lambert, who Jeremiah knew to be a good sailor at twenty-three, the same age as Jeremiah's brother, John, said, "The whole town is involved in gathering weapons."

The Committee of Safety met that afternoon at Reverend Lyon's house. After apologizing for failing to warn his servant of their Sunday plans, Lyon asked, "So, what now?"

"We've had some good fortune," said John Wheaton. "In his haste to withdraw farther downstream to avoid our fire, Captain Moore committed an error when jibing, causing the boom to slam into the shrouds supporting the mast. The main boom shattered, crippling her."

"Where is she?" asked Jeremiah.

"She managed to withdraw and re-anchor at Scott's Point out of musket range," said Wheaton. "Moore has seized Captain Samuel Tobey's sloop from the Bay of Fundy and impressed him onboard the *Margaretta* as pilot since the British crew doesn't know our waters. They also took onboard Robert Avery of Norwich, Connecticut, who had just arrived from Nova Scotia, and the boom from his ship."

"It will take them some time to repair the schooner," said Jeremiah, thinking ahead. "We should take one of Jones' sloops and go after the *Margaretta*."

"Aye, we should," said Lambert, a smile crossing his face.

Later that day, forty men, including all of Jeremiah's

brothers, save the youngest, were chosen to go with him to seize the *Unity*. His father had wanted to go, but at the urging of Jeremiah and his brothers, Morris remained ashore.

Jeremiah's servant, Dick Earle was eager to accompany him, and he didn't have the heart to deny him, for he was a Patriot. Among the crew were Josiah Weston, married to young Hannah, who had brought ammunition from Chandlers Mills, John Wheaton, a fellow member of the Committee of Safety, Isaac Taft, the Machias fisherman, Ben Foster's brother, Ezekiel, three McNeil brothers and a backwoods moose hunter named Jon Knight.

Ben Foster took twenty others, including John Lambert, to borrow the small schooner, *Falmouth Packet*, where it lay at anchor in East Machias. Sometime later he sent a message to Jeremiah saying they had run aground and would, if they could free themselves, catch up and join them.

LATER THAT MORNING, amid the cheers of the town's men, women and children, the *Unity*, still laden with lumber, sailed in pursuit of the enemy. Elizabeth Fitzpatrick, her red hair bright in the sun, was one of those waving to them from the riverbank, along with her sister and brother.

Once underway, Jeremiah ordered the men to build breastworks of pine boards and anything else they could find to screen them from the enemy's fire.

When they first sighted the *Margaretta*, she was headed out to sea, having had a full hour's lead. Jeremiah was determined to catch her. Shouting orders to make sail, the crew responded and the *Unity*'s sails billowed. Running before the wind, they swiftly caught up to the slower British ship.

At that point, the men aboard the sloop realized they had not yet named a captain and, by acclamation, appointed Jeremiah. "You've been our captain all along," said John Wheaton.

"Aye, and a good one," said Isaac Taft.

Jeremiah's first official act was to allow three of the crew, who in the cold light of day had lost their nerve, to depart for the shore in a small boat.

Once they had gone, Jeremiah turned to his crew. "Now, my brave fellows, having got rid of those lily-livered cowards, our first business will be to get alongside of the schooner yonder. The first man who boards her shall be entitled to the palm of honor."

The men smiled their agreement. John's eyes were alight with intent.

It was at that point Jeremiah's youngest brother, Joseph, emerged from his hiding place below deck. "What are you doing here?" Jeremiah asked, miffed. The lad was only sixteen.

"Aw, Jere, I just couldn't be left behind."

"Well, you're here now. Keep out of range of their guns."

Jeremiah urged on his crew whose actions steadily reduced the distance between the two ships. His heart pounded, not just for the battle ahead, but for those waiting onshore. Would they make them proud? Would they succeed?

Turning to look behind them, Jeremiah saw the *Falmouth Packet* in pursuit but trailing. "We cannot wait for Ben," he said to his brother, Gideon, "or we will lose the *Margaretta*."

Captain Moore must have realized he could not outpace the faster sloop, for he cast off the small boats from his stern, releasing them to the choppy waters of the bay. Once within hailing distance, Moore shouted, "Sloop ahoy! Keep off or I'll fire!"

Undaunted, Jeremiah shouted back, "In America's name, I demand you surrender! If you do, we will treat you well."

Moore answered, "Fire away and be damned!" With that, a swivel gun on the schooner's stern opened fire, dropping John McNeil to the *Unity*'s deck. The moose hunter, Jon Knight, manned the small gun on the *Unity* and picked off the *Margaretta*'s helmsman with a ball in his head.

"Well done!" exclaimed Jeremiah.

With the helmsman down, the enemy's quarterdeck rapidly cleared. From the *Unity*'s deck a volley of musket fire followed.

The *Margaretta* broached to under the *Unity*'s bow, causing the sloop's bowsprit to rip through the *Margaretta*'s mainsail, locking the two vessels together. Jeremiah's brother, John, sprang onto the schooner's deck just as the vessels separated, leaving him alone and stranded on the enemy's ship.

Four marines of the *Margaretta*'s crew, appeared ten feet from John and fired their muskets in a deafening volley. Jeremiah looked on, horrified. A thick cloud of gunpowder smoke had erupted with the sharp crack of the marines' shots. When the cloud dissipated, Jeremiah thanked God for the miracle that was John standing, untouched.

The marines, their faces half-obscured by the lingering smoke, fixed bayonets and charged with a guttural shout. John bolted for the stern and leapt into the sea, the water splashing around him as he swam the thirty yards to the *Unity* while bullets from the British crew kicked up sprays of water around him in a deadly hail.

Jeremiah retrieved his brother from the sea, dripping wet but unscathed. "Brother John, you have escaped death and won the palm!" Then, turning to his crew, Jeremiah shouted, "Man the sweeps and lay us alongside once more, and stand ready to fasten on to her."

Jeremiah had appointed twenty of his crew, armed with pitchforks, to board the British vessel. It was their one desperate chance, for they were nearly out of ammunition.

Before they could gain the *Margaretta*'s deck, however, a fight ensued at close range.

Captain Moore mounted the quarterdeck railing, sword flashing in the sun, shouting to rally his men, who must have realized by now the American Patriots were not the ignorant lumbermen they had thought them to be.

Moore began hurling hand grenades onto the *Unity*. One exploded near Jeremiah, the blast's heat singeing his coat. But, like his brother, Jeremiah stood unharmed, his resolve unshaken.

Samuel Watts, the brother of Hannah Weston, raised his rifle and taking careful aim, fired, sending a ball into

Moore's chest. The British captain rocked back. A second ball sent him to the deck.

Maneuvering the *Unity* alongside the schooner's larboard, they lashed the ships together as best they could without grappling hooks. Knowing their ammunition was exhausted, Jeremiah ordered the twenty men he had selected, including his servant, "To your feet, lads! The schooner is ours! Follow me! Board!"

Jeremiah led the charge, his cutlass raised in his hand.

Ben Foster and the *Falmouth Packet*, having caught up to the attack, pulled along the *Margaretta*'s starboard and led a rush down her deck from the bow.

An hour of hand-to-hand fighting followed with men wounded on both sides. Second in command of the *Margaretta*, Midshipman Stillingfleet, wounded and overwhelmed, fled below deck. Unable to reload their muskets in close fighting where the Americans' pitchforks were more effective, the frightened British crew, left leaderless, laid down their arms and surrendered.

Cheers went up from Jeremiah's crew. Ben Foster strode down the deck to congratulate him as Jeremiah looked aloft at the red ensign flying from the schooner's mast. "That must come down," he said and promptly hauled the colors down in triumph.

His crew shouted "Huzzah!"

Ben slapped him on the shoulder. "You may be the first Patriot to bring down British colors, Jere."

Seeing his servant, Dick Earle, standing close by and smiling, Jeremiah went to him, offering his hand. "You fought well, Dick. This is your victory, too."

While some of the *Unity*'s crew took up the *Margaret-*

ta's small boats, others repaired her rigging and put her deck in order. Still others went in search of weapons and ammunition. They found many muskets and cutlasses as well as an ample supply of powder and shot. "We also found these papers on the *Unity*," said John Wheaton to Jeremiah. "You'll want to see them."

Jeremiah quickly scanned the papers, stashed them in his waistcoat and then went with Ben Foster to assess the dead and wounded.

On the *Unity*, two had been killed, John McNeil, whose brothers stood over him, worrying over what they would tell his wife and children, and James Coolbroth, a shoemaker. Eight were wounded, including Ebenezer Beal, hit in his legs by one of Moore's hand grenades, Jeremiah's fisherman friend, Isaac Taft, James Cole and John Berry of Hadley Lake, who took a ball in his mouth that came out behind his ear.

On the *Margaretta*, eight marines and sailors lay dead, as well as the helmsman and Robert Avery, who Moore had impressed aboard, and who was shot in the head on the first volley. Among the wounded were two marines and two seamen. Captain Moore was badly wounded, and Jeremiah ordered his brothers to do what they could to stanch the bleeding from his chest.

He thanked God for bringing all his brothers through the fight unscathed, doubtless due to their mother's prayers and God's grace.

With a favoring wind and tide, the *Unity* set sail with her valuable prize. The *Falmouth Packet* followed. During their voyage upriver, Jeremiah saw that every attention was paid to Captain Moore and the other wounded.

On reaching Machias, amid the cheer from the riverbank, Moore was carried to the house of Stephen Jones where he was cared for. A physician was sent for, as there were none in the village. The rest of the wounded were taken to Burnham Tavern.

Two dozen British were taken prisoner. "When they can travel, we'll see them to the Provincial Congress, along with Ichabod Jones," Jeremiah told Ben. "I expect Midshipman Stillingfleet, a British officer, will be released to Royal Navy officials. The two shipwrights who are among the prisoners, we'll keep at Machias. We will need them to fit out the ships we have, and they will be happier being productive than confined as prisoners."

"The three ships should be Machias' lawful prizes," said Ben.

"An interesting question," said Jeremiah, "since we did not capture them under the colony's orders or any commission. After all, no government supplied the ship that captured the *Margaretta*."

Hours later, a wave of exhaustion washed over Jeremiah from the letdown after the frenzy of battle. Meeting with the families of the dead and wounded, giving what comfort he could, had drained him. But he had yet another stop to make.

The sun had dipped below the horizon, the river aglow with twilight, as he made his way to Reverend Lyon's house—later than he'd intended. Waiting in front was Elizabeth Fitzpatrick, her brows furrowed, her gaze roving over him. "Are you well, Mr. O'Brien...unharmed?"

"I am, thank the Good Lord."

She visibly relaxed. "You are also late. It's going dark."

He was tempted to smile, but noting the worry on her face, he asked, "Were you worried about me, Miss Fitzpatrick?"

"And if I were?" she asked impatiently.

He smiled. "It pleases me, for I can think of no one who I would rather have worry about me than you. Now, I must see Reverend Lyon. Would you come with me?"

She nodded and they walked together into the Lyon house where she and her family were still residing. James Lyon was relieved to hear Jeremiah's report. "I am sorry for those who were killed. I will see the families and prepare a service for them."

"Meanwhile," said Jeremiah, "we need to get word to the Provincial Congress of what has transpired. Since you head our Committee of Safety, it should come from you."

"I will write a report for dispatch on the morrow. Would you go?"

"I'm needed here to oversee the prisoners and prepare the captured vessels for our use. I would send my brother, John, and Ben Foster."

"Very well. London can go with them. The Provincial Congress has moved to Watertown to avoid the British in Boston. It's the safest place to deliver our report of the capture."

"You'll want to see these papers," said Jeremiah. Taking the papers found on the *Unity* from his waistcoat, he handed them to the reverend. "They show Ichabod Jones did not come just to trade. He was a contractor to the British forces in Boston."

"No wonder he hides in the woods," said the reverend. "No matter, we'll find him and confine him with the other prisoners."

Satisfied with the plan, Jeremiah bid them a good night and left to tell John and Ben of the mission they were to be sent upon. He was pleased with the day's events that might leave him with three ships and provisions from the *Unity* and *Polly* to feed the people of Machias. And he was pleased that Elizabeth's eyes never left him as he'd explained the battle to Reverend Lyon.

As he walked along the river, the moon bright in the night sky, the weight of the day settled on him. Victory had come, but at a cost—John McNeil's face flashed in his mind, the man's laughter silenced forever—and the war would not end here. This was only the beginning.

Tonight, all of Machias would celebrate. The air was already filled with the sounds of music, drums, and laughter, the glow of bonfires lighting the riverbank. Glancing behind him, he saw the liberty pole standing tall, its shadow stretching toward the river—a beacon of their defiance reflected in the moonlit waters. The British would seek retribution, and he must be ready.

IN THE DAYS that followed, Ichabod Jones straggled out of the woods to be arrested and held with the other prisoners, viewed by the Patriots in Machias as a traitor. A surgeon, William Chaloner, was brought to Machias from Nova Scotia, and went to work treating the wounded. Jeremiah's father persuaded Surgeon Chaloner to stay and become a part of the community, as the need was great. A Whig, like his friend Reverend Lyon, Chaloner agreed.

Unfortunately, he could not save Captain Moore, who succumbed to his wounds.

The enormity of what they had accomplished soon sank in. Sharing ale at the tavern with Ben Foster, Jeremiah sat back and spoke his thoughts aloud. "We have faced the Royal Navy and her guns with untested, untrained men armed with only a few muskets and pitchforks and won."

Ben pulled his pipe from his mouth to say, "It will go down in history, Jere—the first naval battle of the revolution. And we were a part of it."

"Aye. I shall never forget."

Jeremiah was kept busy fitting out the *Unity* as an armed cruiser using the weapons captured from the *Margaretta*. He'd made his brother, William, with whom he'd always had an affinity, his first lieutenant. His brother, John, had been asked to be first lieutenant to Ben Foster, who for the present was more captain than colonel. Confident the three ships they'd taken would soon be theirs, Jeremiah changed the *Unity*'s name to the *Machias Liberty*.

"Now that you're a captain of your own ship and a celebrated one at that," Elizabeth told him when she came to visit him while he was working on the *Liberty*, "I expect you will no longer be a lumberman."

His mouth twitched up in a grin. "There are enough lumbermen in Machias to keep the mills running so long as we need them. My brother, Gideon, will not leave his mill, but I expect he will rely more on your father. Those in Machias who are able sailors will join those of us going to sea. Our ships will be needed to protect our coast and keep the British merchants from delivering provisions to their soldiers in Boston. Come next month, the fishermen can no longer fish as they have before. Some have already approached me to serve on the *Liberty*. Isaac Taft wants to sail with me as soon as his wounds are healed."

"I remember him," said Elizabeth. "It's sad he will no longer be able to fish."

"There are many fish in the rivers in Machias, so fishing will continue, just not commercially for trade as before. Isaac will be an asset as a skilled seaman when the British come seeking revenge for the *Margaretta's* capture."

Her gaze flitted away as if the prospect worried her. "What will you do if they come?"

"Oh, they *will* come. They will want revenge, and we are conveniently close to the British provinces of New Brunswick and Nova Scotia. When they come, we will meet them."

She turned to go and then looked back. "Will I see you in at services tomorrow?"

"You will. If you think of it, save me a seat next to you. I'd welcome the opportunity to sit beside you, Miss Fitzpatrick. Or, may I now call you Lizzy?" He had heard her siblings call her by that name.

That brought a wide smile to her face. "I will and yes, I suppose you may."

His gaze followed her lithe form as she walked back toward the Lyon house, her long red hair trailing down her back from under her straw hat, catching the sunlight like a river of fire. It was a rare day he didn't think of her.

Weeks later, John and Ben returned from Watertown

with news from the Provincial Congress. Jeremiah was on the *Liberty* working with his crew when they approached.

John's excitement was tangible. "The Congress has passed a resolution thanking you and Ben," he enthused, "and the brave men under your command for capturing the *Margaretta*."

"Those brave men include you," Jeremiah told his brother, who smiled at the compliment.

"Your victory is being hailed as the first naval victory of the war," said Ben. "The Congress has adjudicated and condemned the three ships as lawful prizes and our share of the prize money is twelve hundred pounds."

Astounded at the figure, Jeremiah said, "'Twas your victory, too, and that much money will greatly assist the town and our cause."

"News has spread, Jere," said John. "Everywhere, colonists are stirred to follow your great victory."

Jeremiah was pleased. "That is most welcome news. Did you ask the Provincial Congress for guidance and assistance in preparing for the British threat that will surely come?"

"We did," said Ben, "and they have offered to help with ammunition. They've also promised to coordinate with other coastal towns to watch for British movements."

Jeremiah nodded. "Good."

Ben took a look at the ship's stern and came back to Jeremiah. "I see you have changed the sloop's name."

"Aye, she'll now speak of what we fight for...liberty. She'll be the first armed cruiser of the American Revolution."

"A singular honor," said Ben.

"The Congress has ordered the prisoners be brought to them," said John. "They're sending a Lieutenant Styles of the Continental Army to Machias to accompany them to Watertown."

"We can use the help," said Jeremiah. "Meanwhile, now that you're back, Ben, I think the Committee of Safety should meet to plan the town's defense. As the commander of our militia, perhaps you might post a lookout at the entrance to Machias Bay to provide us notice of any British vessel headed for Machias."

"A good idea," said Ben, nodding. "I will see it done."

THAT SUNDAY MORNING, Machias' Congregational Church was filled with the low hum of voices as Elizabeth slid onto the rough-hewn plank seat beside Annie. Their father and Sean were on Annie's other side, leaving the place next to her free.

The *Margaretta*'s capture had brought a fleeting triumph, but the specter of British retaliation hung over the town like a storm cloud. She sensed it in the furtive looks the people gave the river.

Jeremiah slipped onto the bench beside her just as the opening hymn began, his breath quick, apparently from the rush to arrive.

She glanced at him with a teasing smile, his blue eyes—like her own—sparkling as he removed his cocked hat and set it beside him. "Late again, Captain O'Brien," she whispered, her voice soft but playful, mindful of the reverend's gaze. Like the rest of the town, she had taken to addressing him as "Captain" since his great victory.

He grinned, leaning closer, keeping his reply between them. "My work with the *Liberty*'s crew keeps me running, but I'd not miss a moment with you, Lizzy." His hand brushed hers on the wooden plank, a fleeting touch that sent a warmth through her.

Reverend Lyon began his sermon that spoke of courage and faith in the midst of trials, his steady voice a balm for the congregation, though many continued to cast wary glances toward the river. "They're half-expecting to see British sails on the horizon," she whispered to Jeremiah.

Throughout the service, Lizzy's thoughts drifted between the reverend's words and the worry over what would come next. Ben Foster's lookout at the bay's entrance had yet to report any British ships, but the threat loomed in everyone's mind.

She felt Jeremiah's gaze on her but resisted looking his way. She knew he would see yet another battle at sea, perhaps many. Silently, she prayed, *Lord, keep him and the others safe.*

After the service, as the congregation spilled out onto the grassy area between the meeting house and the river, Lizzy and Jeremiah lingered near the steps. He graciously acknowledged her father and siblings as they passed. Sean's look of adoration for the hero captain was one he had adopted with the *Margaretta*'s capture.

The summer sun was warm, but a cool breeze off the river carried the faint scent of salt and the distant murmur of the falls. Around them, townsfolk spoke in hushed tones, their eyes darting toward the east.

Lizzy retied the ribbon securing her hat, her expression sobering as she turned to Jeremiah. "I can't stop thinking about what you said—about the British coming," she murmured, her voice trembling slightly. "I witnessed the British cruelty in Onslow, and it makes me afraid for you and for all of us."

Jeremiah met her worried gaze. "I'll be careful, Lizzy—I promise," he said softly, his blue eyes steady on hers. "We are prepared to defend the town."

Her heart fluttered at his words, a fragile hope taking root despite her fear.

The familiar voice of Ben Foster called out as he approached, weaving through the townsfolk with a purposeful stride. His voice was low and urgent as he spoke to Jeremiah. Lizzy caught the words "lookout" and "Provincial Congress," her stomach tightening at the reminder of the danger ahead.

Jeremiah nodded, giving Lizzy a warm smile. "I'll see you soon," he said, his voice speaking certainty. As he turned to follow Ben, her eyes followed Jeremiah, his tall, straight form framed against the river, his shoulders squared, and his light brown hair confined in a queue reflecting the sunlight. Here was a Patriot to defy the British.

"We fight, get beat, rise, and fight again."
– John Paul Jones (1778)

CHAPTER 4

ON THE 10TH of July, the lookout Ben had posted at the entrance to Machias Bay came rowing upriver, breathless as he maneuvered his small boat against the wharf. "Captain O'Brien!" he shouted to Jeremiah, who was inspecting the deck of the *Liberty* with his brother, William. Hastily tying off his boat, the lookout said, "Two British schooners, the HMS *Diligent* and her tender, the *Tatamagouch*, are in Bucks Harbor at the entrance of the bay!"

Jeremiah leapt to the shore, his boots thudding on the wharf, and strode toward the lookout. "Tell me more, lad."

"The captain of the *Diligent* went ashore with two marines to inquire about the *Margaretta*. Having been forewarned, the garrison at Bucks Harbor detained them.

The captain made a fuss, but they are bringing him and the two marines to Machias as prisoners."

"Excellent! The garrison is to be commended for quick action." Jeremiah's pulse quickened. The British had come for their revenge, just as he'd predicted.

"Once arrested," said the lookout, "the British captain, Lieutenant John Knight, said he came to take back the *Margaretta* and bring the obstreperous Irish Yankee in for trial."

Jeremiah laughed. "He did, did he?" By now, the *Liberty* was equipped with five guns, ten swivels and a crew of forty ready for battle. Turning to his brother, Jeremiah ordered, "Gather the rest of the crew to be here at dawn tomorrow."

William went off to rouse the crew just as Ben Foster came running. "Is the news correct? We've British schooners in the bay?"

"Aye," said Jeremiah, "we do, and their captain made the unwise decision to go ashore where he was taken into custody by our alert garrison."

Ben lifted his hat and ran the back of his hand over his forehead. Above them the sun was beating down with intense heat, the air still. "Well, that will certainly help, giving us time. I've a small schooner and John waiting in East Machias. If the wind picks up and the tide's in our favor, we'll join you to capture the British vessels."

Jeremiah's jaw was tight with impatience. The British ships were an ever-present threat in Bucks Harbor, but Ben's schooner needed time to be ready for battle and Jeremiah needed to gather and prepare his crew. There was also the wind and the tide to consider. "I will await you tomorrow so we can strike together." Turning to the lookout, Jeremiah said, "Let the village know our plans, and then return to Bucks Harbor to confirm the British ships remain at anchor."

"Aye, aye, Captain."

Over the next two days, Machias buzzed with preparation. Finally, on the morning of the 12th, Ben's small schooner arrived where the *Liberty* was tied up on the river. Meeting onshore, Jeremiah said, "I've been thinking, Ben. Since the British have two ships, let's separate them. You take the tender, the *Tatamagouch*, and I'll take the *Diligent*."

Ben nodded. "Sounds good to me."

Sailing together, they arrived in Bucks Harbor to find the British schooner and its tender still anchored offshore, seemingly unprepared for battle. From what Jeremiah observed through the spyglass his father had gifted him after his capture of the *Margaretta*, the *Diligent* carried eight guns and twenty swivels while her tender, the *Tatamagouch*, carried sixteen swivels.

Jeremiah signaled to Ben, then turned to William. "Bring us alongside the *Diligent*, steady now."

The *Liberty* creaked as the crew maneuvered the sloop into position using the sweeps. The crew who were not needed for the maneuver gripped their muskets in tense anticipation. They had yet to receive any fire from the British schooner when Jeremiah and a contingent of the crew made a bold dash to leap aboard. The rest of the *Liberty*'s crew, who remained under the command of his brother stood ready to return fire.

Onboard the British ship, Jeremiah discovered a fair-haired young lieutenant, pale with shock. "Who's in command here?" Jeremiah demanded, his hand on his sword.

"Lieutenant S-S-Spry," the young man stammered, his eyes darting toward the shore where he'd likely last seen his captain. Then, his gaze shifted to the *Liberty* and Ben Foster's schooner, the crews bristling with muskets. To his inexperienced eyes, such a force must have seemed overwhelming without Knight to lead him.

"Captain Knight has been taken into custody," said Jeremiah. "He'll not be joining you, but you will be joining him. Strike your colors and surrender to the Sons of Liberty!" Jeremiah ordered, his voice ringing with authority.

Spry hesitated only for a moment, then gave over his sword and hauled down the colors, the British ensign fluttering to the deck. The *Diligent* had surrendered without any resistance. Jeremiah glanced across the water to see Ben's schooner alongside the *Tatamagouch*, her colors already struck in a similar bloodless capture.

Jeremiah remained aboard the *Diligent* with part of his crew to weigh anchor and take the schooner into Machias. On the tender, he could see Ben was doing the same.

As the four ships were proceeding up the river to Machias, the sun glinting off the water, they encountered Morris O'Brien and Surgeon Chaloner in a rowboat. "Ahoy!" Jeremiah's father shouted.

Jeremiah leaned over the *Diligent*'s rail. "What brings you here, Father?"

"I thought there might be bloodshed and a need for a surgeon."

Jeremiah grinned. "I thank you for your thought, Father, but there is no need. The British ships surrendered without a fight."

"Praise the Good Lord!" exclaimed his father.

As they arrived at the village, the people of Machias flooded the riverbank, cheering the return of the *Liberty* and Ben Foster's small schooner with the two British ships in tow. Once the prisoners were unloaded, Jeremiah was surrounded by his brothers and the townsfolk shouting their congratulations.

"The praise for our success today," he said to the crowd, "should go to our garrison at Bucks Harbor. Had they not taken the *Diligent*'s captain into custody, we might have faced a very different fight."

Ben Foster joined Jeremiah and, draping his arm over Jeremiah's shoulder, said, "You might as well accept the town's congratulations, O'Brien. Our crews returned unharmed with two British ships. It's a good day's work and, once the admiralty court adjudicates the prize, Machias will be richer for it."

Conceding the point, Jeremiah nodded, a smile tugging at his lips. "Aye, it will be."

It took him some time, but eventually he broke free to go to where Lizzy stood under a sprawling oak with her father, siblings and Reverend Lyon's family, their faces alight with the day's triumph.

"They are calling you the Machias Admiral!" shouted Sean, his face bright with excitement.

"Had the day not gone as it did, they could be calling me much worse," he replied with a grin.

"You've given Machias a victory to rally around," said

Lizzy, a lilt in her voice, "one that will bind us all to the cause of liberty." Jeremiah felt a flicker of warmth at the thought that she shared his vision of the larger fight.

Thomas Fitzpatrick, the only one in his family with brown hair, offered his hand in congratulations. "You've done well, Captain. We are all amazed."

Lizzy's sister, Annie nodded vigorously.

"Thank you," said Jeremiah. "How about the Fitzpatricks and the housebuilding? Does it go well?"

"Very well," said Thomas, "especially now that the mills are not running as much, though I regret that they are not. Gideon is helping me, and I've hired others to speed along construction. By the end of summer, the house should be finished, and I've hired a carpenter to build furniture for us."

Reverend James Lyon, in his role as head of the Committee of Safety spoke up then. "The Committee will be sending you and Foster to General Washington's headquarters at Cambridge with the officers and the news of these additional captures. You can drop off the rest of the prisoners at Watertown."

Jeremiah was excited at the prospect. "I would like to meet General Washington. I've admired him for some time. Perhaps I'll take John and William with me along with some of the crew to guard the prisoners."

"Take good care of your brothers," said Jeremiah's mother, Mary. "Bring them back whole."

"I will," Jeremiah said, as the story of baby John came to mind. Mary O'Brien and others at Scarboro were fleeing from hostile Indians as she carried John in her arms. The townspeople wanted her to leave the baby for fear his cries would be heard. She refused, hugging him tightly to her bosom. No cries were heard, and she saved his life.

"I just received Washington's first remarks to the troops at Cambridge," said Reverend Lyon. "They will be of interest to you." Pulling a paper from his waistcoat, he glanced at it and then looked up. "He declares they are now the Troops of the United Provinces of North America, or the Continental Army, as they're calling it. All distinctions of colonies are to be laid aside, so that one spirit may animate the whole in this great cause."

"A unified force for a unified cause," Jeremiah said, gazing into the distance. The words stirred in him a sense that Machias' fight was part of something greater, a cause that stretched from the rocky shores of Maine to the battlefields of Massachusetts and beyond. "I'll be interested to see how he fits our naval resources into that. If our little fleet can serve the general's vision, we'll make the British rue the day they sailed into Machias Bay."

"I'm quite certain they already do," said Lizzy's father with a smile.

Falmouth, Maine, late July 1775

A FORTNIGHT'S TRAVEL south in a small schooner, sailing cautiously in bad weather and staying close to the Maine coast to avoid British ships, brought Jeremiah to Casco Bay and the seaport of Falmouth one hundred miles north of Boston. As they secured the schooner on the dock, fishing boats arrived accompanied by shrieking gulls.

Jeremiah gazed at the waterfront and spotted a tavern large enough for their purposes. The sign in front of the two-story building with a sloping roof and dormer windows read "Marston's".

He sent John ahead to make arrangements. "A large private room if they have one for the prisoners would suit our needs."

Before heading inside, John pulled him aside. "Jere, on the way here, Isaac Taft spoke with the prisoners and learned three of them were cod fishermen impressed by the British into serving on their ships, one on the *Diligent* and two on the *Tatamagouch*. Isaac doesn't think they should be taken to Watertown."

Jeremiah's brow furrowed as his gaze passed over the three prisoners who stood apart with Isaac. "Do we know where their sympathies lie?"

"Aye, they are New England-born and sympathetic to the Patriot cause."

Jeremiah nodded slowly. "Very well. If they're truly with us, we cannot treat them as enemies, but we must be certain. I'll look for a way to separate them and ensure they're no threat." He turned to Isaac. "Let's keep the three apart from the others for now until we can sort this out."

Isaac saluted. "Aye, aye, Captain."

John ducked inside the tavern and returned a few minutes later. "The tavern has no large room save the common room, but there are empty tables enough for all of us."

"That will serve," he told John. "Keep them bound and together on one side, the officers near the door, well-guarded." Jeremiah followed the others into the tavern. The air smelled of salt, fish and ale, the light dim except for the tables near the windows.

The taproom's hum of conversation ceased as the prisoners filed inside. The customers, who appeared to be seamen and Patriots, sent them curious gazes. "These are British prisoners headed for Watertown," Jeremiah announced, gesturing to the group of sailors and officers, while Isaac kept the three Halifax fishermen to the side.

One customer yelled, "Good place for the king's men!"

Their curiosity satisfied, the tavern's patrons went back to their conversations, and Jeremiah relaxed.

Once the prisoners were seated and the officers under close guard near the tavern door, Ben ordered bowls of fish stew for everyone.

Jeremiah gathered Ben, John, William and Isaac at a corner table with a map of the colony spread before them. "It's taken us longer than expected to get to Falmouth with the bad weather, but now that we're here, we've two roads ahead. The prisoners must be taken to Watertown, except possibly the three you have identified, Isaac, as impressed Patriots. As for the officers, General Washington will want to see them." By now they had Lieutenant Knight, called "Captain" by virtue of his being in command, and Lieutenant Spry from the *Diligent* and Master's Mate Ellis from the *Tatamagouch*. "I say we split up. Ben and I will take the officers to Cambridge by horse to report to Washington. We'll take Isaac with us as a guard. John, you and William with the rest of the crew can take the prisoners to Watertown. With the British ships cruising offshore, 'tis too dangerous to sail south, so you'll have to go overland. 'Twill be longer but safer."

"I agree with your plan," said Ben, nodding. "As head of our militia, I want to meet Washington to let him know all we've done and that we stand ready to support him. The British officers we hand to him might have intelligence on British ships, and the general's men will want to question them. If we ride hard, we can get to Cambridge in three days' time."

A rotund man with chestnut hair, ruddy cheeks and a stained apron over his shirt and breeches approached the table with a tray containing bowls of hot stew. A lass, who came with him, carried a tray with mugs of ale. "My name's Brackett Marston," he said with note of pride in his voice. "This here's my tavern."

"Captain Jeremiah O'Brien and Colonel Ben Foster," Jeremiah said, introducing them, "and Isaac Taft and my brothers, John and William."

The tavern keeper shook Jeremiah's hand as his eyes grew large. "*The* Jeremiah O'Brien from Machias up north? The Patriot who captured the *Margaretta?*"

"Aye, the very one," said Jeremiah, "and Colonel Foster and these with me did their share to assure our success that day."

"'Tis an honor to have you in my tavern. Whatever you need, Cap'n, I'll see you get it."

Jeremiah sat back, a list forming in his mind, as the hearty scent of fish stew whetted his appetite. "We need six horses, as some of us are going to Cambridge to meet with General Washington."

"Aye, we've got horses at the livery on Queen Street.

I'll send a man to fetch 'em."

"Much appreciated," said Jeremiah, taking a large spoonful of the tasty stew. "And we'll need food for the road for those of us riding to Cambridge and more for those taking the prisoners to Watertown."

"Marching them to Watertown? You'll need provisions for a week. By the bye, you should know that on the 19th of July, the Provincial Congress was reorganized as the General Court."

"Well, that marks a new chapter in Massachusetts' governance," said Jeremiah.

The tavern keeper gazed at the prisoners. "For that lot, you'll need bread, salt fish and ale. It's on the house for the cause. You can leave your prisoners in the town jail for tonight. By tomorrow at dawn, you'll have everything you need, including the best route to Watertown to steer clear of the British. For tonight, you and your men can rest here upstairs in the tavern."

Jeremiah smiled at the tavern keeper. "Much obliged. Oh, and we have learned that three of the prisoners are cod fishermen out of Halifax, New England-born Patriots impressed by the British. Might you be willing to hold them here and, if what we heard proves right, release them?"

Isaac gestured to the three, who were sitting by themselves, watched over by a member of the crew. Jeremiah had to admit they looked more like fishermen than British sailors.

"Aye," said the tavern keeper, pursing his lips. "I'll have my man question them. If they prove false, we can turn them over to Cap'n Noyes of our Committee of

Safety. If they prove true, well, they'll be three more to fight the British."

"I am most grateful," said Jeremiah, "as I'm sure are those fishermen."

Isaac leaned forward to Jeremiah, "Thank you, Captain. I will let them know the good news."

"Wait till I tell the missus," the tavern keeper muttered as he walked back to the bar. "The hero of Machias in my tavern…"

John leaned forward. "William and I will gladly take the rest of the British sailors to Watertown, Jere. The crew will help guard them and keep them in line."

William grinned, his expression exuding confidence. "Aye, we've dealt with worse than a few British sailors. We'll see 'em to the Provincial Congress, er the General Court. Will you be joining us in Watertown?"

"We will," said Jeremiah. Clapping his brother on the shoulder, he added, "Colonel Foster and I might even beat you there." To John he said, "Take care on the road. Keep them bound and don't let them talk to any Loyalists. At Watertown, once you hand over the prisoners, take lodging at the Coolidge Tavern. The food's not much and the beds can be buggy, but as I recall, it's close to where the General Court meets. It's also a gathering place for Patriots, so you will be safe there. Nathaniel's widow, Dorothy, runs it now that her husband's gone, and she's generous with the rum. If we get there first, we'll take rooms for you. Once we meet up, we can report to the Congress together."

The next morning at dawn, true to his word, Brackett Marston had the horses, provisions and map for John and

William waiting for them. "You're a good man, Brackett," Jeremiah told him. "America is better for Patriots like you." Jeremiah paid the tavern keeper for the night's lodging and rental of the horses. "If you agree, we'll leave our schooner in your good hands and will claim it when we bring back your horses."

They shook hands and Jeremiah turned to his brothers. "Do you have everything you need?"

"Aye, we're ready," said John.

Jeremiah allowed Captain Knight to mount and then tied his hands. Swinging onto the back of the chestnut he would ride, Jeremiah took up the reins of his prisoner's horse. Ben and Isaac did the same with the two officers they would be taking to Cambridge.

He turned to see his brothers and the crew with the prisoners heading out for Watertown. He said a silent prayer, asking God to watch over them. Then he shouted "Godspeed!" as he and his companions rode off with their prisoners.

Cambridge, Massachusetts, early August 1775

IT WAS JUST after midday when Jeremiah and those with him entered the town center, passing Cambridge Common, a sprawling encampment filled with hundreds of tents and soldiers in all manner of dress. They had ridden hard from Falmouth, taking the safer route through Haverhill, Concord, and Lexington to avoid the British in Boston.

Pausing under the relentless August sun, Jeremiah

wiped the sweat from his brow, adjusted his hat to better shield his eyes, and gazed at the sight before him. Tents and a great company of men were scattered over the ground.

The air smelled of too many men gathered in one place and the faint tang of the Charles River marshes. Despite the hot day, women could be seen bent over cooking fires scattered among the tents. Fife and drum music echoed through the camp as a company of Connecticut militia drilled, their movements uneven.

Some distance on, Jeremiah's gaze narrowed on a young woman near a market stall where they were selling bread. Her red hair, bright as a flame, spilled from beneath her cap as she handed a loaf to a soldier. For a moment, Jeremiah's heart tightened and Lizzy's fiery locks flashed in his mind, her laughter echoing from the riverbank at Machias, a world away from this wartime camp. He could almost see her standing there, her blue eyes sparkling with mischief as she teased him about his latest work on the *Liberty*'s deck, her red curls catching the sunlight.

Their last conversation, just before he'd left Machias, had been brief but charged with a new warmth, giving him hope of a closer relationship when he returned.

Jeremiah and his companions rode on with their prisoners, passing soldiers in hunting shirts and cocked hats cleaning their muskets and mending clothing, while others sat near their tents playing cards. Still others drilled in response to shouted orders from officers.

The soldiers' gazes followed Jeremiah's party, their eyes focusing on the three British officers, whose blue coats were disheveled and dusty from days on the road, their white facings smudged with dirt. A low murmur rose from a group of militiamen nearby, one of them spitting into the dirt as he muttered, "Bloody redcoats."

Knowing they would likely see General Washington this day, Jeremiah and Ben had changed into clean clothes that morning. The comment had not been aimed at them.

Jeremiah shared a look with Ben, thinking he, too, must be wondering what their British prisoners thought of so undisciplined an army. The troops lacked uniforms, their muskets and hunting shirts a far cry from a professional army. But in their eyes, Jeremiah glimpsed a spirit undaunted by their recent loss at Bunker Hill that he and his companions had heard about in the taverns they'd frequented. The Patriots had lost the field to General Gage's British redcoats only because they ran out of ammunition and, unlike the British, their muskets lacked bayonets. Despite that, the British losses were twice those of the Americans, encouraging the Patriots.

And now, they have General George Washington to lead them. Jeremiah's chest swelled with pride at the thought.

Walking their horses along Brattle Street, a half-mile west of the Cambridge Common, they passed grand homes that spoke of Cambridge's wealthier days. From the look of things, many of the houses stood empty, their Loyalist owners having fled, but a few showed signs of life with curtains fluttering in windows and a woman tending a garden, her bonnet shielding her face from the sun. Likely these were now the homes of Washington's officers and staff.

Based upon the description they were given of Washington's headquarters, Jeremiah had no trouble recognizing the handsome two-story Georgian mansion painted yellow with black shutters that was Vassall House.

Jeremiah and Ben dismounted and secured their horses. Leaving Isaac to guard the three officers, they walked to the entrance where a Massachusetts militiaman in a brown coat holding a musket acted sentry. With a stern look, he saluted them. They returned the salute. "Captain Jeremiah O'Brien and Colonel Benjamin Foster with three British naval officers captured off Machias Bay for His Excellency. Colonel Foster and I and our companion, Mr. Taft, would also request a meeting with the general."

"Wait here," said the sentry. He went inside, returning minutes later. "General Gates will be here shortly to accept the prisoners."

A moment later, a stout and slightly stooped man with thinning gray hair, a long nose and ruddy cheeks stepped out. He wore a blue coat with white facings and brass buttons, and white breeches. A pink sash crossed his chest, which Jeremiah had learned marked him a brigadier general. "I am General Horatio Gates. I understand you have some British officers in custody." He glanced at the still mounted prisoners. Lieutenant Knight glared back.

"Yes, General, we do. I am Captain Jeremiah O'Brien and this is Colonel Benjamin Foster, leader of our militia in Machias, Maine. Attending to our horses is our companion, Isaac Taft."

The general smiled. "We know of Machias here. Were you the ones who captured the *Margaretta*?" In the general's voice, Jeremiah caught the hint of a British accent.

"Yes, sir."

"This is the second group of prisoners from Machias we've received," said the general, a note of approval in his tone.

"I transported those prisoners taken with the *Margaretta*'s capture in June," said Ben.

"Very good," said the general, inclining his head. "Ichabod Jones, a Loyalist from your town, has been in our custody since that time. Your actions have struck a significant blow against the British in the north."

"The British officers we bring you now are from two more British ships we have just captured," said Jeremiah.

"Two more ships!" the general exclaimed. "His Excellency will be glad to hear it."

"We captured their sailors as well," said Jeremiah, "but sent them with my crew to Watertown and the General Court. I knew General Washington, or perhaps you, would want to interview these three for what they might know about British ships."

"You were right, and General Washington's orders now require captured officers to be brought to headquarters. I'll get someone to take them off your hands and see to your horses. Meantime, I am certain General Washington will want to meet you."

A pair of Continental soldiers emerged from the house and saluted Gates before leading Knight, Spry, and Ellis away, their expressions grim. Isaac dismounted, handing the reins of their horses to a stable hand, who appeared from the side of the mansion, and then he joined Jeremiah and Ben.

General Gates bid them wait. A short while later, the sentry beckoned them to enter the mansion. Inside, the entry hall was cool and dimly lit, with polished wooden floors and a staircase leading to the upper rooms. A light-colored Negro, who Jeremiah judged to be in his twenties, approached. He wore a fine dark blue jacket with red collar and cuffs. "Good afternoon, gentlemen. I am William Lee, His Excellency's manservant. The main parlor," he said gesturing to the right, "serves as His Excellency's office, his command center. You may go in. He is expecting you."

They were met at the door by an elegant English Foxhound, her manner friendly, her tail wagging eagerly. Jeremiah reached out to pet her, thinking she had met many of the general's guests.

"Let the men in, Sweetlips," said the tall, statuesque man with a prominent nose and strong features, who stood by the window, his powdered hair tied back from his face. He wore a simple blue coat with a light blue sash across his waistcoat, signifying to all he was the com-mander in chief. Jeremiah judged General Washington to be in his mid-forties, of an age with Ben. His blue-gray eyes were sharp as they took in their small group.

"Your Excellency," said Jeremiah. "It is an honor to meet you."

"Liberty, when it begins to take root, is a plant of rapid growth."
– George Washington (1788)

CHAPTER 5

BEHIND THE GENERAL, sunlight from the window fell on a map of Boston and its environs spread across his desk, marked with pins and notes, a testament to the ongoing siege. "Captain O'Brien, Colonel Foster, Mr. Taft," Washington said, his deep voice carrying a Virginia accent that spoke of command. "Welcome. I understand you've brought prisoners from Machias."

"Yes sir," Jeremiah replied, stepping forward. "British officers of the schooner *Diligent* and her tender *Tatamagouch* out of Halifax. We thought they might have intelligence on British naval movements."

"Indeed, they might." Stepping close, the general offered a firm handshake to each of them. "Allow me to thank you and the brave Patriots in Machias. You faced

British guns to keep from Boston the lumber they coveted and, in the process, gained America three ships and now two more. The stories of your daring escapades have followed you, Captain O'Brien. They say you were the first to bring down the British colors on a Royal Navy vessel. Your victories have greatly boosted morale among the troops."

"Thank you, sir," said Jeremiah. "The three of us and our crews participated in the victories. There are many Sons of Liberty in Machias."

"So I hear," said the general, a small smile curving his lips. "Are you three free this afternoon?"

Jeremiah nodded. "Yes, sir, we are at your disposal."

"Then you must join me for dinner." Glancing out the paned window, he said, "Judging by the light, if you hurry, you'll have time to secure lodgings. I might recommend the Blue Anchor Tavern near Harvard Square. Return here at three when my generals and aides-de-camp arrive for dinner."

They thanked General Washington and departed, excited over the prospect of dining with him.

"A rare opportunity," said Ben.

"Just think of who will be there," said Isaac.

Jeremiah considered the men around Washington, the ones he had heard about. They'd already met General Gates. "We might see Major General Israel Putnam, who commands the reserve division. There are other generals, though not all will be in Cambridge. He has several aides-de-camp as well."

A brisk walk brought them to the tavern, a two-story wooden building with a sign hanging out front depicting a blue anchor. A lively place, its taproom was filled with soldiers from the Continental Army, Massachusetts and Connecticut militiamen in homespun hunting shirts and brown breeches, a few officers in uniforms, and a handful of locals. The hum of conversation permeated the air, as well as the clink of pewter mugs and the smell of ale, fish stew and tobacco smoke.

The walls were adorned with broadsides, notices, and a few prints. One picture hanging prominently above the fireplace immediately caught Jeremiah's eye. "Isaac, see about our accommodations, if you will, while I take a better look at this picture of the general."

"Aye, I'll see to it. Ben's ordering us some ale."

Jeremiah walked to the fireplace to stare up at the picture of the man he so admired. It depicted Washington as a colonel in the Virginia militia. The general's blue-gray eyes in a younger face looked into the distance, as if contemplating. He wore the uniform of the Virginia militia, a dark blue coat with red facings and silver trim, a red waistcoat and red breeches. On his left side, he carried a silver-hilted smallsword. On his head of dark hair was perched a cocked hat, and at his back was a musket or a fowler. In the background a blue sky rose above forest and mountains.

As Jeremiah studied the portrait, a man approached. "Afternoon, sir. I understand you are Jeremiah O'Brien. I'm John Haskell, the proprietor. I see ye are admiring the general's portrait."

"Yes, indeed," said Jeremiah, still staring up at Washington. Turning from the portrait to the tavern keeper, a man in his forties with dark hair and a weathered but friendly face, he said, "I'd like to have such a print for my home in Machias. It'd mean a lot to our people, knowing we're part of something bigger."

Ben and Isaac joined them. "It's a fine thing to have his image here," said Ben.

"The colors are not as bright at the original portrait," said Haskell, "or so I'm told, but I think 'tis a good likeness of the great man."

"Having seen him, I can agree," said Jeremiah.

Wiping his hands on his apron, the tavern keeper's face took on a pleased look. "Ye're in luck, Cap'n. I've got a few more copies in the back. Bought 'em from a peddler who came through last week, straight from a printer in Watertown. They're two shillings each, unframed, but I'll throw in a bit of cloth to keep it safe on yer journey. A man like yerself, who's taken British ships, ought to have the general's likeness to show for it."

Jeremiah pulled out a few coins and handed them to Haskell. "Done. I'll take one, and I'll see it hangs proud in Machias. America's army is fortunate to have so worthy a leader. Washington is an inspiration to all of us."

Haskell fetched the print from a back room and handed it to Jeremiah wrapped in a piece of coarse cloth. "Here ye are, Cap'n. Safe travels, and give the British hell when ye get back to Machias."

As Haskell walked away, Jeremiah carefully tucked the print into his satchel and accepted a tankard of ale from Ben. "I'll fight all the harder knowing his face is watching over us."

"We've rooms for the night, Jere," said Isaac, returning to them.

"Thank you," said Jeremiah.

A half-hour later, they returned to Brattle Street and Vassall House, arriving at three by the sun's descent. An amiable man, who appeared to be in his thirties, greeted them. Like Jeremiah, he had blue eyes, but his hair, tied back in a queue, was a darker brown. Beneath his blue jacket, across his chest he wore a green sash, which marked him an aide-de-camp to Washington. "You must be our guests," he said, "Captain O'Brien, Colonel Foster and Mr. Taft from Machias."

"Yes," replied Jeremiah, "and honored to be here."

"I am Colonel Joseph Reed, His Excellency's Military Secretary. Allow me to escort you into the parlor where the general is gathered with a few of his officers and staff."

"We are not late, I trust," said Jeremiah, worried such might be the case.

"Oh, no. Some met with the general earlier and others are yet to arrive."

In the parlor, General Washington, attired as he was earlier that day, stood on one side of the room, a glass of what appeared to be Madeira in his hand. A servant brought a tray to Jeremiah and his two companions, offering them some of the wine, which they accepted.

Washington's gaze turned to Jeremiah. Speaking in his deep voice, he said, "Captain O'Brien, Colonel Foster and Mr. Taft, welcome back. I have told those here of your victories over the British, though they were not unfamiliar with them. Before we dine, I would propose a toast to your bravery in Machias." Raising his glass, he said, "The capture of the *Margaretta* last month, and now the *Diligent* and *Tatamagouch*, have struck a blow against the British that echoes far beyond Maine. You've brought us not only prisoners but a spark of hope and ships to serve the cause of freedom."

The men in the parlor raised their glasses to the three of them. "To your bravery!"

Jeremiah inclined his head in acknowledgement, the words echoing in his mind, the commander in chief's commendation humbling him.

General Washington continued. "Allow me to introduce the men you see here who serve the cause of liberty with me. You have met General Gates, I believe." Gates, who had accepted their prisoners, lifted his glass to them. "Next to General Gates is Major General Israel Putnam, our reserve commander." Putnam who looked to be the oldest of Washington's generals, perhaps in his fifties, wore a purple sash, designating him among the highest ranking of them. Not a tall man, Putnam's silver curls framed his round face.

Jeremiah had heard of the general they called "Old Put", known for his courage under fire. The story was told he once tracked a wolf into his den to make sure the beast would never kill another of Putnam's chickens.

"General Charles Lee may join us later," said General Washington, "as he's riding in from Medford for tomorrow's council. Meantime, I want you to meet my aides-de-camp. You have met my Secretary, Joseph Reed, an accomplished lawyer and my right arm when it comes to communications. The other two standing with him are Major Thomas Mifflin and John Trumbull." All three men wore green sashes over their waistcoats.

Mifflin was of an age with Jeremiah, with dark eyes,

striking against his powdered gray hair confined to a queue. "Major Mifflin has been assisting with our quartermaster duties," said Washington, "and will soon take on that role officially. A very important post.

"Young Mr. Trumbull," said Washington, "is a talented artist and skilled at making maps so essential to our siege of Boston." Trumbull smiled at the general's praise. A handsome young man with dark hair and sparkling eyes, Trumbull was not yet twenty by Jeremiah's reckoning.

A servant entered from a side door and nodded to the general, at which point Washington led his staff and guests from the parlor to the dining room, a modest but welcoming space. The late summer air drifted through an open window, carrying the faint sounds of the encampment. The walls were lined with portraits of the house's former Loyalist owners, their stern gazes softened by the afternoon's warm light filtering in through the windows.

The large table was set with a simple meal: roast mutton, boiled potatoes, green beans, hasty pudding—a cornmeal mush with a drizzle of maple syrup—and brown bread. There were also two pitchers of ale. The aromas set Jeremiah's mouth to watering. The meal was likely the best the army's strained supplies could offer, but the blue and white Chinese porcelain on which the food would be eaten was elegant, perhaps left by the Vassalls.

As they took their seats, Washington's servant, William Lee, stood to one side, overseeing all.

General Washington sat at the head of the table, his demeanor reserved but attentive. To his right sat General Gates, his pink sash bright under his dark blue coat, his thinning gray hair catching the candlelight. To Washington's left was General Putnam, his broad frame filling the chair, his weathered face creased with a hearty smile as he recounted a tale from Bunker Hill.

Colonel Reed, Washington's secretary, sat next to Gates, his quill and notebook at hand, ready to jot down any pertinent details Washington would want to record.

Jeremiah and Ben sat mid-table across from each other, Jeremiah next to General Putnam. On Jeremiah's other side was a vacant seat, presumably held for General Lee.

Major Mifflin occupied a seat near the end of the table, his polished manners and easy smile putting the guests at ease. Isaac was seated next to Ben and across from Mifflin, his quiet presence a testament to his role in the Machias victories.

The youngest aide-de-camp, John Trumbull, sat at the far end of the table.

Sweetlips, Washington's foxhound, padded into the room just then, her black-white-and-tan coat gleaming as she sniffed the air, her tail wagging. She nudged Jeremiah's leg, prompting a chuckle from Putnam.

"Looks like Sweetlips has taken a liking to you, Captain O'Brien," Putnam said, his voice booming. "She's a fine hunter, just like her master. Ain't that right, General?"

Washington's lips curved into a smile as the hound returned to his side. The general reached down to pat her. "She's been with me since Virginia," he said. "A loyal companion in these trying times."

William Lee, who the general called "Billy" poured the first round of ale. General Washington then offered a prayer of thanks for the food. When the prayer ended, he gestured to the table with a nod. "Gentlemen, let us begin."

Taking up a carving knife, he sliced into the roast mutton and placed a few pieces on his own plate before passing the platter to Putnam, who followed suit. The guests, taking their cue, began serving themselves from the dishes before them.

General Putnam heaped a generous portion of potatoes onto his plate, grinning as he offered the platter to Jeremiah. "Good New England fare, eh, Captain O'Brien?" he said, his voice warm.

Jeremiah nodded. "Aye, reminds me of home, except these days we most often have pork." He added potatoes to the mutton he had already placed onto his plate, its savory aroma whetting his appetite.

Washington, ever the attentive host, spooned a small serving of hasty pudding onto his plate and passed the dish to Gates, who took a modest portion. "A fine meal for a soldier's table," Washington remarked, his tone appreciative, "though I daresay we'll need more than maple syrup to sweeten our prospects against the British."

Jeremiah savored the mutton, its simplicity a stark contrast to the elegant porcelain, and washed it down with a sip of ale. He added a portion of potatoes and a small helping of green beans onto his plate.

Across the table, Ben passed the green beans to Isaac, remarking on their freshness.

The shared meal, though humble, fostered a sense of camaraderie, the clink of forks and the murmur of appreciation filling the room as the men began to discuss the war's next steps.

General Gates leaned forward, his expression serious. "Captain O'Brien, Colonel Foster, I'd like to hear more about your capture of the *Diligent* and *Tatamagouch*. The officers you brought us may have valuable intelligence on British naval plans, especially with the threat to our coastal towns."

Jeremiah nodded, setting down his mug of ale. "I will gladly recount that capture, though you might be disappointed as it bore little resemblance to the violent taking of the *Margaretta*. On the 12th of July, we spotted the *Diligent* off Machias Bay, a British schooner under the command of Lieutenant Knight. She was accompanied by her tender, the *Tatamagouch*. We suspected they had come for revenge and to retake the *Margaretta*. The *Diligent*'s captain made a fatal mistake coming ashore. Our garrison at Bucks Harbor took him prisoner."

Ben picked up the story at that point. "With the two British ships anchored in Bucks Harbor, we took the sloop we'd captured earlier, renamed by Captain O'Brien, the *Machias Liberty*, and a small schooner we'd armed after the *Margaretta* affair—and gave chase. Mr. Taft, recovered from the wound he received while capturing the *Margaretta* is with us today and now serves as one of Captain O'Brien's crew."

"When we arrived in the harbor," said Jeremiah, "the two schooners, though armed, appeared unprepared for a fight. I boarded the *Diligent* first with Mr. Taft and a few others, leaving the rest of my crew ready with their muskets. After words with Lieutenant Spry, who'd been left in command, I demanded he lower his colors and surrender to the Sons of Liberty, which he did."

"Impressive," said General Gates.

"The lieutenant left in command is young," put in Jeremiah, "and in the absence of his captain and facing our guns, was ill-prepared for a fight."

"It was the same for the *Tatamagouch*," offered Ben. "We then took the two ships back to Machias to the cheers of our people waiting on the riverbank."

"The General Court will want a full report," said Reed, pausing to butter a piece of bread, his quill resting beside his plate. "But the officers you brought us may know of British plans to retaliate against Machias or other ports. Falmouth is thought to be in their sights."

Washington's gaze sharpened. "Falmouth's vulnerability is a concern. The British navy has the means to strike our coastal towns, and we lack the ships to counter them. Your actions in Machias have given us a small advantage, but we must be prepared for their response."

The door opened, and a tall, lean-frame man entered clad in a blue coat with a purple sash, his hawkish features set in a determined expression.

"General Charles Lee," said Washington, "meet our Patriots from Machias."

General Lee offered his hand to Jeremiah, Ben and then Isaac. "Apologies for my tardiness, Your Excellency," he said, his British accent evident as he took the vacant seat near Putnam. "I just rode in from Medford. Are these guests from Machias the ones who captured the *Margaretta?*"

Washington inclined his head. "Indeed they are. Captain O'Brien and Colonel Foster and Mr. Taft have brought us three British officers recently captured in

Machias, along with news of their latest victory. We were just discussing the implications."

Lee's eyes gleamed with interest as he turned to Jeremiah. "Another naval victory, eh? I've long argued we need a proper navy to challenge the British at sea and to cut off their supply lines." Taking some mutton and potatoes onto his plate, he said, "Tell me, Captain—how did you manage to take these latest ships?"

Jeremiah quickly recounted the tale, and the table came alive with discussion, the clink of mugs and the warmth of shared purpose filling the room. Sweetlips rose and resettled at Washington's feet, her presence a quiet reminder of the man behind the general, while the conversation turned to the war ahead and the role Machias might yet play in it.

As the afternoon wore on, the light through the window softened, casting long shadows across the table. William Lee and a servant quietly cleared the empty platters, leaving space for the next phase of the meal. Washington's men appeared content to linger over their ale, as the conversation deepened while they debated strategies for the siege and the potential for a Continental Navy.

"The ships we have," said Jeremiah, "will be at the disposal of the Massachusetts General Court to defend the coast and seek out British merchants."

"Ah," said Joseph Reed, "privateers supporting the cause of freedom!"

"Precisely," said Jeremiah, "though we have yet to receive a commission."

His face taking on a contemplative look, Reed said, "I

have been considering a flag for such ships. Isn't the pine tree one of New England's symbols?"

"It is," interjected Ben. "A symbol of the Colony of Massachusetts since the 1600s."

"Many of the flags flown by the Patriots at Bunker Hill had a green pine tree on them," added General Putnam.

"The pine tree on a white background is the naval ensign of New England merchants," said Jeremiah.

Turning to General Washington, Reed said, "Perhaps it would make a good flag for the cruisers you are contemplating, Your Excellency. And I might suggest we add the phrase 'An Appeal to Heaven' from John Locke's treatise describing the right of revolution where there is no appeal on earth."

Washington nodded, his blue-gray eyes sharp. "The pine tree would make an excellent symbol for a privateer flag, and I like the phrase you would add, Joseph, since it is God to whom we appeal for victory in our cause for liberty."

Reed smiled. With a glance at John Trumbull, he said, "I shall ask our resident artist to sketch such a flag to hold in reserve."

"The Continental Congress in Philadelphia has yet to authorize a navy," said Washington, "though I've urged them to do so. Until then, privateers like you, Captain O'Brien, must needs be our navy. Every British ship you capture weakens their hold on the coast and brings us cannon, powder, and provisions we desperately need. What, may I ask are your challenges?"

"Mostly it's money to pay our crews and ammunition for our weapons," said Jeremiah. "The last two months we've been consumed with defending the coast, taking men from their regular jobs. We also need to raise a company to guard our port."

Major Mifflin nodded vigorously. "We recently discovered we have only enough ammunition for nine rounds per man. A truly alarming situation."

"That is something we keep close," cautioned Washington. "We would not want the British to know. And we are working diligently to remedy this with messages sent all over the colonies asking for ammunition and urging the conservation of what supplies we have."

"We will speak of the army's situation to no one," said Jeremiah.

Across from him, Ben nodded in agreement. "When we get to Watertown, which is where we'll go from here to meet up with our crew, we intend to ask the General Court for needed funds and ammunition ourselves."

"They should be receptive to your requests," said General Gates, "though I expect they are also low on ammunition."

"We also need funds for our men who were wounded in the battle to take the *Margaretta*," said Ben, "and for the town surgeon, who has recently joined us and will be bringing his family to Machias. In one case, we've a crew member's widow and six small children to care for."

"Our business used to be lumber and fishing," said Jeremiah, "which provided well for us, but with Boston's trade ended and the Fisheries Act barring our fishermen from the waters of Nova Scotia, Newfoundland and our coast, that has changed. Now, our mills are silent much of the time, and our fishermen must find other ways to feed their families. Mr. Taft was one of our best fishermen before joining my crew."

All eyes turned to Isaac. His expression serious, he said, "Captain O'Brien speaks the truth."

Washington, a hint of admiration in his smile, said, "Your courage is an example to us all. The British navy may rule the seas, but men like you can make those seas a perilous place for them." With a glance at his secretary, Joseph Reed, he said, "I'll write to the General Court and urge them to issue letters of marque—official commissions for privateers—to men like yourselves."

Reed scratched away on his pad.

Jeremiah said, "We would be most appreciative, sir."

Washington sat back, nodding slowly. "We need a fleet of such vessels to harass their supply lines, to capture their ships, and bring us the resources to sustain this army. You've already done much, but I suspect your work has only begun."

Jeremiah nodded his head in agreement, for he had the same thought.

As the conversation turned to the broader war effort, William Lee served apple dumplings from a large tray, the warm scent of baked apples and pastry filling the room. Washington poured a small glass of Madeira for each man, the golden liquid catching the light of the candles, which had been added as the afternoon faded into evening.

"Here in Cambridge," said Washington, "we face a siege that may last months. The British are fortified in Boston, and we lack the artillery to drive them out. Though young Henry Knox, who is with General Ward, has an idea to obtain some." Pausing, his gaze fixed on

Jeremiah, he said, "My men are brave, Captain O'Brien, but most are farmers, shop keepers, laborers and craftsmen, not soldiers. Discipline is poor, and diseases, such as dysentery and smallpox, are taking a toll. We need victories to sustain their spirits."

"In Machias," said Ben, "my men in the militia praise your leadership, and that of the officers serving you. They believe, as Captain O'Brien and I do, that with God's help, you will lead America to victory."

Jeremiah nodded. "We've got sailors and shipbuilders who know the coast better than any British captain, Your Excellency. Even the *Margaretta's* captain had to take a local captain onboard to navigate our waters with their mudflats and rocks. If we are given the authority to act as privateers, we will continue to capture their merchant vessels."

"I believe you will," said Washington. "And I'll do all I can to support you. In time, the Continental Congress will come to see the value of privateers in this fight. For now, know that your actions have not gone unnoticed. I'll ensure your report reaches Philadelphia, and I hope to dine with you again, perhaps after another victory on the sea." Raising his Madeira, he said, "To the men of Machias, and to the privateers who will help us win this war. May your sails be swift, your aim true, and your courage unwavering."

"To victory for America and to liberty!" said Jeremiah, raising his glass with Ben and Isaac.

Echoes of "To victory and to liberty!" sounded around the table.

Not long after, Jeremiah and his companions left Vassall House, buoyed with the encouragement they had received. The dinner had stretched on nearly three hours, and by the time they left, the sun had begun its descent in the western sky, casting a golden glow over Cambridge.

As he stepped into the cooler evening air, Jeremiah felt a renewed sense of purpose. Washington's words had lit a fire within him, making him determined to secure the support they needed in Watertown.

The next morning dawned warm and hazy, the sun climbing into a cloudless sky as Jeremiah, Ben and Isaac set out from Cambridge on horseback. They rode west along the dusty road to Watertown. The heat of the day began to build, the humid air thick with the drone of cicadas and the scent of goldenrod blooming vibrantly along the roadside.

The journey would be a short one, just four miles, and within an hour, the landscape shifted from Cambridge's scattered homes and encampments to the rural outskirts of Watertown, one of the earliest of the Massachusetts Bay Colony settlements. Fields of ripening corn and hay already harvested stretched out on either side, shimmering under the August sun, while orchards heavy with early apples offered patches of shade.

As they neared the town center, the road widened into a dusty thoroughfare, bordered by the Watertown Common, a grassy square shaded by ancient oaks. The tall steeple of the First Parish Church, the temporary seat of the Massachusetts General Court, pierced the sky, rising above a cluster of modest wooden buildings.

The town hummed with activity. Men in militia coats and homespun shirts moved purposefully toward the church doors, some carrying papers or muskets, while townspeople, a woman with a basket of vegetables, a farmer driving a cart of hay, went about their tasks. A group of boys chased each other across the Common, their laughter mingling with the low murmur of conversation from a cluster of delegates outside the church.

The air was heavy with the earthy scent of the nearby Charles River and the dust kicked up by passing horses. Jeremiah reined in his horse, wiping his brow as he took in the scene. It had been four days since he'd bid his brothers, John and William, Godspeed in Falmouth, where they'd all arrived by schooner with the British prisoners. The memory of their parting, the weight of their shared mission, lingered in his mind. "If they held to the schedule, John and William should arrive by tomorrow," he said, glancing down the road behind them.

Ben adjusted his hat, squinting against the sun. "Watertown's a busy place for a small town," he observed, his gaze sweeping over the modest wooden buildings that appeared to be homes, but there was also a tavern with a faded sign and a blacksmith's shop with smoke rising from its chimney. "'Tis likely they're feeling the war here as much as we are in Machias."

Isaac, ever quiet, nodded, his eyes on the church. "That's where we'll make our case," he said softly.

Jeremiah nodded, turning to look at the place where the General Court met. "We'd best secure our lodgings at the Coolidge Tavern first. I told John we'd be staying there."

He urged his horse forward, the trio riding past the Common toward the cluster of buildings along the main road. Jeremiah's mind was fixed on their mission. They must secure the support needed to continue their fight against the British, and to ensure the sacrifices of the people of Machias were not in vain.

"The battle, sir, is not to the strong alone; it is to the vigilant"

– Patrick Henry (1775)

CHAPTER 6

A MILITIAMAN IN a blue coat, leaning against a fence, looked up as Jeremiah and his companions reined in their horses. "Need a place to stay, sirs?" he called, his voice friendly but tinged with the weariness of a man accustomed to war.

"Aye," Jeremiah replied. "Can you direct us to Coolidge Tavern? It must be close."

The militiaman nodded, gesturing down the road. "Just a bit farther, on your right. Look for the wooden sign with a mug of ale on it. Plenty of folk there, what with the Congress in session."

"Thank you," Jeremiah said, tipping his hat. The trio continued down the road, the sound of their horses' hooves hitting the packed dirt. Within moments, they spotted the tavern: a two-story wooden building, its white paint weathered, with a sign bearing a mug of frothing ale swinging gently in the breeze. A few horses were tied to a post outside, and the sound of laughter and conversation spilled from the open windows.

They dismounted, tied up their horses, and stepped inside. The taproom of Coolidge Tavern was a warm, dimly lit space, the air thick with the scent of ale, roasted meat, and wood smoke from the hearth. Wooden tables and benches were scattered about, occupied by a mix of locals, militiamen, and a few men in finer coats, likely delegates to the General Court.

A woman in her late forties, with a sturdy frame and graying hair pinned neatly under a cap, approached them from behind the bar. Wiping her hands on her apron, her brown eyes took them in with a practiced glance.

"Welcome to Coolidge Tavern," she said, a faint smile softening her weathered features. "I'm Dorothy Coolidge. You'll be needing a room, I reckon?"

"Aye," Jeremiah said, removing his hat. "More than one if you have them, Ma'am. I'm Captain Jeremiah O'Brien, and these are my companions, Colonel Benjamin Foster and Mr. Isaac Taft, from Machias."

Dorothy's eyes lit up with recognition at the mention of Machias. "Machias, you say? I've heard of your victories. The *Margaretta*, wasn't it? Word travels fast in these parts, especially with the Congress meeting here."

"Kind of you to say so," said Jeremiah. "Yes, we are from that Machias. We'll need a room beginning tonight. My brothers, John and William, and some of our ship's crew should arrive tomorrow. They are bringing prisoners for the General Court from British ships we recently captured."

The widow's smile widened. "You'll find a warm welcome, Captain. I've got a room upstairs you and your companions can share, and I'll have the stable boy see to your horses." She gestured to a serving girl, who hurried over with a tray of mugs. "First ale's on the house for Patriots like yourselves. And tomorrow we'll find rooms for your brothers and crew."

"Thank you," Jeremiah said, accepting a mug with a nod. The ale was cool and bitter, a welcome relief after the hot ride. Ben and Isaac took their mugs as well, the three of them settling at a table near a window, where they could keep an eye on the street.

As they drank, the hum of conversation around them painted a picture of Watertown's wartime reality. At a nearby table, two militiamen spoke in low tones about the Siege of Boston, their voices tense. "General Washington's got the British pinned, but he needs powder," one said, shaking his head. "All the colonies are being asked to send more."

Across the room, a man in a dark coat, likely a delegate, argued with a companion about the need for a navy. "Washington's right," he said, his voice rising. "We can't let the British control the seas. Privateers like those Machias men could turn the tide." Jeremiah exchanged a glance with Ben and Isaac, a flicker of pride in his chest at the mention of their efforts.

After finishing their ale, Jeremiah stood, adjusting his coat. "We can leave our satchels upstairs in our room and then make ourselves known to the General Court. I expect they'll want to make arrangements for the prisoners arriving tomorrow."

The trio left the tavern a short while later and walked back to the First Parish Church, the heat of the day still pressing down despite the shade of the oaks along the Common. Before they reached the church, Jeremiah brushed his coat free of the dust he had gathered from the road.

At the church door, a young militiaman in a blue jacket stood guard, his musket resting against his shoulder. He straightened as they approached, eyeing them from beneath his cocked hat with a mix of curiosity and caution.

"We're here to see the General Court," Jeremiah said, keeping his tone respectful. "I'm Captain Jeremiah O'Brien of Machias, with Colonel Benjamin Foster and Mr. Isaac Taft. We've come to report on our captures of British ships and to let the delegates know our prisoners will arrive tomorrow."

The guard nodded, stepping aside to let them enter. Inside, the church was simple but spacious, its wooden pews filled with delegates in discussion, their voices echoing off the high ceiling. A clerk, about Jeremiah's age, thin and with spectacles perched on his nose, approached them from a table near the pulpit, a quill in hand.

"O'Brien, you say? Captain Jeremiah O'Brien?" the clerk asked, peering at them over his spectacles. "We've had word of your actions in Machias. You've caused quite a stir. I'm Samuel Freeman, newly appointed Secretary to the General Court. President James Warren is in session now, but I can arrange for you to speak with him tomorrow, once your prisoners arrive. How many are you bringing?"

"There are fourteen left now," said Jeremiah. "We have already presented the officers to General Washington in Cambridge, and there were three who were New England-born and impressed by the British, who we released. My brothers, John and William, are escorting the rest from Falmouth, along with some of our crew."

Freeman nodded, jotting a note in his ledger. "Very well. We'll make provisions for the prisoners and expect you tomorrow. In the meantime, I suggest Coolidge Tavern as a fine place to stay, if you haven't already found it. It's General Washington's favorite."

"We have secured rooms there, thank you," Jeremiah said, tipping his hat. "We'll return tomorrow."

As they stepped back into the sunlight, Jeremiah pondered the next day. They would make their case to the General Court, a case that could shape the future of Machias. "Tonight," he told his companions, "we should prepare a petition that details our situation in Machias, including our needs and a tally of expenses we've incurred."

Back at the Coolidge Tavern, over dinner Ben transcribed Jeremiah's words to the court that described their desire to guard their port and protect their coast. He documented their need for powder and ball to render a credible defense. Jeremiah concluded with, "We humbly pray your Honors would supply us with two hundred weight of powder and balls in proportion."

"I've been keeping an account of the charges we've incurred to transport the prisoners to Cambridge and

Watertown," said Ben, "to which we'll add John and William's expenses. We can ask the court to reimburse us."

"Aye, we must give the court a complete accounting, including the expenses of fitting out the sloop and schooners," said Jeremiah, "and of keeping the crews employed."

"We should ask for the estate of Ichabod Jones," said Ben, "so that it can be sold to help the widow of John McNeil and his six children left destitute, as well as others wounded in the seizure of the *Margaretta*."

"I agree," said Jeremiah. "And there are the expenses of obtaining a surgeon to tend the wounded."

Isaac nodded his agreement, as Ben scratched away with quill and ink.

"I've another thought," said Jeremiah. "Our visit with General Washington reminded me that our officers need commissions as well as our ships, so that we act with authority, else if we are taken by the enemy—and I pray it never happens—we will be treated as pirates. With the proper papers, the British can never deny our status as prisoners of war."

"A good idea," said Ben.

When the petition was completed and the list of expenses drawn up, Jeremiah signed the document and Ben added his signature.

"We must pray the court grants our petition and reimburses us for expenses and wages," said Jeremiah, "so we can pay the men and provide the defense of Machias." Content he had done all he could, before he crawled into bed, he asked God to give them favor in the eyes of the court. Despite his anxiety for the next day and the biting insects that always annoyed at this time of year, he fell fast asleep.

The next day at noon, John and William arrived in good spirits and with all the prisoners in tow. Most were seamen, their faded blue and gray jackets torn and dirt-streaked, their trousers worn from the journey. Among them, two marines stood out, their red coats, once bright with white facings, were now faded and dirt-smudged, a stark contrast to the blue and homespun of the Machias men who flanked them.

Relieved at seeing his brothers and the crew, Jeremiah said, "You've done well. Did you have any problems?"

"No," said William. "The route the Falmouth tavern keeper provided was a good one, and the prisoners gave us no trouble."

Smiling, John added, "Better to be fed by us than loosed into a countryside filled with Patriots."

Jeremiah laughed. "Indeed."

Ben turned to John and William. "The General Court said they would make arrangements for the prisoners, so we might as well deliver them now."

Once Jeremiah and his companions were refreshed with ale and his brothers' expenses added to those already tallied, they marched the fourteen prisoners back to the First Parish Church, their footsteps heavy on the dusty road as the midday sun beat down on Watertown. Jeremiah kept a watchful eye on the group, ensuring his crew maintained a firm but fair grip. "Keep them moving," he said to John, his voice low but steady. "We'll not mistreat them, but they'll not have a chance to bolt either."

As they walked to the church, Jeremiah noticed militiamen in blue and homespun coats patrolling the streets, their muskets slung over their shoulders, while a group of women hurried past with baskets of bread, perhaps heading to feed the growing number of refugees fleeing Boston. The air carried whispers of British reprisals, the name "Falmouth" on more than one tongue, causing Jeremiah to worry about the vulnerability of the coastal towns.

At the church door, the young militiaman again stood guard. He straightened at the sight of the prisoners, his eyes narrowing as he took in the marines' red coats among the seamen's faded maritime garb. "Captain O'Brien," he said, recognizing Jeremiah from the day before, "are these the British you promised?"

"Aye," Jeremiah replied, his tone firm. "We're here to deliver them to the General Court."

The guard stepped aside, calling into the church, "Mr. Freeman, the Machias men are here with the prisoners."

Moments later, Samuel Freeman emerged, his dark coat slightly rumpled from what must have been hours at his desk, his spectacles glinting in the sunlight. At his side was a militia captain, a tall man with a strong face beneath his cocked hat, his blue coat adorned with a single epaulet. Freeman introduced him. "This is Captain Wheeler. He'll take charge of the prisoners."

Wheeler surveyed the group with a stern gaze, then gestured to a squad of militiamen waiting nearby, their muskets at the ready. "We'll house them in the old Thompson barn on the edge of town," he said, his voice gruff. "They'll be under guard until the court decides their fate. Could be a prisoner exchange, if the British are willing." He turned to one of the marines, a broad-shouldered man with a sunburned face. "Any word of British ships off the Massachusetts coast?"

The marine shook his head, his voice low. "None that I know."

Wheeler grunted, seemingly unconvinced, but waved his men forward to take the prisoners. "They'll be secure," he said, turning back to Jeremiah.

"The court will want to hear from you, Captain O'Brien," said Freeman. "Did you have a petition you want considered?"

"We do," said Jeremiah, "and an accounting of our needs and expenses." Taking the papers from his waist-coat, he handed them to Freeman.

Freeman nodded, adjusting his spectacles. "Wait just inside while I show these to President Warren."

Jeremiah and those with him stepped inside the cool interior of the church. The hum of voices from the delegates filled the air as they debated powder, militia, and the war's next steps. Jeremiah felt the weight of the moment settle on his shoulders as he steeled himself to face the court, knowing their support could mean the difference between survival and ruin. Turning to Ben, he said, "I am glad Warren will take time to read what we have brought him. Perhaps he might even speak on our behalf."

He had asked Mrs. Coolidge that morning about Warren and learned that he was a merchant and a gentleman farmer from Plymouth, a close friend of John and Samuel Adams. "A radical Patriot," the widow described him.

It was not long before the clerk returned with a man of dignity and stature beside him, his face serious beneath a gray wig. He wore a long green coat over black waistcoat and breeches.

"President Warren," said Freeman, "these are the men from Machias whose petition you hold."

Jeremiah shook Warren's hand and introduced those with him. "My brothers, John and William, the leader of our militia, Colonel Foster, and members of my crew."

"Please come with me," said Warren. "We can speak better over here." He led them to one side of the room where an alcove provided some privacy. "I was not the president when you brought the first group of prisoners from the capture of the *Margaretta*, but I know of the enthusiastic reception your news received. Now you bring us more and two additional ships captured. This is splendid news. With your permission, I will set these facts and your petition before the court for their action."

"Of course," said Jeremiah. "We would be most grateful."

"Whatever you suggest," added Ben.

"Can you return in a few hours? All will be ready for you by then."

Jeremiah agreed, and he and his men returned to the tavern to hear from John and William about their travel to Watertown. It was clear from their enthusiasm that his brothers and his crew were proud of their achievement.

Two hours later, they retraced their steps to the church. The air inside was thick with the scent of wood polish and sweat in the heat of the day as the delegates continued to debate.

James Warren sat at the head of the room, his gavel resting on the table before him as he listened to a delegate arguing. "We need heavy guns to fortify Dorchester Heights," the delegate insisted, his voice urgent. "Without them, General Washington cannot hope to drive the British from the harbor!"

Samuel Freeman stood nearby, his quill scratching notes in a ledger, his spectacles reflecting the light streaming in through the windows.

When Freeman announced the Machias men, the room quieted, all eyes turning to Jeremiah and Ben, as they stepped forward, John and William joining them while Isaac and the other crew members stood behind them.

Jeremiah felt the weight of the men's gazes before him. He stood tall, his hat in hand. The brown woolen coat and ivory waistcoat he wore were a testament to his father's fine tailoring, and though weathered from his travels, told all he was a gentleman. "Mr. President, honored delegates," Jeremiah began, his voice clear despite the tension in his chest, "I am Captain Jeremiah O'Brien of Machias, here with Colonel Benjamin Foster, my brothers, John and William, and some members of my crew. We've come to report our captures of the British ships *Diligent* and *Tatamagouch*, subsequent to our capture in June of the *Margaretta*, and to present a petition for the defense of our town and the support of our privateering efforts. We have just come from Cambridge where General Washington gave us his endorsement."

"General Washington's letter of support arrived this day just before you returned," said Warren, his voice carrying over the murmurs of the delegates. "You and your men have done a great service to the cause. Machias stands as a bulwark on our eastern frontier, and your privateering has brought great victories. I have reviewed your petition and all seems in order. Your requests appear most reasonable. Why don't you review the details for the members of the court?"

Jeremiah nodded, stepping forward. "We humbly pray for two hundred weight of powder and balls to defend our port and continue our fight against the enemy. We've incurred significant expenses transporting prisoners to Cambridge and Watertown, fitting out the captured vessels, employing crews, and securing a surgeon for the wounded. We seek reimbursement for these costs and wages for our men. We also request commissions for our officers and ships, so we may act with authority and not be treated as pirates if ever we are captured. Finally, we ask for the estate of the Loyalist Ichabod Jones to be sold, the proceeds to support the widow of John McNeil, who was killed, and others wounded in the *Margaretta* affair."

The delegates murmured among themselves, some nodding in approval, others frowning at the mention of powder. A delegate in a dark coat stood, his tone measured. "The captures at Machias are a testament to the courage of these men. I move we grant their requests, though our powder stores are stretched thin. Half the amount—one hundred weight of powder and balls in proportion—can be spared to be delivered to them by the Committee of Supplies."

Another delegate, who Jeremiah thought a farmer with his sun-browned face, rose. "The expenses and wages should be paid. And these men must be recognized as lawful privateers protecting our coast under our authority."

A third delegate, possibly a merchant who had a sharp gaze, added, "The estate of Ichabod Jones should be confiscated and sold, as requested, to support the Machias widow and injured. It's a just use of a Loyalist's property."

Warren nodded, his expression one of careful consideration. "There is more to consider," he said, his voice firm. "The actions of Captain O'Brien and his men have shown the value of a naval force on our eastern coast, particularly as we can anticipate British revenge for these victories. I propose we appoint Captain O'Brien as a Captain of the Marine of the Massachusetts Colony, and name him Commander in Chief of the vessels *Machias Liberty* and *Diligent*, to be fitted out under his supervision at Machias and employed to cruise against the enemy's vessels along the New England coast, thus making him the commander of the first American naval 'flying squadron' of the War of the Revolution."

The room erupted in a chorus of "ayes," and a delegate in the back called out, "And let us pass a resolution of thanks to Captain O'Brien, Colonel Foster, and their men, for their bravery in taking the British ships!" This proposal was met with more affirmations, the delegates' voices rising in agreement.

A lump formed in Jeremiah's throat and he pressed a hand to his chest. God had answered his prayer, for they had given him more that he expected. So much more.

Warren banged his gavel, sealing the decision. "The petition is granted," he declared, looking to Jeremiah with a rare smile. "Be it resolved, as follows: There be paid out of the public treasury of this colony to Captain O'Brien, for the purpose of guarding the sea coast, the sum of one hundred and sixty pounds lawful money of this colony for supplying the men with provisions and ammunition, and there be delivered to said O'Brien one hundred weight of powder, one hundred cannon balls of three pounds weight each and two hundred swivel balls. Commissions for Captain O'Brien's officers and ships will be issued. Captain O'Brien is hereby appointed a Captain of the Marine of this colony, and Commander in Chief of the *Machias Liberty* and *Diligent*, to cruise against the enemy along our coast. The estate of Ichabod Jones is approved for sale, the proceeds to be used as proposed. Finally, this Congress passes a resolution of thanks to Captain O'Brien and his men for their service to the cause of liberty."

The delegates stood as one and applauded, a rare moment of unity in the fractious assembly. Half the powder they requested might not be enough. It would force them to stay close to the coast, but that would mean more time in Machias and more time with Lizzy, God willing. The commissions, the command, and the resolution of thanks filled him with pride, and the reimbursement would keep his crews paid and his mission alive. Raising his head, he said, "Thank you, Mr. President, honored delegates, we'll not let you down."

As they gathered their belongings to depart, Samuel Freeman approached, his ledger tucked under his arm. "Captain O'Brien, Colonel Foster," he said, his voice warm, "a word before you go."

They turned to give him their attention. Freeman

adjusted his spectacles. "Since Machias lies so far north, the court deems it fitting to establish an admiralty court there…a judge who, with the assistance of merchants or town leaders, can adjudicate your prizes expeditiously."

"That is wonderful news," said Jeremiah. "We have men like Colonel Foster here, who could serve."

"Excellent. And mark this," he said to Ben, "the proceeds are one-third to Massachusetts, one-third to the ship owner, and one-third to the crew."

Jeremiah nodded, committing it to memory.

Beside him, Ben said, "Sounds right."

"Do you return to Machias now?" asked Freeman.

"Yes, but first we must stop at Falmouth," Jeremiah replied. "We've a schooner to retrieve, and a few errands to see to before we return to Machias."

Freeman's expression shifted, a flicker of concern crossing his face. "Falmouth is my home," he said softly, his gaze distant. "I fear for it, Captain. The British won't take kindly to our resistance. All our coastal towns are at risk. They'll seek revenge, mark my words. I pray you'll find it safe when you arrive."

Jeremiah nodded. "We'll be vigilant, Mr. Freeman. And we'll do our part to keep the coast secure."

Freeman offered a small, grateful smile. "Godspeed, then. And give my regards to the folks at Marston's Tavern. Tell Brackett I'll be home soon, if the war allows."

As they left the church, Ben clapped Jeremiah on the shoulder, a grin on his face. "A Captain of the Marine, and Commander in Chief of a flying squadron," he said. "You've earned it, Jeremiah."

"Aye," John added, his eyes bright. "And with the *Liberty* and *Diligent*, we'll make the British rue the day they sailed near our coast."

Jeremiah nodded, a question on his mind. "Ben, would you have wanted to be named a commander as well?"

"No, Jere. The militia is my calling. I'll remain on land and make sure our garrison is ready for action while you and your brothers go to sea. And with your many captures, my role as admiralty judge will keep me busy. However, there is a man I would recommend to take command of the *Diligent*—John Lambert. You know him to be a worthy captain with experience, and I believe he will accept the position."

"Aye, he would be a good choice," said Jeremiah. Lambert was young but experienced. Turning to his brother, John, he asked, "Would you be willing to serve under him?"

"I would," said John without hesitation.

"Then before we leave, I will add his name to the list of those for whom we seek commission," said Jeremiah.

"Yes," added Ben, "he'll need one."

Satisfied, Jeremiah's thoughts turned to the journey ahead. They'd provide a list of officers for Freeman and make arrangements to receive the ammunition and money, then head to Falmouth where they would retrieve the schooner they'd left with Brackett. As he thought of the bustling port of Falmouth, a few things came to mind that he still had to do before returning to Machias.

A week later, they arrived in Falmouth as the sun was dipping low. Weariness was written on the faces of his companions. They were all exhausted from the trip from

Watertown. Some of them rode and some walked, often trading positions for fairness.

Jeremiah dismounted as the rotund tavern keeper came outside to greet them wearing a broad grin. Brackett Marston had changed little in the time they'd been gone, except his apron bore further evidence of his serving food for his customers.

Jeremiah dismounted, as did Ben and John. "I told you we would return the horses," said Jeremiah, "and here we are."

"Good to see you back, Cap'n." The tavern keeper's eyes scanned the men with Jeremiah and Ben. "I thought it was about time you'd be coming our way again. We'll stable these horses—glad to have 'em returned safe." Summoning a boy to take the horses, he said, "Have your men take a seat inside and I'll see they have ale."

Following Jeremiah into the tavern, Brackett wiped his hands on his apron and asked, "How was the trip?"

Jeremiah couldn't resist a smile thinking of all they had accomplished. "Very successful."

Beside him, Ben said, "O'Brien is too modest. The General Court named him Commander of the *Machias Liberty* and the schooner *Diligent*, and, in recognition of his exceptional abilities as a naval officer, made him Captain of the Marine of Massachusetts Colony, so his title is now official."

"More importantly," said Jeremiah, "they granted our petition for ammunition and our expenses."

"Very good," said Brackett. "I expect you're all famished."

"Aye, it's been a long day," said Jeremiah, as the group

settled at a large table in the common room, the air thick with the scent of wood smoke and roasting meat.

"Then I'll see you fed well, and I think I can find rooms for all of you, but some will have to share."

"Sharing rooms will not be a problem," said Ben. "We did it in Cambridge and Watertown."

Brackett brought out a hearty meal: a steaming pot of boiled cod laced with chunks of salt pork, a roasted leg of mutton seasoned with thyme, and sides of boiled potatoes, corn on the cob, and stewed beans. Two pitchers of hard cider were placed in the center of the table. For a touch of sweetness, Brackett offered a bowl of blueberries.

Isaac, who'd walked most of the way, grinned as he dug into the mutton. "Worth the trek, this is," he said, passing a plate to William, who'd taken a turn riding.

John nodded, sipping his cider. "Aye, and a fine welcome."

Brackett stood watching them as they began to eat, his hands on his hips. "Just so you know, Cap'n, you'll not be paying for tonight. The food and the rooms are on the house for all you have done for the cause."

Jeremiah was humbled by the tavern keeper's generosity. "You are more than kind, Brackett. My men and I thank you. And by the way, Samuel Freeman, the clerk at the General Court, asked me to give you his tidings. He hopes to join you soon."

"He is a good friend," said Brackett. Then the tavern keeper pulled up a chair next to Jeremiah. "Ye can sing for your supper, meaning I want to hear about your visit with General Washington and your meeting with the General Court."

"A fair bargain," said Jeremiah. Whereupon he and Ben recited as much as they could recall of their dinner with Washington, omitting the part about the severe ammunition shortage. When they got to the story of meeting with the General Court, Jeremiah's brothers and the crew chimed in with their contributions.

"The court must have been impressed with your petition," said John, "for they granted you all you asked for."

"Not all," said Jeremiah. "Only half the ammunition, but these are hard times."

"We didn't ask for the accolades," put in Ben. "Those were freely offered."

Brackett appeared to enjoy their stories. He thanked them and, as he rose to leave the table, Jeremiah said, "Brackett, I would ask your help in a matter."

"Anything," he said.

"I need to find a surgeon to join the crew of the *Machias Liberty*. We'll be sailing into dangerous waters in the months ahead, and we'll need to be prepared to treat our wounded. Is there a man who might meet our need and be interested?"

Brackett's brows furrowed as he thought. Finally, he said, "Enoch Freeman, who leads our Committee of Safety will know. I'll send him word of your need and tomorrow morning we'll see what he says."

"The women of America have at all times
exhibited a vigor of mind, a firmness of resolution,
and a degree of patriotism, which will do honor to
their character in all future ages."
– Abigail Adams (1777)

CHAPTER 7

THE NEXT MORNING, Jeremiah broke his fast with his companions in the taproom of Marston's Tavern. The scent of fresh-baked bread and boiled oats mingled with the salty air of the nearby harbor, a reminder of the sea that awaited them. The sun streamed through the windows, casting its light across the rough-hewn tables.

Brackett Marston bustled about, serving steaming bowls to the handful of early risers, including Jeremiah, his brothers, John and William, Ben Foster, Isaac, and the half-dozen crew members, all enjoying the beginning of their day of rest before the journey back to Machias.

A tall man entered, dressed in a brown jacket and

breeches, his golden hair tied back at his neck under a cocked hat. Brackett approached him, wiping his hands on his apron. "Are you here for breakfast, sir?"

"Nae, I've already eaten, thank ye," the man replied, his voice carrying a light Scottish accent, the vowels soft and the "r" sounds gently rolled. Jeremiah detected a faint echo of the Highlands. "I'm here to see Captain O'Brien."

Jeremiah rose and crossed the few steps to the two men, his bowl of oats forgotten. "I'm Jeremiah O'Brien," he said, studying the taller man's honest, open face. "Who might you be?"

"Donald McDonald, a surgeon by trade." His tone was clear but with a subtle lilt. "I was born in Scotland, on Islay, but now I'm an American, trained in Philadelphia. Enoch Freeman tells me ye're lookin' for a surgeon to join your crew on the *Machias Liberty*. A fine sloop, I hear, with a name for takin' British ships."

Jeremiah liked the man's steady gaze, one that spoke of sincerity and resolve. "Aye, the *Machias Liberty* has taken more than one British ship. Did Mr. Freeman explain what we're about?"

"Aye, he did," McDonald replied, a spark of enthusiasm in his eyes. "He said ye're a privateer captain, named Commander of the *Machias Liberty* and the schooner *Diligent* by the General Court, tasked with protectin' our coast and huntin' British ships for the liberty of these colonies."

"You have it right," Jeremiah said, nodding. "It's dangerous work, but there's prize money in it if we take more ships."

"I've seen enough of British tyranny to want a wee

piece of 'em myself," McDonald said. "My grandsire lost his lands after Culloden, and I've watched the Crown press men into service here. I'll keep yer lads patched up, and I'm not afraid of a fight. When do we sail?"

His enthusiasm brought a smile to Jeremiah's face. "If Mr. Freeman recommends you and you're willing, I'd welcome you as one of my officers, commissioned alongside the rest of us by the Colony of Massachusetts." Jeremiah made a mental note to write the General Court asking for another commission. "My crew has today to rest. Tomorrow, we sail with the tide on the schooner tied at the dock, but when we return to Machias you'll be surgeon on the *Machias Liberty*."

McDonald gave a sharp nod. "I've a few things to tend to and a patient to see, but I'll be here early on the morrow, Captain."

They shook on it, McDonald's grip as firm as his resolve, but before he left, Jeremiah turned to his companions, raising his voice over the hum of the tavern. "Lads, meet our new surgeon Donald McDonald, whose job it will be to keep us whole on the *Machias Liberty* and the *Diligent!*"

The crew raised their mugs of cider in a hearty cheer, welcoming the Scot into their fold.

Jeremiah had a few errands before he set sail. Spotting Brackett conversing with a customer at the counter, he bid his companions a good day and crossed the room to the tavern keeper. "Is there a place in Falmouth where I might find a lady's gewgaws like hair ribbons?"

The tavern keeper considered for only a moment. "Aye. Moody's on Fore Street, not far from here. Nathaniel Moody runs the place himself. Just keep walking north along the waterfront and you'll see it."

The sun's rays shone on the wharves of Falmouth as Jeremiah stepped out of Marston's Tavern, the air still cool in the early hour. The waterfront bustled with activity—sailors hauling crates, fishermen mending nets, and merchants haggling over the last of their wares in a town on edge.

Jeremiah's pace was lively as he thought of Lizzy's smile upon receiving his gift. But he was too much the older brother not to realize he couldn't return to Machias with a token for Lizzy alone, not when her siblings meant so much to her.

Making his way along Fore Street, the salty breeze tugging at his coat, he reached Moody's store, a modest clapboard building wedged between a chandlery and a cooper's shop. The store's sign swung gently in the wind, its faded letters promising "Dry Goods & Sundries." Inside, the air smelled of molasses and tobacco, the shelves lined with barrels of flour, bolts of homespun cloth, and a jumble of goods for sailors and townsfolk alike.

A stout man with a ledger in hand, presumably Mr. Moody himself, glanced up from behind the counter. "Morning," he said. "What brings you in? Powder's scarce, but I've got some fair rum if you're stocking a ship."

"I'm Captain Jeremiah O'Brien, in Falmouth just for a day."

"Captain O'Brien! Your success against the British precedes you. Welcome to my store. How can I help you?"

"I'm after a few things," Jeremiah said. "First, a satin ribbon—green, like the pine tree that graces the flags of many Patriot ships. Something fine for a pretty lady, if you've got it."

Moody raised an eyebrow, a faint smile tugging at his lips, and gestured to a small wooden box on the counter. "Not much call for finery these days, with the British prowling the coast, but I've a few bits left from better times." He opened the box, revealing a tangle of ribbons—red, blue, and, nestled beneath, a length of green satin, its sheen catching the light streaming through the window. "This one's a shilling. Came from Boston before the war turned sour and 'tis long enough to wrap around a lady's straw hat. Best I've got."

Jeremiah ran his fingers over the green ribbon, its vibrant hue reminding him of the pine tree Joseph Reed had proposed for Washington's naval ensign, a symbol of their fight on the sea. It was perfect for Lizzy, a token of hope and resilience. "I'll take it," he said. Then, thinking of Lizzy's siblings, he added, "I'll need another—for her younger sister—blue, if you have it."

Moody rummaged through the box again, pulling out a narrower ribbon in a deep blue, the color of a calm sea. "This one's sixpence," he said, laying it beside the green. "It'll do nicely for a young lady."

Jeremiah nodded, the blue a fitting match for Annie's steadfast nature, always there to support Lizzy. "And one more thing," he added, glancing around the store. "A game for a boy, their ten-year-old brother. Jackstones or knucklebones, I think they call them, if you've got a set."

Moody scratched his chin, then stepped to a shelf

behind him, retrieving a small leather drawstring pouch. He opened it, spilling out six pewter jacks and a tiny wooden ball, their surfaces glinting dully in the light. "Pewter jacks, made by a tinsmith in Portsmouth last year," he said. "The pouch keeps 'em together—two shillings for the set. Boys go mad for 'em."

Jeremiah smiled, imagining Sean's delight as he scattered the jacks on the floor of their new Machias home. "Perfect," he said, counting out the coins—three shillings and sixpence total—as Moody wrapped the goods. Jeremiah's heart warmed at the thought of the Fitzpatricks' smiles.

The store owner handed him the package, and Jeremiah tucked it into his coat pocket. His gaze drifted to the street outside, where a group of militiamen hurried past, their muskets slung over their shoulders. "Heard any more of British ships?" he asked.

Moody's expression darkened. "Aye, word is Captain Henry Mowat's been spotted off Cape Elizabeth. He's none too pleased with Falmouth since he was taken prisoner here back in May by a band of militiamen. 'Twas Colonel Thompson's doing. Folks are saying Admiral Graves will make good on his threats of revenge for our privateers' successes. You'd best be quick about your business, Captain."

Jeremiah thanked him and stepped back into the bustle of Fore Street, the gifts a small comfort against the storm he knew was coming. God willing, he'd spend the afternoon obtaining supplies and provisions for Machias and tomorrow sail without incident. But as he stepped into the street, Falmouth's uneasy air lingered, making him glad to be leaving.

Machias, Maine, late August 1775

LIZZY STROLLED ALONG the riverbank, her gaze fixed on the sun dancing on the water of the Machias River as she and Annie, sewing baskets in hand, made their way to the sewing circle at Mrs. Spencer's house. The group of congenial women and older girls, who gathered three afternoons a week to stitch clothing for their families and furnishings for their homes, had become a cornerstone of Lizzy's new life in Machias. Sean was at the old schoolhouse on Main Street, practicing his letters with the other children, leaving Lizzy and Annie to their work.

Lizzy's attention was suddenly diverted to a bald eagle swooping over the river, its huge wings spread wide as its talons snatched a trout from the water. "Annie, did you see that?"

"I did. Made me think of Jeremiah and his crew capturing the *Margaretta*. It must have been like that to hear the men speak of it."

Lizzy agreed. "It was very courageous of them to do that, facing British guns and redcoats with few weapons and little ammunition. Given what transpired, I can only think God was protecting them."

They reached the *Machias Liberty* tied up at the wharf, the sails reefed and the sloop's mast stark against the late August sky. Lizzy's thoughts drifted to Jeremiah. He'd been gone nigh on six weeks, having left in mid-July to deliver the British prisoners from the *Margaretta* to the Provincial authorities in Watertown. Surely it wouldn't take so long, even with the delegates' deliberations. Her father had finished their new house, a sturdy two-story frame with a view of the river, and she longed to show it to Jeremiah, to see his blue eyes light up with that ready smile she missed so dearly. Beyond that, if she were honest, the uncertainty of war gnawed at her. Each day without word deepened her worry for Machias and for him, though she clung to the hope he would soon return.

The crewmembers who had stayed behind to finish their work on the *Liberty* waved to her from the deck, their sleeves rolled up as they scrubbed planks, coiled ropes and mended sails. "Afternoon Miss Fitzpatrick!" called a ruddy-faced sailor, his hands busy with a tarred brush.

She waved back, her spirits lifting at their cheerful greeting, and noticed one handsome young crewmember, a lad with tousled chestnut hair, flash a shy smile at Annie. "'Lo, Mistress Annie," he said, tipping his cap.

Annie blushed beneath her straw hat and returned the young man a small wave, her cheeks pink as the roses blooming along the riverbank. With each year, Annie had grown more beautiful. They had made friends in Machias, not just among the women but among the young men, especially those looking for wives in a town where women often married young and bore large families. At sixteen, Lizzy thought Annie too young to marry, though Hannah Weston had married at seventeen.

Lizzy paused to gaze up at the bare mast of the sloop as an idea came to her. "Does the *Liberty* fly no colors?" she shouted to the crewmember who had greeted her.

"Not yet. When Captain O'Brien returns, he'll decide, he will. Same with the *Diligent* where some o' the lads are mendin' sails now, and her tender, the *Tatamagouch* bein' loaded with provisions downriver."

Beside her, Annie tilted her head up toward the mast, her blue eyes curious. "What are you thinking. Lizzy?"

"I'm thinking of making a flag for Jeremiah's ships. Something to show who we are, what Machias stands for. Something to bring pride to him and his crews."

Annie drew her brows together. "What will it look like?"

"Well, Machias is a lumber town, surrounded by pine trees, isn't it? I've seen some of the merchant ships flying a white flag with a green pine tree in the center. No words, just the tree. They say it tells folks in port the ships have New England fish and lumber to trade. The pine tree represents Machias, too, and our roots in this land."

Annie's eyes sparkled with enthusiasm. "It would be simple enough to sew the white flag. The hard part will be the pine tree. I'll help you."

"You were always good at drawing," said Lizzy. "I'll be glad for your help."

When they arrived at the Spencers' house, the women were already busy with their sewing, their needles flashing in the sunlight pouring through the open windows. The air smelled of dried lavender, a comforting smell that mingled with the hum of conversation. Mrs. Spencer was a widow whose husband had died a few years before. With her children grown, she welcomed the women of Machias into her home, and they were glad to come.

Lizzy was happy to see Mrs. O'Brien was there, her light brown hair laced with gray framing her face. It was in the sewing circle that Lizzy had learned Mrs. O'Brien met her husband while working in his tailor shop in

Kittery, Maine, and that her father had been a merchant captain. "He helped teach the boys to sail," she told Lizzy. The women of Machias admired Jeremiah's mother, who was wise in many ways and had endured much as a young mother to bring her family safely to Scarboro and then to Machias.

After greeting the women and settling into a chair, Lizzy eagerly shared her idea. "I have an idea to make pine tree flags for Captain O'Brien's ships. A white field with a green pine tree, to show we're of Machias, of New England, standing tall against the British."

"A wonderful thought!" said Mrs. Spencer, her gray eyes crinkling with a smile. "We'll all help, won't we ladies?"

"I've some green broadcloth you can use for the tree," offered Mrs. Oakes, a matronly woman with a knack for finding scraps of fabric in her stores. "It's sturdy enough for a flag."

"And I can hem the edges," chimed in eighteen-year-old Sarah Libby, her fingers nimble from years of quilting.

So, Lizzy's project was adopted by the group, their laughter and chatter filling the room as they set to work. Annie sketched the pine tree's silhouette on paper, its branches spread wide, then traced the shape onto the green cloth with a piece of chalk. The women cut and stitched, appliquéing a tree onto each of the white fields with careful stitches, their hands moving in seeming unison as they shared stories of their men and their fears of the war that loomed over them all.

By the end of the afternoon, they had fashioned two pine tree flags, one for the *Machias Liberty*, one for the

Diligent, their green trees bold against the white. Lizzy was so pleased to see them finished. "I hope Jeremiah likes them," she told Annie as they walked home. "If he wants one for the *Tatamagouch*, I can make another."

Annie's words were encouraging. "He will be proud of you for thinking his ships needed colors."

The first days of September brought a crispness to the Machias air, the river sparkling under a pale blue sky as Lizzy stood on the wharf, her heart pounding with anticipation. Annie and Sean flanked her, their eyes fixed on the horizon where the small schooner's sails had just come into view. The pine tree flags were folded carefully in her basket, a surprise she'd waited weeks to share with Jeremiah.

The schooner glided to the dock, her crew bustling as they secured lines and furled sails. The *Liberty* waited nearby, freshly scrubbed and ready for her captain's return. Jeremiah shouted an order to unload the provisions, then leapt ashore, his cocked hat tilted against the sun. His face broke into that ready smile Lizzy had missed so dearly. "Lizzy! Annie, Sean!" he called, striding toward them with the confident gait of a man who'd faced the sea and returned whole.

"We've missed you, Captain O'Brien," Lizzy said, her voice warm as she met his gaze, her worries of the past weeks melting away. She waved to Colonel Foster and Jeremiah's brothers, John and William. "Father's finished the house. I can't wait to show you. But first, I've something for you." She set down her basket, unfolding the first flag with a flourish, the green pine tree catching the light against the white cloth. "The women of Machias helped me make these for your ships. A pine tree for our town and for New England, to show who we are and what we stand for."

Jeremiah's eyes widened, a mix of surprise and admiration flickering across his face as he took the flag, running his fingers over the careful stitches. "Lizzy, this is...it's perfect," he said, his voice thick with emotion. "The pine tree's a symbol of our fight, you know. Merchant ships have flown it for years, and now it's ours, too. It was discussed with approval among Washington's generals in Cambridge. I'll fly this on the *Liberty* with pride, and the other on the *Diligent*. They'll be a beacon for liberty wherever we sail."

Annie beamed. "I helped draw the tree."

"'Tis a fine one," said Jeremiah.

Sean stood by his hero, an eager expression on his face. "Can I help raise it, Captain?"

"Aye, lad, you can," Jeremiah said. He turned to his crew, who had finished unloading boxes and barrels on the wharf. Next to them stood William and a tall, golden-haired man Lizzy hadn't seen before. Jeremiah held up the flags. "Our new colors, lads, sewn by Miss Fitzpatrick and the women of Machias, to fly proud on every voyage!"

The crew cheered, their voices echoing over the river, and Lizzy felt a swell of pride as Jeremiah handed the flag to Sean, who scampered onto the *Liberty* and, with a sailor's help, sent the pine tree flag up the mast. It caught the breeze, the green tree prominent against the white field.

Jeremiah stepped closer to Lizzy, his voice low. "You've given us more than a flag, Lizzy. You've given us a piece of Machias to carry into battle, a symbol of our fight for freedom. I'll think of you every time I look at it."

She smiled, her heart full, knowing that wherever Jeremiah sailed her stitches would fly with him, a reminder of home.

Gesturing to the tall, golden-haired man, Jeremiah said to her and Annie, "Meet Surgeon Donald McDonald. He joined us in Falmouth and will be an officer on the *Liberty*."

Turning to the young doctor, Lizzy said, "I am Elizabeth Fitzpatrick and this is my sister, Annie, and my brother, Sean. We welcome you to our town, and hope you will like it here."

The doctor smiled at them, his eyes narrowing on Annie with a flicker of interest. "I ken I will, Lass," he said, his voice carrying a gentle lilt.

As the pine tree flag caught the breeze above the *Machias Liberty*, Lizzy watched Jeremiah's face. A wistful look crossed his features, and he spoke softly, almost to himself. "I can see it now, the *Liberty* in that fight with the *Margaretta* back in June, this flag flying proud as we chased her down. We had no colors then, just our grit and the will to be free, but this...this makes it real, Lizzy. It's what we were fighting for, even if we didn't know it yet."

Lizzy's heart swelled at his words, imagining the scene as he described it, the *Liberty*'s sails taut, the roar of the muskets as they fired, the pine tree flag snapping in the wind as Machias' sons defied the British Crown. It was a vision of the past made new, a symbol of their fight that would carry them into the battles yet to come.

Jeremiah picked up his satchel and they began the

walk toward his home. Sean ran ahead. Annie and Surgeon McDonald walked behind them, Lizzy's sister telling the new surgeon of the town's history.

"I want to hear everything about your trip," said Lizzy. "Pastor Lyon has invited everyone to his house this evening to hear of your adventures."

Jeremiah nodded. "Ben and I will be happy to tell them. It was a very good trip." Leaning close, he added, "I've something for you, Lizzy, and for Annie and Sean. Small tokens that reminded me of you when I was gone." He reached into his satchel, pulling out a length of green ribbon that shimmered in the sunlight, handing it to Lizzy with a tender smile. "For you, long enough for your straw hat if you wish."

Lizzy smiled, her heart warming to think he'd remembered her in the midst of his important doings. She had never received such a gift from a man who was not her father. "It's beautiful. I'll wear it proudly," she said, already imagining it woven into her hair for the evening at Pastor Lyon's.

Turning to Annie behind them with the surgeon, Jeremiah pulled a blue ribbon from his satchel. "This is for you, Annie lass."

Lizzy's sister's eyes grew wide. "For me?" She took the slender ribbon between her fingers. "It's lovely! Thank you, Captain."

"'Tis a perfect match for yer eyes," said the new surgeon, bringing a blush to Annie's cheeks.

Sean came running back to admire the ribbons. Jeremiah pulled a small leather pouch from his coat pocket. "I didn't forget you, lad. A game of knucklebones when you've free time from your lessons."

Lizzy had observed Sean playing the game in Onslow with older boys, but he didn't have a set of his own, not until now. Her brother's mouth dropped open as he peered into the leather pouch. "Jacks!"

"Don't forget to thank the captain," Lizzy reminded him gently.

Sean looked up, his expression sheepish. "Thank you, Captain O'Brien. I really like 'em."

The new surgeon watched with a pleased expression. "Thoughtful, Cap'n."

That evening after supper, Lizzy stepped into Pastor Lyon's house with her family, the warmth of the fire and the glow of candles welcoming them on this crisp September evening. She'd draped her shoulders in a shawl with green threads and woven Jeremiah's green ribbon into her hair. Smoothing her skirt, her gaze took in the gathered townsfolk.

Annie, her blue ribbon tied neatly at her throat, stayed close, while Sean clutched his new knucklebones pouch, eager to show it off. The room buzzed with chatter. Mrs. Spencer and Mrs. Oakes sharing a bench, Sarah Libby whispering with other girls, and Colonel Foster nodding to Jeremiah's brothers, John and William, who stood near the hearth. Jeremiah's other three brothers, Gideon, Dennis and Joseph, sat farther away. Gideon's wife, Abigail, who Lizzy had only just met sat with her young daughter, Mary, who was just a toddler.

Surgeon McDonald stood near the door, his golden hair catching the candlelight, his gaze flickering to Annie with a shy smile.

Lizzy leaned into to her sister. "The new surgeon is staying with Jeremiah for now."

Annie's gaze lingered on the tall Scot, giving Lizzy a thought for the future.

Reverend Lyon, his lined face bearing a kind expression, raised a hand for quiet. "Friends, we're here to give thanks for the safe return of Captain O'Brien, Colonel Foster and those who accompanied them on their successful trip. While they were away, as some of you know, the Committee of Safety sent Captain Stephen Smith with a privateer and forty militia to capture the British brig *Loyal Briton* at Saint John, Nova Scotia. We were informed that ship was to be loaded with cattle and supplies for the British Army in Boston. We must pray for their safe return and success. I'll open us in a prayer to the Good Lord and then we can hear from Jeremiah and Ben on their journey to Cambridge and Watertown."

The reverend then bowed his head. "Father, we thank you for protecting our men who have fought for Machias in the name of liberty, and for their success not only in the waters of the bay but in their travels and meetings with General Washington and our leaders in Watertown. And we ask your protection and success for Captain Smith and his crew at Saint John. May our conversations tonight give you the glory. Amen."

"Amen" was repeated by all in attendance.

Jeremiah thought Smith was a good choice for the task the Committee of Safety had given him. In his late thirties, Smith was a respected member of the militia and, like Jeremiah, an experienced captain of privateer vessels.

Ben Foster took his place in front of the fireplace next

to Jeremiah, whose blue eyes were bright with purpose as he began to speak. "We had two missions on this trip: to deliver the British officers to General Washington at his Cambridge Headquarters, and to deliver the other prisoners to the General Court in Watertown. We decided it was most efficient to separate into two groups. Ben Foster, Isaac Taft and I took the British officers to Cambridge, and my brothers, John and William, along with some of the *Liberty*'s crew, many of whom are here tonight, took the British seamen and marines to Watertown."

At that point, Ben Foster spoke. "General Washington received us with kindness, inviting us to dine with him and his officers. In their presence, he lavished us with praise for the captures of what are now five ships, the *Margaretta*, Ichabod Jones' two sloops, the *Unity*, renamed the *Machias Liberty*, and the *Polly*, and most recently, the *Diligent* and her tender, the *Tatamagouch*. Specifically, His Excellency praised Jeremiah for his bravery as a privateer for the cause of freedom."

Lizzy smiled, remembering the battle in June and the *Liberty*'s bare mast now flying her pine tree flag. She glanced at Mrs. Spencer, whose gray eyes shone with happiness, and Mrs. Oakes, who nodded firmly, her matronly presence a steadying force. On the face of Mary O'Brien, Jeremiah's mother, was a look of fierce pride.

Jeremiah didn't acknowledge the praise he received, as Lizzy knew he wouldn't. Instead, he said, "Washington even sent a letter of support to the General Court, praising Machias' efforts, which likely bolstered our standing when we petitioned that body for ammunition, funds and supplies. The petition was granted, though they could spare only half the ammunition we asked for. They have allowed us to sell the house of Ichabod Jones and use the proceeds to help the widow McNeil and the wounded. They have also allowed Ben Foster to serve as judge in Machias' new vice admiralty court to adjudicate prizes more quickly. A good choice, don't you agree?"

"A great choice," said Reverend Lyon, to which the crowd responded with smiles and applause.

Ben modestly dipped his head. "I am honored."

Jeremiah continued, "As Ben, John and William will confirm, Watertown's abuzz with talk of war. With the siege of Boston now into its fifth month, folks are ready to fight."

Standing next to the fireplace, John and William nodded.

Ben chimed in, his voice gruff. "Jeremiah is too modest to tell you this, but I will. The General Court has appointed him a Captain of the Marine of the Massachusetts Colony, and named him Commander of the vessels *Machias Liberty* and *Diligent*, to be fitted out under his supervision here at Machias and employed to cruise against the enemy's vessels along the New England coast, making him commander of the first American naval 'flying squadron' of the War of the Revolution."

Gasps of awe sounded from the people. Lizzy's eyes were filled with tears, overwhelmed by all Jeremiah had accomplished. The room erupted in applause as everyone expressed their appreciation for this honor paid the eldest son of Morris and Mary O'Brien, who had been watching from the side blinking back tears.

When the applause quieted, Ben said, "The General Court passed a resolution thanking Jeremiah and his men for their service to the cause of liberty."

"It doesn't get any better than that," said Reverend Lyon.

"In Falmouth," said Ben, "we secured our new ship's surgeon Donald McDonald, the handsome Scot who you see standing by the door."

The young Scottish surgeon was, indeed, handsome, a fact noted by many young women in the room. He smiled and dipped his head in acknowledgment of his new role.

"A welcome addition to our ships' officers," said Ben.

"We also secured provisions before heading home," added Jeremiah. "I have to say, we were glad to depart Falmouth. The port town is tense with worry for a British reprisal, and there are whispers of British ships being sighted off the coast."

"It's not just Falmouth," said Ben. "While you were securing provisions, Jere, I asked around and discovered all the coastal towns from Marblehead north are on alert."

Jeremiah nodded. "I am not surprised. With our success in taking British vessels, Machias will be a special object of British retribution, but Ben and I have anticipated this and will be working to ready Machias for any attack. As head of our militia and now judge of our vice admiralty court, Ben has asked to remain on land where he can best oversee our preparations for defense. That should give all comfort. Anticipating I would need a new captain of the *Diligent*, I asked the General Court to commission John Lambert, hoping he would accept. Upon my return today, I spoke with him and am happy to report he is most willing."

"I was honored to be asked," said John Lambert, from where he stood behind Jeremiah's brothers, arms crossed. "'Twill be my privilege to serve under Captain O'Brien."

Lizzy studied Lambert's weathered face, tanned and lined by the sun. He was a man who, though young, had clearly spent years battling the sea. A dark beard framed his jaw, and his deep-set brown eyes held a steady, unyielding gaze, like a man who'd faced storms and lived to tell of them. His shoulders, strong and unbowed, spoke of a sailor in his prime, ready for the fight ahead.

"It will be my privilege to serve as your First Lieutenant, Cap'n Lambert," said John O'Brien, stepping forward with a proud grin, his resemblance to Jeremiah clear in his blue eyes, though his hair was a shade darker. Lizzy smiled at the sight of another O'Brien ready to fight for Machias, side by side with his brother. William, too, served Jeremiah as his First Lieutenant aboard the *Liberty*.

The room erupted in cheers. Lizzy joined in, her heart racing with both pride and fear. She watched Jeremiah, his broad shoulders steady as he answered more questions, his voice carrying the confidence of his leadership. The war felt closer now, its shadow looming over Machias, but in that moment, surrounded by her new family of Patriots, Lizzy felt a fierce hope they would fight and prevail. In her mind, she pictured the pine tree flags flying high on the *Liberty* and *Diligent*, her stitches carrying Machias' spirit into battle, knowing she would stand with Jeremiah, no matter what loomed before him.

"The spirit of freedom is not confined to the battlefield; it thrives in the hearths of our homes."
– Attributed to Mercy Otis Warren (circa 1779)

CHAPTER 8

ONE MORNING A few days after the gathering at Reverend Lyon's, Jeremiah walked with Lizzy along the riverbank, heading toward the Fitzpatricks' new home. It was early autumn but Jeremiah could feel the change in the air, a crispness that wasn't there a few weeks before.

"I am anxious to show you our house now that it's finished," she said, her blue eyes alight with anticipation.

Built with help from Jeremiah's brother, Gideon, and the townsfolk, the two-story house was nestled near the Machias River, not far from Gideon's house.

Standing before the Fitzpatricks' home, Jeremiah thought its clapboard sides and steeply pitched roof with its central door would serve the family well, a testament to their new roots in Machias. "'Tis a fine house viewed from here, Lizzy." Noting the paned windows on both floors, he said, "The windows must give a lot of light."

"They do, good light both upstairs and down. We can read in the day in every room. Father got the pane windows from a man in Machias who'd bought more than he needed in Boston before the troubles began."

She led him inside to the main room, its stone hearth already blackened from use, and its fresh-cut timbers still smelling of pine. Rays of sunlight flowed into the room from the windows.

Annie, wearing a white apron over her blue dress, descended the stairs to join them. "Isn't it wonderful? Father made some changes from the one he built in Onslow, more windows and a larger second story."

Jeremiah nodded his agreement. "'Tis a splendid house."

"Father sleeps there," said Lizzy, gesturing to a half-open door on one side of the room, revealing a good-sized bed. "He likes to be on this floor to tend the fire at night." She pointed to the staircase. "Up there's where Annie, Sean, and I sleep. We've plenty of room."

Thomas Fitzpatrick came in from the outside, wiping his hands on his work apron. "What do you think?" he asked.

"You've done solid work here, Mr. Fitzpatrick," said Jeremiah. Gazing at the table with its six chairs and sideboard set with dishes and glasses, the pots and pans that hung inside the large hearth, and the candles on the mantel, he added, "The house really looks like a home now." There was even a small hearth rug in front of the fireplace.

Looking at the ceiling, Thomas said, "I must thank you, Jeremiah, for your help in raising the roof."

"I was glad to do it. My neighbors helped me when I built my house."

Sean came through the front door, his cheeks rosy from the morning air, making Jeremiah think he must have been running. "Do you like our new home, Captain?"

"I do. It's a fine home," said Jeremiah. "And you have a good location on the river."

"Now that your ships' flags are finished," said Lizzy, "Annie and I are making curtains for our windows." Her gaze flitted about the room. "We brought as many of our things as we could from Onslow. Some were our mother's and are very special to us."

Annie picked up a beautiful pewter candlestick, part of a set sitting on the mantel, and turned it in her hands. "These were hers," she said, her voice saddened with the memory of a mother much missed. "I was young when she passed. I remember her mostly from the stories Father and Lizzy have told me." Her voice trailed off as she looked into the glowing embers in the hearth.

Thomas put his arm around Annie. "Your mother was a wonderful woman and she loved you all very much."

Sean said nothing in response to his father's words. Jeremiah thought the boy likely didn't remember much about his mother. For him, Lizzy had been mother, her steady hands shaping his world since he was a young child. The boy eagerly lifted a small wooden boat to Jeremiah, perhaps wanting to move from a difficult subject. "I carved it myself, Captain, with help from

Gideon."

"Gideon is very good at carving," said Jeremiah. "A worthy teacher for you." Jeremiah turned the small boat in his hand, admiring the fine workmanship. "A grand beginning you've given it. We'll have to add a sail."

Staring at the carved boat with adoration, Sean said, "I'll sail my wooden boat on the river one day, like you, Captain."

Jeremiah chuckled. "You will. And one day, when you're older, you can accompany me on a cruise if your father approves." Some of Jeremiah's crew were young, not even eighteen. It would only be a few years until Sean was old enough to join them.

When it was time to go, Jeremiah bid Thomas a good day and, saying goodbye to Annie and Sean, followed Lizzy outside to the riverbank where they stood for a moment admiring the water glistening in the morning light. The air was crisp with the promise of autumn. "The apples on my trees are nearly ripe enough to eat. We're harvesting plums now."

"I will help you pick them if you like," she said.

"I would like that very much. 'Tis always a joyous occasion."

Just then, the trill of a black-capped chickadee echoed through the woods. Lizzy turned toward the sound where the small bird sat on a nearby branch. "We have many chickadees around our new house," she said.

"If you listen carefully, you will be able to tell the difference in their calls. Some signal a predator, like an owl, is nearby."

She smiled at his suggestion she could learn to distinguish the calls of the tiny bird. "You know much of Machias, and I have much to learn."

"There is time," he said. "You were close to your mother," he said, thinking of their conversation in their new home.

"I admired her greatly. She was my example. She taught me to stand tall, even when the storms came."

"And with her death, you took on the responsibility for your sister and brother."

She nodded, a flicker of pride breaking through. "There was no one else. I've carried them since I was barely more than a girl, through all we faced at Onslow." Turning to face him, she said, "I'm grateful, Jeremiah, for Machias taking us in and showing us hospitality, for giving my father a new beginning, and for all you have done. You and your family have showed us kindness."

"You don't need to carry the whole burden of your family, Lizzy. We can help you." And then with emphasis, he said, "*I* can help you."

Meeting his gaze, he thought he saw a spark of hope in her eyes. "Perhaps you can. Time will tell. But after Reverend Lyon spoke of Captain Smith's mission to Saint John, and your mention of the threat to the coastal towns, I can't help but worry. The British won't let your success pass. What if you aren't here when they come?"

Jeremiah's eyes met hers, understanding in his voice. "You're right, they won't forget about Machias, and I won't always be here; it is my job to see our coast is protected. But Ben Foster will make sure the militia is prepared for any attack."

Squaring her shoulders, she said, "I will stand with the

women of Machias if such an attack comes, ready to defend the town."

"That, I never doubted." Jeremiah admired her courage and hoped the time would come when she didn't feel the need to stand alone. "I must sail on the morrow, Lizzy, but I'll be back soon." Their hands brushed as he spoke, a lingering touch that sent a warmth through him. "Stay strong," he added softly, their fingers parting with a shared glance that promised more than words. They stood a moment longer, the weight of his pledge and her quiet strength binding them, before he turned to go.

THAT AFTERNOON THE sun dipped low over Machias, its golden rays filtering through the trees that would soon change to the brilliant colors of red, gold and yellow. Lizzy and Annie joined the women of the sewing circle in a small barn near the river, the air heavy with the scent of melting tallow.

A fire crackled beneath a large cast-iron pot where pork fat bubbled. Lizzy watched as Mary O'Brien, Jeremiah's mother, stirred the pot with a steady hand, her gray-streaked hair tucked beneath a linen cap. Her presence was a quiet strength among the women, who had asked her to come because of her expertise in candle making.

A short while later, with the scent of bacon fat very strong, Mrs. O'Brien directed the women helping her to strain the tallow of its impurities. Once the impurities were removed the tallow was poured into a large kettle.

It was time to dip the wicks.

Lizzy worked with the women placing the candle rods—slender sticks about eighteen inches long—across two parallel poles. Each candle rod was hung with six cotton wicks.

The women worked with deft hands, taking turns dipping cotton wicks into the hot tallow. After each dip, they returned the rods to the rack, the wax cooling and hardening until, with the final set dipped, they turned to the first rod. "Time to begin again," Lizzy reminded them. The candles grew fatter as they were repeatedly dipped and cooled.

As they dipped the candles, their chatter filled the barn, a familiar blend of town gossip and family news. Machias families were large and births were a constant topic.

"Ben and Beth Foster's new son, Asa, will be a handsome lad," said Mrs. Carter.

"That makes fourteen," Mrs. Spencer noted, "though the oldest two were by his first wife who passed."

"Beth says Asa will be their last," Mrs. Carter informed them. "One can hardly blame her."

Many heads nodded at that.

"Wooden Foster and his wife seem to be competing with Ben and Beth," said Mrs. Spencer. "They just had that adorable daughter, Ruth."

"You think all babies are adorable," remarked Mrs. O'Brien with a smile.

Mrs. Spencer nodded. "I suppose I do."

As the birth talk waned, they turned to a discussion of candles.

"I remember the whale oil candles we used to make

before the British closed off whaling with their blockade," said Mrs. Oakes. "Like beeswax, the wax from that oil produced a brighter light without tallow's odor."

Lizzy nodded, twisting a wick. "Tallow's all we have for now unless we want to send the children to pick bayberries. Those candles have a pleasant smell. Whale oil's a memory since the British closed the seas. But Jeremiah's *Liberty* and *Diligent* might bring us something better. Often, he finds luxuries among the goods intended for the British. He's sailing tomorrow. Perhaps he'll find beeswax candles among the British goods."

"I remember beeswax candles in Onslow," said Annie. "They burn so clean."

Mrs. O'Brien paused her stirring, her voice warm with memory. "Aye, we had them in Kittery, too, before the war. A fine light they gave, but I like your idea to gather bayberries, Lizzy, for our next effort."

The barn door creaked open wider and Jeremiah stepped in, his coat damp from the mist outside. "I heard that," he said with a grin. "And I remember, Mother, you always had a fondness for beeswax."

"Can we do something for you, Captain?" Lizzy asked him, curious at his visit but heartened by his appearance.

"No," he said, stepping closer. "Just passing and thought to say hello before I sail. Now that I know you favor beeswax candles, I'll keep an eye out."

"The families of Machias will appreciate any you find," said Mrs. O'Brien.

"We'll need many candles for the coming winter," said Mrs. Spencer, "or we'll be reading only by firelight."

"It looks like you have made a fine start," said Jeremiah, his gaze shifting to the store of candles cooling on one side of the barn. "You ladies are a credit to Machias."

"We're trying," Mrs. Carter replied, wiping her brow.

"I won't interrupt more," Jeremiah said with a nod to Lizzy. "I'll wish you a good afternoon and thank you in advance for the candles I'll be reading by."

The women laughed, their spirits lifted as they resumed their work, the growing stack of tallow candles a small stand against winter's darkness. Lizzy's fondness for the man had only increased with their morning conversation on the riverbank.

TWO DAYS LATER, the air in Machias buzzed with anticipation, the early September breeze carrying the scent of the sea. Lizzy stood at the wharf with Annie and Sean, her shawl wrapped tightly around her against the chill. The townsfolk had gathered when word spread that a ship was coming. Shouts echoed across the water as the brig *Loyal Briton* came into view, her sails taut and her deck alive with the bleating of sheep and the lowing of cattle. On her deck stood Captain Stephen Smith, his weathered face making him look older than his thirty-six years. His expression displayed his pride, his forty militiamen waving as the brig neared the dock. Behind the brig was the schooner that Smith had sailed to Nova Scotia.

The crowd cheered loudly, throwing their hats high as ropes were tossed to secure the brig. Lizzy's heart raced with a mixture of joy and awe. Machias had struck another blow against the British, just as Reverend Lyon had prayed for.

"It's Captain Smith!" Sean shouted, tugging at her sleeve, his blue eyes wide. "He's got animals—look!"

"You're right," said Lizzy. "And it looks as if the crew has their hands full in trying to control them."

Next to Lizzy, Annie's eyes grew wide as she watched the commotion. "So many!"

Stephen Smith stepped ashore, his chestnut hair visible beneath his cocked hat. His boots thudded on the wooden planks as he raised a hand to quiet the crowd. "We've taken the *Loyal Briton* from Saint John," he called, "loaded with cattle and sheep meant for the British army in Boston. And there's also casks of molasses."

Mrs. O'Brien smiled. "Molasses will serve us well." And then, with a twinkle in her eyes, she added, "once our new admiralty judge, Ben Foster, determines the prize was lawfully taken, of course."

"We burned Fort Frederick, too," said Captain Smith, "a message to the British they won't soon forget!"

The townsfolk roared their approval. Lizzy joined in, clapping her hands as she glanced at Annie, whose cheeks flushed with excitement. Sean stood with them, his gaze fixed on the crew struggling with the animals.

Colonel Foster pushed through the crowd, clasping Smith's hand. "You've done Machias proud, Captain. The Committee of Safety will hear your full report, but first, let's get these beasts ashore."

The men set to work, herding the livestock down makeshift ramps, their bleats and moos filling the air. Lizzy stepped forward with the other women—Mrs. Spencer, Mrs. Oakes, and Sarah Libby among them—to help sort the provisions and list them for Ben Foster's adjudication. In addition to molasses, there were hogsheads of sugar, making Lizzy think of apple tarts.

She ran her hands over a sheep's thick wool, imagining the blankets they could weave for the coming winter, while Mrs. Oakes said in her matronly voice, "This beef when salted will add to the town's stores and keep us fed through the cold months." Then with a glance at Lizzy, "It will be enough for Captain O'Brien's crew when he returns."

"We'll cook up a good feast for them," said Lizzy, imagining all they could serve up with so much beef.

As the work continued, the town organized a small feast on the grassy bank near the wharf, tables laden with fish stew, for it was a fine autumn day. Once the prize was adjudicated, they would have cuts of fresh beef from some of the captured cattle.

Reverend Lyon offered a prayer of thanks, his voice carrying over the chatter. "For Captain Smith and his men, for their courage in Saint John, and for this bounty that strengthens Machias in our fight for liberty, we praise you, Lord."

The townsfolk echoed his "Amen," and the feast began, laughter and songs rising into the afternoon sky.

Lizzy sat with Annie and Sean, their father nearby, a wooden plate balanced on her lap, her gaze drifting to the *Loyal Briton* moored at the dock. She thought of Jeremiah, on the *Liberty* and John Lambert on the *Diligent*, facing the same British forces Smith had defied. And she thought of Annie and Sean, who she watched over like a mother. Machias was growing bolder, its defiance a fire that warmed her heart. But she knew the British would answer, and soon. As the sounds of celebration filled the air around her, she silently prayed for Jeremiah's safe return.

JEREMIAH STOOD AT the helm of the *Liberty*, the salt spray stinging his face as the sloop sliced through the waves, the *Diligent* keeping pace on their starboard under John Lambert's steady command. It was early September when they had sailed from Machias, the New England coast stretching out before them, a jagged line of pine and rock under a gray sky.

For weeks, they'd patrolled the waters off Maine, the crew's eyes sharp for any sign of enemy merchantmen, their spirits high after the victories at Machias. Their pine tree flag snapped in the wind above, a defiant banner. His orders from the General Court burned clear in his mind: guard the coast, seize enemy vessels, and cut off supplies to the British in Boston.

It was now weeks later, and finally, their vigilance paid off. A lookout's cry broke the morning calm. "Sail to the north, Cap'n!"

Jeremiah's gaze locked on a small British sloop, her sails taut as she hugged the coastline, likely bound for Boston with provisions. "Signal Lambert to close in," he ordered, his voice steady over the creak of the rigging. The *Liberty* and *Diligent* moved like hawks on the hunt, their speed outmatching the sloop's.

A warning shot from the *Liberty*'s bow cannon sent the British crew scrambling, and within the hour, they struck their colors, surrendering without a fight.

Jeremiah boarded the prize, his boots thudding on the deck as he inspected the hold—barrels of salted pork, flour, and rum, enough to ease Machias' hunger for a month. "Send her back to Machias with a prize crew," he told William.

As the captured sloop turned toward home, Jeremiah's thoughts drifted to Lizzy, wondering what she would think when the ship came back without him. She would know they had been successful and sailed on.

The sea, he knew, held darker challenges than a merchant sloop. By October, they'd sailed south into Gloucester Bay, near the Massachusetts coast, where the waters teemed with British activity. The HMS *Falcon*, a sloop-of-war, had been spotted in these parts, her smaller boats harrying fishermen and scouting for rebel ships.

On a foggy morning, the lookout's shout roused Jeremiah from his thoughts. "Schooner dead ahead, Cap'n, flyin' British colors!"

He recognized her lines at once—a Gloucester fishing schooner, taken by the British weeks before, now turned against her own. "She's ours to rescue," he growled, his eyes narrowing on his prey. "Signal Lambert to take the *Diligent* to her port side. We'll box her in."

The *Liberty* and *Diligent* surged forward, their guns run out and their cannon fire echoing across the bay as they targeted the schooner's rigging.

The British crew fired back with muskets, but their resistance faltered under the Americans' relentless volleys, and soon they struck their colors. The schooner was America's once more.

As Jeremiah's men secured the schooner, a new threat loomed through the mist—a British cutter and two barges, their marines' red coats stark against the gray sea.

The cutter's small cannon barked, a ball splintering the *Liberty*'s rail, and musket fire peppered the deck.

"Hard to starboard!" Jeremiah shouted, his voice cutting through the chaos. "Signal Lambert to take the *Diligent* to their flank. We can't let 'em escape!" The *Liberty*'s crew returned fire, their three-pounders roaring as they aimed for the cutter's sails, while the barges rowed desperately to close the distance.

Across the water, the *Diligent* answered the signal, her bow turning sharp as Lambert's crew opened fire on the barges, their muskets cracking like thunder. One barge took a direct hit, splintering its side and sending redcoats diving into the sea, while the other faltered, its oarsmen pinned down by the *Diligent*'s steady volleys.

Musket balls whizzed past Jeremiah, one grazing his sleeve. He stood firm, continuing to direct his men.

A sudden cry pierced the din. One of his gunners, a young man named Daniel Cole, fell to the deck, a musket ball through his chest, his brown eyes wide with shock. Two others clutched wounds, blood seeping through their coats, but the crew fought on, their faces grim with determination.

With a final volley, the *Liberty*'s cannon shredded the cutter's mainsail, and the barges faltered, their oars tangling in the swell. The British lieutenant, a wiry man with a red face and a snarl, threw down his sword, his men following suit.

"Secure the prisoners!" Jeremiah ordered, his voice

hoarse as his men bound the thirty-five British crew and redcoats, the lieutenant spitting curses as he was hauled aboard the *Liberty*. The cutter and barges were lashed to the *Diligent*, their small cannon silenced. The captain of the rescued schooner shouted his thanks as his ship was freed to go on her way.

The fog was just lifting as Jeremiah knelt beside Daniel Cole's body, his heart a leaden weight. Closing the lad's eyes, he whispered, 'You fought bravely, Daniel,' his voice catching as he pictured Cole's family in Machias. The sea's cold embrace was all he could offer the young man now—weeks from port, with no way to preserve his body without risking the crew's health or the mission. Regret gnawed at him, but he knew this was best, a sailor's end under God's sky.

Rising, he ordered Cole's body to be wrapped in a weighted canvas shroud for burial at sea. This done, he called the crew together, his tone thick with grief. "We commit Daniel Cole to the deep and into God's hands," he intoned. Then recalling the services Reverend Lyon had performed, he said, "And we remember what Jesus said… 'I am the resurrection, and the life: he that believeth in me, though he were dead, yet shall he live: And whosoever liveth and believeth in me shall never die.' Go with God, Daniel Cole." He signaled to his crew. The splash as they lowered him to the water was a quiet thunder. Jeremiah stood silent, head bowed, the salt spray mingling with the sting in his eyes.

The two wounded men, James Reed, shot in the shoulder, and Isaac Holt, with a gash on his leg, groaned as Surgeon McDonald tended their wounds, his hands steady despite the blood. "Will they recover?" he asked Donald.

"Aye, they will."

Jeremiah returned to the helm, the weight of command pressing down like an anchor. They'd struck a blow against the British, aye, but the cost was steep—Cole's young life a bitter price—and Jeremiah knew it'd only grow steeper. With the prizes in tow, he turned the *Liberty* north, followed by the *Diligent* and their prizes, the coast of Maine a faint promise on the horizon.

THE LATE OCTOBER wind howled through Machias, rattling the shutters of the Fitzpatricks' house and lifting the curtains. Lizzy sat by the hearth, close to the crackling fire, as she mended a tear in Sean's breeches. The fire cast a warm glow over the room, where her father whittled a spoon by candlelight, his brow furrowed in thought. The mills were silent now and the winter harvest of trees had yet to begin.

Annie sat close, finishing her embroidered sampler that included the lines Lizzy had admired,

While Innocence is all our pride
and virtue is our only guide,
women would scorn to be defied
if led by Washington.

Sean, on the hearth rug, stared into the fire, humming a seafaring tune, his toy boat beside him and an open book he had been reading in his lap.

Nearly two months had passed since Jeremiah had

sailed from Machias, taking the *Liberty* and *Diligent* south. Though he had sent back a captured British sloop with a prize crew, Lizzy worried for his safety and that of his men, his absence as heavy as the autumn chill.

A sudden shout from a neighbor broke the quiet, followed by the clamor of boots on the path outside. Lizzy set down her needle, her pulse quickening as she rose. "Stay here," she told Annie and Sean, glancing at her father, who nodded and rose to go with her. Grabbing her shawl, she hurried out, joining a growing crowd of townsfolk moving toward the river.

A short way down the riverbank, they saw a small schooner had tied up, its sails tattered. A man stumbled ashore, his face gaunt and blackened with soot. Lizzy recognized him as a fisherman from Falmouth, who sometimes came north to deliver what supplies could get through.

"What news?" Colonel Foster called out, weaving his way through the crowd, his voice steady but tense. Mrs. Spencer and Mrs. Oakes stood nearby with Mr. and Mrs. O'Brien, their faces pale, while Reverend Lyon stood with his wife, Martha, holding hands, their faces mirroring the concern everyone felt.

The fisherman's voice trembled as he spoke, his words tumbling out like a flood. "Falmouth's gone, sir, burned to ash by the British. Mowat's fleet—four ships, they were—sailed into the harbor on the 16th with one hundred marines aboard besides the crews. The next day, they gave us two hours to flee, demanding we surrender our arms and swear allegiance to the king, else they would 'burn, sink and destroy'. This he delayed until the next morning.

Many fled west, and we hid our weapons. Come morning, when we refused to surrender our weapons, the British bombarded us with cannon and fire for twelve hours."

At this point there were gasps from the listening crowd. Mrs. Oakes said, "The homes, the shops the people!"

Lizzy's hand flew to her mouth, her knees weakening. Her father placed an arm around her shoulders, his strength a comfort.

"That wasn't enough for Mowat," said the fisherman. "He sent landing parties to fire the town, till nothing was left but a smoldering heap. Hundreds of buildings, including the church, and near all thirteen vessels in port were destroyed. Over a thousand souls are homeless. And winter is coming," he added, shaking his head.

Protests rippled through the crowd. Lizzy trembled as the fisherman's words sank in.

"They said it was to punish the Rebels for the Patriot victories in Cape Ann and Machias," the fisherman continued, his voice breaking. "For the *Margaretta* and Saint John. They said we'd pay for defying the Crown."

Mrs. Oakes let out a choked sob, and Mrs. Spencer gripped her arm, her eyes filled with fear.

Lizzy's mind raced to Jeremiah, out there on the sea, facing the same British wrath that had razed Falmouth. Her chest tightened, a cold dread settling in her bones.

Her father answered her unspoken question. "He'll be all right."

Foster's face darkened, his jaw tight. "Machias will be next if we aren't prepared." Turning to the men of the militia who had come to stand around him, he said,

"Double the garrison at Bucks Harbor and the patrols, day and night. Make sure the riverbank is fortified. I want every able hand ready."

The men nodded, eager to go to work.

The fisherman said, "The Continental Congress has added two cruisers to Washington's new privateers and issued a prize law to seize British ships."

"This is a call to fight, lads," said Ben Foster.

The men nodded, their faces grim, as the crowd began to scatter, some running to fetch tools, others to spread the word.

Reverend Lyon raised his voice, calling for calm. "Let us pray for Falmouth's people, and for our own safety," he said, adding, "This cruelty will turn even doubters to the cause. Independence is the only path now."

Lizzy barely heard him, her thoughts a jumble of fear and resolve. She went to Martha Lyon and asked, "What should we do to help the people of Falmouth?"

"We can share with them what we have, dear," said the reverend's wife. "When the fisherman returns to Falmouth, we'll send him with provisions and blankets."

Lizzy nodded. Her father was already discussing with the men what measures to take. Telling him she was returning to their house to begin gathering things for Falmouth, she hurried back, thinking of what they could contribute.

Her breath came in sharp gasps as she explained to Annie and Sean what had occurred. "You can help me find things we can spare for the poor folks in Falmouth."

They made a pile on the table of clothing and blankets and food they could spare, even some of their precious candles. Lizzy was pleased with what they had managed to find. Included were things they could have used themselves, but now others had a greater need. "When Father returns, we'll take these to Mrs. Lyon."

"It feels good to know we are helping them," said Annie, her expression revealing her fear.

Grabbing a quill and paper from her father's small desk, Lizzy forced a smile directed at her siblings. "It will be all right," she encouraged them with her father's words, though her voice was shaking.

"What are you doing?" asked Annie.

"I need to write something for Jeremiah." She sat by the fire, the paper resting on a book in her lap as she dipped the quill in the bottle of ink on the small side table, the words spilling out like a prayer.

> *My dearest Jeremiah, news has come of Falmouth's burning. The British commander Mowat gave the town only hours to flee, then he razed hundreds of buildings, even the church, leaving a thousand without homes. The man who brought us the news says it's because of the Machias victories. I fear they'll come for us next. I pray you're safe, that the Liberty and the Diligent shield you from their wrath.*
>
> *I hold your green ribbon close, a promise of your return, but I'd give anything to know you're whole. Stay safe, dear captain.*

She folded the letter, her tears smearing the ink in one place, and tucked it into her apron pocket. She would have said more, but the time to fully share her heart had not yet come. She could not send the letter, for she did not know where he was. But writing it eased the ache in her chest, if only a little. As though he were there to confide in.

The fire crackled, and she looked at Annie and Sean, their faces pale but brave, and knew she had to be strong for them. The war was closing in, its shadow darkening their door.

"We knew these days would come," she told them, "but Reverend Lyon says we must pray, and we can help Mrs. Lyon do what we can for Falmouth. The fight for liberty will not be easy, but with God's help, it is winnable."

"A free people ought not only to be armed, but disciplined; to which end a uniform and well-digested plan is requisite…"
– George Washington (1790)

CHAPTER 9

THE FIRST LIGHT of November broke over Machias, the river glistening like a ribbon of silver under a pale sky, the air sharp with the bite of early winter. Lizzy stood at the riverbank, her cloak pulled tightly around her against the cold wind as she watched the horizon with a hope she scarce dared to name. Since her mother's death years ago, she'd learned to shoulder her family's burdens—feeding Annie and Sean through lean winters, guiding them through their fears—yet today, the promise of Jeremiah's return stirred a joy within her.

The town had been abuzz since early that morning, word spreading that Jeremiah's *Liberty* and *Diligent* had been sighted off the coast, returning from their cruise with prizes in tow. The news of Falmouth's burning still hung heavy over Machias, the doubled patrols at Bucks Harbor and the fortified riverbank a constant reminder of the British threat. But today they could celebrate.

A cheer rose from the wharf as the *Liberty* came into view, her pine tree flag waving in the wind, the *Diligent* sailing close behind. Trailing them were what Lizzy assumed were the spoils of their cruise: a British cutter, and two barges, their red-coated prisoners under guard on the *Diligent*'s deck.

Lizzy's breath caught as she spotted Jeremiah standing amidships on the *Liberty*, his broad shoulders steady as he barked orders, his face weathered but whole. She clutched the letter in her apron pocket, her fingers tracing the folded edge—a plea she'd written through her tears after Falmouth—and wended her way through the gathering crowd. Somewhere behind her trailed Annie, Sean and their father.

The shore bustled with activity as the ships moored, the townsfolk surging forward to welcome the men and hear the news. Colonel Foster strode down to meet Jeremiah, his voice carrying over the din. "Well done, O'Brien! I see you've struck another blow for Machias and for liberty!"

The crowd roared, men clapping each other on the back as the captured goods were unloaded, barrels of pork, flour, and rum—a lifeline for the town as winter loomed—and crates of muskets. Thirty-five British prisoners, their clothing stained with salt and grime, were marched off under militia guard, the lieutenant's blue coat ripped in one place. His scowl met with jeers from the townsfolk. After the burning of Falmouth, few were sympathetic to British prisoners.

Reverend Lyon stood nearby, offering a prayer of thanks for the safe return of Machias' seamen, while Mrs. Spencer, Mrs. Oakes and Mrs. O'Brien passed out mugs of cider to the crew, their faces beaming with pride as they nodded their thanks to the women.

Jeremiah stepped ashore, a folded newspaper tucked under his arm, a satchel slung over his shoulder. Close behind him a crewman carried a crate. His eyes scanned the crowd until they found Lizzy. Her heart leapt as she ran to him, heedless of the mud spattering her skirts. She stopped before him, her smile wide as she took in his appearance. His face was tanned and he smelled of the sea, and he was whole. "You're back." Then with a smile, "Late as usual, but back all the same."

"Aye. I'm here, Lizzy," he murmured, his voice rough with emotion. "And I have something for you." Waving the crewman forward, he pointed to the crate. "Found this in the hold of one barge—beeswax candles, stashed beside casks of rum. The candles are for you, to brighten your nights. There's enough to share with your candlemakers. I'll have the value of the candles taken from my share of the prize."

"Thank you! The women will be delighted. I'll save some for your family, too."

Jeremiah asked the crewmember to take the crate to Lizzy's father, who was standing nearby with Ben Foster. The crewman hefted the crate, grinned at her, and strode off.

Searching Jeremiah's face, Lizzy detected no sign of

injury. "I've been so afraid, Jeremiah, ever since the news of Falmouth. I thought…" Her voice broke, and she reached into her apron pocket, pulling out the letter. "The day we learned what Mowat did at Falmouth, I wrote this for you. I couldn't send it, but I needed you to know." She pressed the letter into his hands, her fingers trembling.

Jeremiah unfolded the paper, his eyes softening as he read her words, the ink smudged with her tears. He looked up at her, his expression tender. "We got news of Falmouth when we made port at Gloucester." Tapping the newspaper under his arm, he said, "It was there I picked up a copy of the *Providence Gazette*. The paper tells the sorry tale." Opening the paper, he read, "Washington called the bombardment of Falmouth an 'outrage exceeding in barbarity and cruelty every hostile act practiced among civilized nations,' and John Adams says it's 'proof we must break from the Crown for good.'" He paused for a moment, and then said, "Just think, Lizzy, Massachusetts is going to create its own naval force! Coastal towns from here to the Carolinas are fortifying themselves. From the look of things as we sailed in, Ben and the militia are doing that here in Machias." He shook his head, his jaw tight. "Mowat's a ruthless man, but we'll make him pay. We took the cutter back from the British along with their barges, and brought back thirty-five of their sailors to trade for Patriots." His expression darkened. "But it came at a cost. We lost a good lad in the fight, Daniel Cole."

"Oh, Jeremiah." Lizzy's heart ached, her mind flashing to Cole's young son. "Daniel was married with a young son. His wife, Margaret, will be devastated."

"Before I go to my house, I must speak with Cole's widow, to tell her of his bravery and the service we gave him before burying him at sea."

"Do you want me to go with you?"

"Aye, if you're willing. It might help to have a woman present."

She took the newspaper from him, glancing at the bold headline: *Falmouth Burned by British Tyranny—Independence Now!* Despite the fear in her chest, she encouraged him, "You're doing what's right for Machias, for all of us."

He smiled, a flicker of warmth in his storm-blue eyes. "Thank you. How did Captain Smith's raid go?"

"It went well. His capture of the *Loyal Briton* was a blessing. He returned a few days after you left with the captured brig and a deck full of sheep and cattle."

"I would have liked to have seen that. We need all the victories we can get, and now that Ben Foster is judge of our vice admiralty court, the prizes can be judged and determined to be lawful when they are returned to Machias."

"In your absence," said Lizzy, "Dick Earle and London Atus harvested your apples with some of the townspeople. Annie, Sean and I helped. It was wonderful to see all those baskets full of apples."

"Thank you for helping. I had completely forgotten about the harvest."

"We sent some of the apples to the people of Falmouth," said Lizzy. "I hope that was all right. Some took shelter in the woods before leaving for nearby towns."

"Of course," said Jeremiah. "We should help them."

They stepped aside from the crowd, the water lapping gently at the river's edge.

Lizzy returned the newspaper to Jeremiah, and he tucked the letter she'd given him into his waistcoat. Taking her hand, he said, "I thought of you every day. The memory of your smile kept me going through the worst of it. We've a long fight ahead, but knowing you're here…it means a lot."

The tension in her chest eased for the first time in weeks. The war was far from over, but in that moment, with Jeremiah holding her hand and his blue eyes gazing into hers, she felt a glimmer of hope. "I'm glad you're home," she told him.

For a moment, they lingered, two hearts bound by a growing fondness and a shared fight for liberty, ready to face whatever came next.

Finally, he broke the silence. "Come, let us find Margaret Cole. 'Tis a sad duty but it must be done."

The wind tugged at their clothes as they walked toward the meeting house where a group of women stood with Martha Lyon around the sobbing widow.

THE SNOW FELL gently over Machias on Christmas Day, blanketing the town in a hush of white as the late December wind whispered through the pines. Inside the Fitzpatricks' house, a fire burned steadily in the hearth, casting a warm glow over the room where Lizzy helped Annie and Sean string dried apples to weave through greenery for the community gathering at Reverend Lyon's home. The air carried the scent of pine boughs and the faint sweetness of molasses, a rare treat her father had bartered for with some of the extra firewood he'd cut for the winter.

The town's share of the captured goods from Jeremiah's last cruise—barrels of pork, flour, and rum—had been rationed carefully. Her father's hunting had added to the Fitzpatricks' store of food. Winter's bite was expected to be fierce, and the town clung to every scrap to see them through until spring.

Lizzy kept a few of the beeswax candles for her family, gave some to Jeremiah's family and distributed the rest to the women who had made tallow candles with her, the "candlemakers" as Jeremiah called them. Lifting her gaze to the mantel, she smiled seeing the special candles set in her mother's pewter candlesticks. Tonight, she would light them.

Tying her green ribbon in her hair, Lizzy's thoughts drifted to Jeremiah, who had returned just days before from a short patrol along the coast with his Flying Squadron. The *Machias Liberty* and *Diligent* stood ready at the wharf, their masts stark against the snowy sky, a reminder of the war that loomed even amid the celebration of the holy day.

She glanced at Annie, whose sampler now hung on the wall, its stitched lines about Washington added to by a prayer for liberty. Sitting by the fire, Sean clutched his carved boat, humming a tune Jeremiah had taught him. "Will Captain O'Brien be at the reverend's, Lizzy?" Sean asked, his eyes hopeful.

"I believe he shall," Lizzy replied, her heart lifting at the thought. She put on her cloak, pulling it tightly around her, then she made sure Sean's coat was secured against the cold. Together with her father, she organized all of them for the walk to the Lyons' home, their greenery carried in a basket. The day before, she and Annie had helped Martha Lyon and the ladies of the sewing circle bake a few treats, and she was anxious to share them.

The families that lived close enough to the village would gather at the Lyons' home. Their faces might be etched with the strain of war, but the joy of the season would cheer them all. The British had not harassed Machias since Falmouth was burned, for great was the outrage all over the colonies. Even Britain was shocked at the destruction of an entire town. Apparently the revenge of Vice Admiral Graves would be delayed, Lizzy hoped forever.

As the Fitzpatricks entered the Lyons' home, the scent of cedar and candle wax wafted through the air, combined with the pine wood burning in the hearth and the spice of mulled cider. Setting down the basket near the door, Lizzy glanced at the table. It held what the community could spare—cornbread, smoked fish, and a precious pot of clam chowder, made with clams dug from the river, bits of pork from the captured stores, and a small portion of milk from one of the two cows that had survived from the *Loyal Briton*'s capture. The creamy chowder steamed gently in the cool air, a symbol of the town's resourcefulness. For dessert there were baked tarts with dried blueberries, for along with the beeswax candles, Jeremiah had found a hogshead of sugar aboard one of the barges and claimed it as part of his share when the prize was adjudicated. A punchbowl of mulled cider graced one end of the table.

Reverend Lyon stood by the hearth, his wife Martha at his side. Children, including their own, confined because of the weather, ran about. The reverend raised his hands for quiet. "We worshiped together yesterday," he began, "but as this Christmas falls on Monday, we again give thanks for the Savior, born to bring us God's gift of Salvation. We also give thanks for our safety in these times of war, and the victories and protection of America's brave leaders and men. Lastly, we thank God for the food we are about to eat."

The prayer was not long but it reminded all that God had not forgotten them, and that their leaders in Philadelphia and General Washington sought the Almighty's guidance every day.

When the prayer ended, Reverend Lyon said, "I have written to General Washington this very morning, proposing a plan to take Nova Scotia for the Continental Congress. We know from our friends there they are with us and would welcome such an effort. I have named our own Colonel Foster, Captain O'Brien, Captain Smith, and Mr. Shannon as men to lead such a venture, for Machias stands ready to strike another blow for liberty. It remains to be seen if General Washington has troops to spare for the effort."

Murmurs of approval sounded in the room. Lizzy's gaze met Jeremiah's across the crowd, his blue eyes sparkling with a quiet intensity. He may not have known of the reverend's letter, but his expression told her he approved.

Christmas greetings were followed by discussion as the townsfolk shared the food. Then Reverend Lyon led them in the hymn "Hark! The Herald Angels Sing," their voices rising together in the song of praise. When the chorus quieted, Jeremiah approached Lizzy, a small package in his hands, his expression hesitant. "I have carved this for you, Lizzy," he said, unwrapping a small wooden heart, its edges smoothed with care. "A token of my regard, to let you know you are in my heart this winter." Lizzy's cheeks flushed as she took the heart into her palm, her fingers tracing its curves, her own heart swelling with a fondness she scarce dared name. "It is beautiful, Jeremiah," she whispered. Gazing into his blue eyes, she added, "I shall treasure it."

Lizzy reached into her apron pocket, retrieving the dark blue-green woolen scarf she had stitched for him over the past weeks. Using scraps of green wool, dying some with elderberries and a touch of indigo, she had worked by candlelight to create a simple but sturdy scarf, hoping it would keep him warm on the cold decks of the *Liberty*. "And I have this for you, Jere," she said, her voice soft with emotion as she handed him the scarf. "To keep you warm on your voyages this winter, and to remind you of my fondness for you."

Jeremiah's eyes softened as he took the scarf, running his fingers over the careful stitches, the deep green hue a fitting match for the pine tree flag flying from his ship. "Lizzy, this is a thoughtful gift," he said, his voice full of gratitude. "One I sorely need, too. I shall wear it with pride, knowing it came from your hands." He draped the scarf around his neck and offered her a smile that warmed her more than the fire.

They stood together by the hearth, the glow of the

coals illuminating their faces, two souls bound by a growing fondness amidst the uncertainty of war. As snow fell outside, Lizzy silently asked God to keep Jeremiah in her life.

THE FIRST WEEKS of January 1776 brought a biting chill to Machias. The river was edged with ice and the wharf dusted with frost. Word had arrived days before that the Colonial Navy of Massachusetts had finally become official on December 29, 1775. There were to be uniforms for its officers and seamen, and its ships would fly the pine tree flag with the words "An Appeal to Heaven." Jeremiah had invited everyone to his house to see the new uniforms, and Lizzy, who had never been inside his house, was eager to go.

Bundled in their winter cloaks, Lizzy walked with Annie and Sean along the riverbank. The house, which fronted on the south side of the river, was similar in appearance to the home of Jeremiah's father, two stories with a gambrel roof and, like most houses in Machias, Jeremiah's was painted red, the iron oxide said to preserve the wood.

The large size of both houses as well as Gideon's, were among the conditions dictated by the grant of township as Jeremiah's sister, Mary Burnham had told her.

A row of poplar trees stood sentinel from the house nearly to the water's edge. In the summer months they would give welcome shade, but now their limbs were bare of leaves. Jeremiah had both plum and apple orchards on either side of the house.

People wearing winter cloaks against the cold were filing into the house as they arrived. Lizzy and her siblings followed them in. Stepping over the threshold the aroma of hot mulled cider welcomed them, the enticing scent of cinnamon and cloves wafting in the air. Candles and a blazing fire in the hearth added to the light reflecting off the snow that streamed into the large parlor.

As they were shedding their cloaks, she heard Jeremiah, who had yet to notice them, shout to his servant above the crowd, "Dick, can you fetch another cask of cider from the cellar?"

"Aye, I'll see to it," Dick replied.

Jeremiah's sister, Mary Burnham, came to greet them. "Hello to you!" she said. "Is Thomas coming?"

"Father will be along a bit later," said Lizzy. "He had an errand to do for the tree harvest beginning next week."

"You must try the cider," said Mary. "It's mulled with spices. Jere's very proud of it since it's made from his own apples."

Lizzy glanced at her brother whose eyes were bright. "Yes, please," he said.

"Go join your friends," she told him, which was all the encouragement he needed to scamper off. She watched him join a group of boys standing near the table in the center of the room where Mrs. Spencer and Mrs. Oakes appeared to be handing out something.

"There's food," said Mary, watching the boys. "Enough to keep the young ones happy."

"I had no idea Jeremiah was planning a party!" remarked Lizzy as the din in the large parlor increased with more arrivals.

"I think it's wonderful," said Annie. "There's not much to do except read and sew on days like this."

"He wanted to do it for his crews and their families," said Mary. "The bulk of the uniforms won't arrive until spring, of course, but at least he can show them what they will look like."

With that, Mary urged them toward the end of the table where Martha Lyon was serving cider from a large punchbowl. Jeremiah stood with Reverend Lyon a short distance away, each with a tumbler of cider in hand. Above the fireplace mantel was a man's portrait, an officer by the look of his uniform. He was not anyone she had met. Next to it hung a coat of arms with three lions, half-gold and half-silver, on a red shield, the same O'Brien coat of arms that hung in the home of Morris and Mary O'Brien. Beneath the shield was a phrase in a language she did not recognize but presumed was Irish, *Lámh Láidir an Uchtar*. She made a mental note to ask Jeremiah about both the portrait and the coat of arms.

Just then, Jeremiah caught sight of them. "The Fitz-patricks have arrived!"

Lizzy met his gaze, her heart quickening at the warmth in his eyes. He was wearing her woolen scarf. She and Annie walked to the two men. "Good day to you, sirs," said Lizzy. "My father has yet to arrive, but he will be along soon. This is a wonderful party, Captain O'Brien."

"Most welcome on a winter's day," said the reverend. "Martha is serving the hot mulled cider; you must have some."

"Come," said Jeremiah, "I will go with you. I could

REGAN WALKER

use a second tumbler."

Reverend Lyon waved them on and they crossed to where Mrs. Lyon was serving the cider. "A splendid event, isn't it?" she asked Lizzy and Annie.

"It is," said Lizzy, stealing a glance at Jeremiah.

Mrs. Lyon poured them each a tumbler and refilled Jeremiah's.

Surgeon McDonald approached Annie, greeting her with a broad smile. She had just turned seventeen and suddenly looked very much the young lady to Lizzy. Annie offered to introduce him to her friends. When he appeared pleased at the suggestion, the two walked away, leaving Jeremiah and Lizzy alone but surrounded by people.

"You are looking lovely this day, Miss Fitzpatrick."

"Why, thank you, Captain." Then, with a small smile, she added, "I'm very fond of the ribbon you gave me and my family admires it in my hair. And the wooden heart is very special."

"I am fond of my scarf," he said stroking the wool with his hand. "It keeps the chill off my neck."

Holding her tumbler in both hands to warm them, she took a sip. "Your cider is very good, a fitting beverage to toast the new navy."

"Aye," he said with a pleased look. "We are official now."

Shifting her gaze to the portrait over the mantel, she asked. "Who is that officer?"

Jeremiah turned to it. "General Washington. I purchased the print in Cambridge."

"He's a fine-looking man," said Lizzy.

174

"And a great leader," added Jeremiah. "He wears a different uniform now that he is Commander in Chief of the Continental Army, and his hair is often powdered."

"The coat of arms next to it is the O'Brien shield, is it not?"

"Yes. The motto in Irish means 'the strong hand uppermost'."

Lizzy laughed at the irony. "Do you know the motto of the Fitzpatricks?"

He shook his head.

"It's *Fortis sub Forte Fatiscet* in Latin and means 'the strong will yield to the strong'."

That brought a smile to his face. "Well, then, I would say we are inherently compatible."

Reverend Lyon came to them. "Now would be a good time, Jeremiah."

Jeremiah said to her, "It's time to show our officers and the crews what they'll be wearing come spring."

Lizzy's father entered just then, and she carried a tumbler of cider to him.

Jeremiah took his place before the hearth flanked by John Lambert and Reverend Lyon. Crowded in front of them were the officers and several members of the crews from the *Liberty* and the *Diligent* and their families. Annie was standing to one side with the golden-haired surgeon. Looking on was Colonel Foster and a few of the militia.

Jeremiah began. "Thank you for coming. It was my thought to celebrate this day, for we are now officially a part of the new Massachusetts Navy. Soon, we will have uniforms and official colors flying from our masts."

His lieutenants and crew nodded, their smiles eager,

their loyalty to their captain unwavering.

"Finally!" said John O'Brien.

"In his capacity as leader of the Committee of Safety," said Jeremiah, "Reverend Lyon has brought the first shipment of uniforms to show us. The rest are being made and will hopefully arrive in the spring."

From behind him, Reverend Lyon reached into a neatly stacked pile of clothing, pulling out a dark green woolen coat with buff facings and pewter buttons. Holding it up for all to admire, he said, "This officer's coat will be paired with a matching buff waistcoat and breeches, and a white cravat. Due to a shortage of metal, the buttons are pewter at this time, but eventually they will be brass. There is also this," he said, pulling out a cocked hat bearing a small pine tree flag stitched onto its side.

Everyone applauded. "Green is a fitting color for our colony," said Ben Foster. "'Tis a handsome uniform for our naval officers."

Jeremiah set his scarf down and took the dark green coat from Reverend Lyon and slipped it on, the buff facings catching the firelight. He adjusted the white cravat and placed the cocked hat on his head, the small pine tree flag insignia gleaming proudly. Lizzy's breath caught at the sight. He looked every inch a captain of the Massachusetts Navy, a leader ready to defend their cause.

"The seamen's uniforms," Lyon announced to the gathered crowd as he lifted more clothing from behind him, "consist of red striped jerseys, white pantaloons and black neckerchiefs, to which will be added cutlasses for charging the British."

The seamen smiled their approval. "Impressive," said Isaac Taft. "The British will spot us a mile away."

"All the better," said Jeremiah. "You will strike fear in their hearts."

Isaac's young daughter tugged at her father's sleeve. "You'll look fine, Papa!" she said, her eyes wide with excitement, drawing smiles from those nearby.

"As you know," said Reverend Lyon, "thanks to the sewing skills of the Machias women, our ships fly the pine tree flag from their masts. The new colors, you will be happy to learn, are the same but with the added phrase 'An Appeal to Heaven'. This is the same flag that will fly from the privateers General Washington commissions."

Lizzy immediately thought of some black cloth she had that could be used for the new motto that she would add to the existing flags. Her father leaned close. "You should be proud of your idea for the pine tree flag, Lizzy."

Lizzy nodded, her thoughts drifting to the motto 'An Appeal to Heaven.' It was a plea for divine aid in their struggle, a hope she held for Machias, and for a future with Jeremiah. Happy to participate in something so grand, she resolved to stitch the words with care, each letter a prayer for their victory.

The crews cheered and the crowd applauded. Lizzy felt a swell of pride as she joined in, her eyes on Jeremiah, a leader men could be proud of, and a man she could love.

"Perseverance and spirit have done wonders in
all ages."
– George Washington (1776)

CHAPTER 10

THE LATE JANUARY wind brought Jeremiah and his
ships to Newburyport, south of Falmouth and north of
Salem. The wind howled through the docks, carrying the
bite of winter as he stood amidships on the deck of the
Liberty, his dark green woolen scarf wrapped tightly
around his neck. The *Liberty* and *Diligent* were moored
side by side, their crews loading what meager provisions
they had secured, but a palpable tension hung over the
men. Jeremiah's eyes scanned their faces, noting the
furrowed brows and muttered complaints as they worked.

The news had come earlier that day: the Massachusetts General Court intended to maintain the Flying
Squadron's wages at their initial rate, scarce enough to
feed a man, let alone a family, and the payments, already

months overdue, had yet to arrive.

Isaac Taft tossed a sack of flour onto the deck with more force than necessary, his voice rising above the wind, his weathered face contorted in a frown. "We risk our lives for the Patriot cause, Captain, and the colony will not pay us a proper wage. And what it does pay is not paid on time! My children go hungry while the General Court dithers. We should not sail another day under these terms."

A murmur of agreement rippled through the crew, and Jeremiah's first lieutenant, his brother, William, stepped forward, his expression grim. "They are near to abandoning the service altogether, Jere," he said quietly. "We shall be left in the lurch if this continues."

Jeremiah's jaw tightened, his heart heavy with the weight of their words. Believing the General Court would treat them fairly, he had promised his men wages equal to those of other seamen sailing vessels in the colony's service—eight pounds a month for captains, three for seamen—a fair rate for the dangers they faced. But the General Court's refusal to honor this promise, paying them only half, threatened to unravel the loyalty of the very men who had fought so bravely under his command. "I hear your grievances," he said to his crew, his voice carrying the length of the deck. "They are just." His voice was steady despite the storm brewing within him. "I shall not see you wronged. I shall travel to Watertown this very day at my own expense and plead our case before the court. You are the heart of this fight, and I shall ensure you are paid what you are owed."

The men nodded, their anger tempered by their trust

in him as their captain, though Jeremiah sensed their unease lingered. Turning to William, he said, "See that the provisions we have purchased are loaded and secured. In addition to proper pay, I will ask for more gunpowder, as we have but a fraction of what we need, barely enough for a single engagement. Explain all to Captain Lambert on the *Diligent*. I shall return as soon as I am able."

William saluted, his face resolute. "Aye, aye, Captain. We shall hold fast until you do."

As the crew dispersed to their duties, Jeremiah descended the companionway to his small cabin aboard the *Liberty*, the flickering light of a single lantern casting shadows on the bulkheads. The gentle sway of the moored sloop was a constant reminder of the sea as he sat at the narrow desk, pulling a sheet of parchment and quill from his satchel.

He first drafted a petition for the General Court, pleading their case with specificity. When that was done, his thoughts turned to Lizzy. Her face, framed by her red hair glistening in candlelight, filled his mind. Would she think he had failed his men? Dipping the quill in the ink, he began to write, his words a blend of duty and longing.

> *My dearest Lizzy, I find myself in Newburyport, seeking provisions and ammunition for the squadron, but a grave matter weighs heavily upon me. I had promised my crew wages equal to those of other vessels in the colony service, for they risk their lives as bravely as any Patriot. Yet word has reached us that the General Court intends to keep our pay at the first establishment, scarce enough to feed their families. The men are near to abandoning the service altogether, and I fear I shall be*

left in the lurch. I have no choice but to travel to Water-town, and I will do so at my own expense, to plead their case before the court. I shall not see the men wronged, for they are the heart of this fight. Pray for us, Lizzy. Gunpowder is scarce here, and the road to Watertown is long.

He paused, his quill hovering over the page as he pictured Lizzy reading his words, her brow furrowed with worry. Perhaps she would question his leadership that he had allowed things to come to this. He longed to tell her more—to speak of the hope she gave him, of the future he dreamed of with her, but duty called, and he could not linger on such thoughts when his men could not buy bread. He added a final line, his heart in every word: *Keep me in your prayers, as I keep you in mine.*

Sealing the letter, Jeremiah entrusted it to a passing courier headed north, then gathered his cloak to leave for Watertown. The road ahead was uncertain, the war's shadow ever present, but the thought of Lizzy, and the justice he owed his men, gave him the strength to press on.

THE FEBRUARY CHILL lingered in the Fitzpatricks' house near the river. Lizzy was grateful for the warmth of the hearth and its bright glow as she sat at the table, her hands holding a letter just arrived from Newburyport. Her father sat across from her, cleaning his hunting rifle, while Annie read by the fire, and Sean played with his knuckle-bones on the floor, exclaiming in delight when he picked

THE IRISH YANKEE

up all the jacks. Her brother's joy was a counterpoint to the worry in Lizzy's heart.

The letter, penned by Jeremiah in late January, had taken weeks to reach Machias. It was now nearing March. She unfolded the parchment, the faint scent of saltwater still clinging to it, and silently read the letter, trembling at the grim picture painted by Jeremiah's words. Her eyes lingered on his words.

> I had promised my crew wages equal to those of other vessels in the colony service, for they risk their lives as bravely as any Patriot. Yet word has reached us that the General Court intends to keep our pay at the first establishment, scarce enough to feed their families.

She set down the letter, her eyes glistening with unshed tears as she stared into the fire, the weight of Jeremiah's burden heavy on her heart.

"What news from Captain O'Brien?" asked her father. She turned to see his attention was still on his rifle.

"The *Liberty* and *Diligent* are in Newburyport where Jeremiah and Captain Lambert have been obtaining provisions and ammunition for the squadron. The crew complains of poor wages, slowly paid, and expressed their deep unrest in no uncertain terms. It seems the colony has failed to pay both Jeremiah and his crews the same wage as other captains and crews. He feels responsible."

Her father looked up, his expression stern. "As the captain of the flying squadron, he *is* responsible, Lass. But the colony's coffers are strained by the war, and the General Court faces many demands. 'Tis said General Washington has had to petition the court for weapons for

183

his army. It's a heavy burden for any man to bear with so many lives counting on him."

Letting out a sigh, Lizzy said, "Yes, I suppose so, and it has become a grievous burden for Jeremiah. Using his own funds, he has gone to Watertown to plead their case before the General Court." Setting the letter down, she said, "He risks so much, Father. He asks for prayer." Her voice was thick with emotion. "The General Court may refuse him, and the gunpowder he needs is scarce."

Thomas set down his rifle, his face softening with understanding. "We will pray for him. Jeremiah is a man of honor, Lass. He fights for his men as fiercely as he fights the British. The General Court will see reason. They must, for men like him are the backbone of the Massachusetts Navy."

Lizzy nodded, though she still worried. Beside her on the table lay the black cloth she had been using to cut out the words "An Appeal to Heaven" for his ships' colors. She tucked the letter into her apron pocket and resumed her sewing, silently praying for the man who held her heart.

Annie looked up, her eyes wide. "Will the captain be back soon?" Lizzy knew her sister worried for the *Liberty*'s surgeon.

"I hope so, sweet," Lizzy replied, forcing a smile. "He is doing what is right, and we shall pray he and his crew return safely."

From the floor by the hearth, Sean said, "I will pray for him, too."

Thomas rose, placing a reassuring hand on her shoulder. "I have seen the way he looks at you, Lizzy," he said in a quiet voice. "When he returns, I shall speak with him about his intentions. A man who fights so fiercely for his crew shall surely fight for the woman he loves."

Lizzy's cheeks flushed, her heart lifting at the thought, though the shadow of war still loomed large. "But Father, if he must spend his own wages to meet the needs of his men, perhaps he is not ready to take on...more responsibilities."

"You may be right," said her father, "but he has a position with rank and a fine home. I doubt he will be deterred. Perhaps when he returns for the St. Patrick's Day celebration, we shall have cause to celebrate more than our Irish heritage."

That brought a smile to her face. As the fire crackled and the wind howled outside, Lizzy set down her sewing and felt in her apron pocket for the carved wooden heart Jeremiah had given her at Christmas. Holding it tightly, she thought of him on the cold road to Watertown. She admired his sense of justice, his willingness to bear the cost for his men, but she could not dismiss the war's dangers. She prayed that spring would bring him back to her, whole and with good news.

MARCH BROUGHT THE first hints of spring to Machias, a welcome change after the long winter. Jeremiah stood outside the meeting house where the townsfolk were gathering to celebrate St. Patrick's Day, a day of joy for the many Irish families like the O'Briens and Fitzpatricks who had made this rugged coast their home.

He had returned from Newburyport yesterday, the

sixteenth of March, his spirits high as his mission to secure fair wages for his squadron had been successful. He had not received the full amount of gunpowder he'd asked for due to its short supply, but they had enough for their next cruise.

When he arrived, he called first upon Lizzy to tell her his good news, not just for his success in Watertown, but of the good news coming from Boston. General Washington had fortified the hills of Dorchester Heights above the town. The clever idea of Colonel Henry Knox to obtain artillery, which General Washington had alluded to at the dinner in Cambridge, had worked.

"In one night in the early days of this month," he told her, "the Patriots hauled at least twenty cannon up the hills to loom over Boston. Providence then intervened with a storm to prevent the British from attacking Dorchester Heights. Taken by surprise, General Howe could no longer defend the city. He sent word to Washington, telling him the 120-ship British fleet would be leaving Boston with thousands of Loyalists and their families."

"Truly this St. Patrick's Day will be an Independence Day for Massachusetts," Lizzy had replied.

With a smile he told her, "You will love what General Washington did next. He issued orders that anyone wishing to pass the sentries guarding the army's camp on St. Patrick's Day must give the special password, 'Saint Patrick'."

Lizzy loved that. "Wait until I tell my father."

"And mine," replied Jeremiah.

With a good night's sleep, he looked forward to the

town's celebration today, as he strode over the grass leading to the meeting house, his servant Dick by his side. The whole area was alive with music and laughter. A fiddler played a lively jig as children danced and women set out tables laden with soda bread, smoked fish, and bowls of colcannon—mashed potatoes mixed with kale, a nod to their Irish roots. The *Liberty* and the *Diligent* were anchored in the river not far away, their pine tree flags fluttering in the breeze. The motto "An Appeal to Heaven" was proudly displayed in black letters, a testament to Lizzy's careful stitching.

Jeremiah released Dick to enjoy himself, then took a stance near the edge of the crowd, glad for his dark green woolen scarf, for it was still cool despite the milder weather. He smiled as he watched the festivities. Soon, his brothers joined him along with John Lambert. They congratulated Jeremiah again on his success at Watertown, and then began to talk about General Washington's success in Boston. One of the girls who worked in Burnham Tavern brought them tankards of ale.

"I expect they are celebrating in Boston today," said Jeremiah, "cheering and weeping for the joy of seeing General Howe's flagship, *Chatham*, his ships-of-war and his army leaving with the Loyalists."

"Aye, it would be a spectacle," said John Lambert.

"To where would Howe be sailing?" asked Gideon, his expression curious.

"It is thought he would take the Loyalists to Halifax, Nova Scotia," said Jeremiah, "before turning his army to New York."

"Reverend Lyon will be dismayed to hear that," said

John. "He had hoped Nova Scotia would join the cause for liberty."

When Jeremiah's eyes met Lizzy's across the crowd, the noise of the celebration faded. Handing his empty tankard to his brother, William, he crossed the grass to her. She had on a pretty green dress, one he'd not seen before. "You look radiant today, Miss Fitzpatrick," he said, his voice low and earnest. "It's only been one night and already I have missed you dearly."

Lizzy's cheeks flushed. "And I you, Captain O'Brien. I am glad to see you celebrating with your men."

"There is much to celebrate this day."

Before Lizzy could respond, her father approached, his face lit with a smile. "Captain O'Brien," he said, clapping Jeremiah on the shoulder. "A word, if I may."

"Of course," said Jeremiah. Excusing himself, he stepped aside with her father, leaving Lizzy to join Annie and Sean, who stood nearby, clapping along to the fiddler's tune.

Thomas spoke quietly to Jeremiah, his tone firm. "You have proven yourself a man of honor, Jeremiah, not only in battle but in your care for your men. I know you carry the burden of command and have experienced deprivations from the General Court's failures, but I have seen you rise above those to triumph. All that is to your credit but that is not why I asked to speak to you."

Jeremiah fixed the older man with a steady gaze, suspecting the subject Thomas wanted to discuss.

"For some time now, I have noticed the way you look at my daughter. I have observed the growing affection between the two of you. It is my duty as her father to ask what your intentions are toward Elizabeth."

Jeremiah met Thomas' gaze unflinchingly. "I love her and wish to marry her, to build a life with her here in Machias, if she will have me. The war brings uncertainty, and my role as commander of the Flying Squadron will often keep me away. The General Court has restricted our operations to the Massachusetts coast, but that extends over five hundred miles. If she can accept that I would not always be at home, that there may be weeks, if not months, I would be at sea, I would swear to protect and provide for her, as I have for my crew."

Thomas nodded, his approval showing in his eyes. "Then you have my blessing. A wedding in autumn, perhaps after your next cruise, would be a pleasant occasion. Go to her, and may you find joy together amidst these troubled times."

Jeremiah thanked him and they shook hands. He returned to Lizzy, his step light for the task ahead. He held out his hand. She placed her hand in his, and he led her to a quiet corner on one side of the meeting house, the mottos of their families running through his mind—*Lámh Láidir an Uchtar* for the O'Briens, "the strong hand uppermost" and *Fortis sub Forte Fatiscet* for the Fitzpatricks, "the strong shall yield to the strong". They were indeed compatible, as he had said at the gathering in his home. He hoped she thought so, too.

The music faded into the background as he faced her. "Lizzy," he began, softening his voice, "these past months have shown me the depth of my feelings for you. Your courage, your kindness, and your steadfast heart have sustained me through every trial. I have spoken with your father, and he has given me his blessing to ask, will you do me the honor of becoming my wife?"

Her eyes shone with tears of joy. "Yes, Jeremiah," she said, her voice steady. "I shall be your wife, and I shall stand by you through all that the war may bring."

"You know the war and my duty will often separate us?"

"Yes." She smiled, adding, "I have already experienced that. But I am proud of you for your commitment to America and to the cause of liberty. We will trust God for the rest."

Jeremiah drew her close, pressing a gentle kiss to her lips, mindful of the crowd nearby.

"I love you, Lizzy Fitzpatrick."

"And I love you, Jeremiah O'Brien."

"Come," he said drawing her back to the crowd. "This is a glorious day. Let us announce our engagement."

The fiddler struck up a new tune, as they rejoined the celebration, hand in hand, the future uncertain but their love a beacon of hope as spring dawned in Machias.

At sea off the Massachusetts Coast, June 1776

THE JUNE WIND carried the tang of salt and the promise of summer as Jeremiah stood on the deck of the *Liberty*, his eyes scanning the horizon as the sloop cut through the waves with a steady rhythm. Beside her sailed the *Diligent*, under the command of John Lambert, the two vessels patrolling the coastal waters of Massachusetts together.

A shout from the lookout broke into his thoughts.

"Sail ho! Off the starboard bow!" Jeremiah raised his spyglass, narrowing his eyes on a small schooner flying British colors, her sails taut as she made for a cove near Cape Ann. "A supply runner, likely," he said to William, standing at his side. "Signal the *Diligent* to come about—we'll take her."

"Aye, aye, Captain." William barked the orders and the crew sprang into action. The sails of the *Liberty* billowed with wind as they bore down on the schooner, their guns primed but unneeded, for the smaller vessel struck her colors after a single warning shot across her bow.

The schooner's captain, a grizzled Loyalist, glared at Jeremiah and his crew as he brought down his flag, muttering curses under his breath.

Within the hour, the *Liberty*'s crew had boarded her, securing a cargo of flour, rum, molasses and a small cache of muskets—meager but welcome provisions for Machias and muskets for the militia. The air grew thick with the sharp scent of rum leaking from a breached barrel.

As the prize crew took control, Jeremiah leaned against the rail, his dark green woolen scarf a comfort against the wind. His thoughts turned to Lizzy, as they so often did on these long patrols. In Machias, she would be preparing for their wedding come autumn, filling the hope chest her father had crafted for her. Before he sailed, she had told him she'd not been preparing for such an event, so consumed she had been caring for her siblings. He pictured her stitching clothing and linens for her trousseau, her head of red hair bent over her needle. The promise of their life together, amidst the uncertainty of the war, was an island of joy, giving him strength to press on.

William joined him, wiping sweat from his brow. "A good day's work, Jere. Ben Foster will be pleased with the prize when it arrives in Machias, and I wager the men are already dreaming of their share."

Jeremiah's jaw tightened. "Aye. The one-third of the proceeds promised to them must suffice for the present, though the allure of privately owned vessels, offering higher rewards and higher pay for the crew, grows apace." Jeremiah was well aware of the whispers that promised better pay drawing sailors away from colony ships.

Turning his gaze back to the horizon, Jeremiah murmured, "Soon we will return to Machias, and I will make Lizzy my wife. Then, perhaps, we shall see what the future holds for the squadron."

William's brow furrowed. "The cry for independence stirs in the colonies, Jere. Rumors of bold resolves from Philadelphia have begun to drift northward. I hear it in the crew's talk."

Boston, Massachusetts, mid-July 1776

THE *MACHIAS LIBERTY* rocked gently at the wharf in Boston, her crew granted leave to go ashore after a grueling patrol along the Massachusetts coast. The port, freed from British control since March, buzzed with renewed life, its taverns alive with the clamor of Patriots celebrating the city's nascent independence.

Walking a few streets from the harbor, Jeremiah

stepped into the Green Dragon Tavern, his dark green naval coat dusted with sea salt. He breathed in the scent of ale and pipe smoke as the hum of voices grew louder around him. He and his brothers, John and William, joined John Lambert, Donald McDonald and a few crewmen at a rough-hewn table where they were served ale. "This is where they planned the dumping of England's tea," whispered his brother, William.

"Aye," said Jeremiah, "and the Sons of Liberty still call it home."

A grizzled merchant, his face flushed with drink, slammed a broadsheet onto their table. "Hear ye, Captains!" Then, looking around him, he said, "Hear ye, all! Word from Philadelphia has just arrived. A declaration of our independence has been adopted!" He pointed to the ink-still-damp paper.

Jeremiah leaned forward, his eyes scanning the lines as he read aloud for the benefit of those around him. "A Virginian, Richard Henry Lee, moved for independence on the seventh of June, calling for separation from the British Crown, a move to form foreign alliances, and a plan for confederation. In response, Congress formed a committee to draft a Declaration of Independence, assigning the duty to Thomas Jefferson. The committee presented the final draft to Congress on the 28th of June, and on the fourth of July, Congress adopted a Declaration of Independence." Looking up, Jeremiah added, "The alarm for freedom was sounded by the bell in the Pennsylvania State House in Philadelphia."

The merchant pointed his long finger at the last lines. "Do ye see that? A Declaration of Independence from Britain has been adopted!"

Jeremiah looked up, staring at his brothers sitting across from him whose faces were frozen open-mouthed. The tavern erupted in cheers, tankards clashing and loud huzzahs sounding as the Patriots reacted to news.

A sailor at the next table began a rousing chorus of Yankee Doodle, the tune spreading through the tavern like wildfire.

John and William lifted their tankards to toast Jeremiah's. "We're a new nation, Jere!" said John.

"Our privateering has helped secure this day," added John Lambert, raising his own tankard.

Jeremiah nodded, pride swelling in his chest as tears welled in his eyes. The months at sea, the captured prizes, the stories of their privateering—everything that had gone before paled beside this moment. He rose from his chair and lifted his tankard to his officers and crew in toast, "To America and to freedom!"

"To America and freedom!" they echoed.

As he sat down, he wondered, did Lizzy know? Would she and those in Machias be celebrating? His father had lived for this day. "I must write to Reverend Lyon and to Lizzy," he told John and William.

Rising, he went to the tavern keeper and borrowed quill and paper. As the celebrating continued around him, Jeremiah began a letter to Reverend Lyon, his hand steady despite the tavern's din.

> To the Reverend James Lyon, pastor of the Congregational Church of Machias, Maine:
>
> I pen this from Boston, where I have just learned of the Continental Congress' bold decree of the fourth of July, declaring America's independence from Britain.

All are celebrating here as I hope you are in Machias, for you have done your part, as have the people there, in bringing about this day. The war is not over, but this marks a momentous advance. We are no longer colonies, dear reverend, we are newly declared independent states!

There is no turning back now and I am glad for it.

We will be a few days in Boston's port and then will resume our cruise for British ships. In the meantime, I will send this north to you by the first ship headed your way. Do tell my parents and my brothers still at home the good news.

Enclosed is a note for Elizabeth, that she may share this joy with me. I shall return to Machias ere long, God willing, to wed her as planned. Pray for our success against the foe.

Jeremiah O'Brien

Before Jeremiah folded the parchment, he slipped inside a smaller sheet bearing his words to Lizzy.

My dearest Lizzy, the colonies—now states!—are free, and my heart yearns to celebrate with you. This news strengthens my resolve to return by autumn for our union. Keep the symbol of my heart close, as I hold you ever in my heart.

Jere

Sealing the letter and its enclosure, Jeremiah entrusted them to the captain of a fishing boat headed north, his spirit lifted by the promise of independence and the love that awaited him.

"I retain an unalterable affection for you, which neither time or distance can change."
– George Washington to Martha Washington
(1775)

CHAPTER 11

Machias, Maine, August 1776

THE SUN FILTERED through the open windows of the Spencers' home in Machias, casting its light on the circle of ladies gathered to sew. It was a warm summer day, and they were all thankful for the breeze off the river.

Lizzy took her place in the circle, her fingers nimbly stitching a linen shift for her trousseau. Their father had made Lizzy a hope chest of fine pine wood to store the things she was making for her new life with Jeremiah, and she was eager to see it filled.

Annie, sitting next to her, glanced at the shift. "I'll be happy to embroider some flowers on the neckline if you like."

"Oh, yes, I would like that," said Lizzy, "your stitches are so fine. You have the prettiest sampler of all those I've seen."

The other women worked on their own projects, their voices excited for the news that had reached the town concerning independence. "The news from Captain O'Brien has lifted our spirits," said Mrs. Oakes. Lizzy had shared the contents of Jeremiah's letter delivered by courier, and then just yesterday they received a copy of the actual declaration sent to every town from Philadelphia.

"Why don't you read it for us?" Mrs. Oakes asked Mrs. Lyon. The reverend's wife set down the piece she was working on. "My sewing can wait. I'd be pleased to read the new declaration instead." Whereupon she picked up the printed copy and began to read, "The unanimous declaration of the thirteen united States of America…" She stopped and said, "Just think, we are now states, no longer Britain's colonies."

"It's as if we are embarking on a journey uncharted," said Mrs. Spencer. Heads nodded as fingers continued to stitch.

Mrs. Lyon read on, repeating the words, "We hold these truths to be self-evident, that all men are created equal, that they are endowed by their Creator with certain unalienable rights, that among these are life, liberty and the pursuit of happiness."

"I like the sound of that," said Mrs. Spencer.

Mrs. Lyon read more and then said, "The declaration lists 'repeated injuries' the colonies have endured at the hands of the King of Great Britain." She then read the list any Patriot would agree with. It was a long list.

The ones that stayed in Lizzy's mind were Britain's cutting off trade with all parts of the world, imposing taxes without the colonies' consent and, in many cases, depriving the colonies of the benefits of trial by jury. But when the reverend's wife read the next items, all the women were noticeably affected. "He has plundered our seas, ravaged our coasts, burnt our towns, and destroyed the lives of our people."

Lizzy shuddered, recalling the news of the burning of Falmouth.

At the end of the list of grievances, Mrs. Lyon read, "A prince, whose character is thus marked by every act which may define a tyrant, is unfit to be the ruler of a free people."

Heads nodded and Lizzy joined them. Mrs. Lyon then read the part that dissolved all political connection between the new states and Great Britain, finishing with, "And for the support of this Declaration, with a firm reliance on the protection of divine Providence, we mutually pledge to each other our lives, our fortunes and our sacred honor."

Lizzy thought of the flag that flew from the masts of Jeremiah's ships. "'Tis the Appeal to Heaven that speaks from the colors flown on Machias ships."

"It certainly is," said Mrs. Oakes.

Annie, her cheeks flushed with excitement and tears in her eyes, set down her needle. "We are a free nation! And to think Jeremiah and his crews helped secure our liberty with his squadron." Her eyes darted to the window. Was she thinking of Donald McDonald, the surgeon who'd caught her fancy?

"The path ahead will prove arduous, I think," said Mrs. Spencer. "The Crown will not take us seriously until and unless we win the war."

"With General Washington leading our army and our navy fighting on the seas, and God granting them favor, it is winnable," said Lizzy. "We must continue to pray for them."

The discussion went on with both praise and worry being expressed. When they finally finished their sewing, Mrs. Spencer rose and said, "We have blueberry tarts and cider to celebrate."

Happy to set aside her sewing, Lizzy joined Annie at the table where the tarts were set out, their golden crusts bursting with the season's bounty. Beside them were two pitchers of cider, which she and Annie poured for the others.

Hannah Weston, Josiah's wife, who had made a special trip to be with them today, raised her tumbler. "To America and our new freedom!" she declared, her voice ringing with conviction.

The women echoed her toast, their laughter mingling with the clink of tumblers as they savored the blueberry tarts. The young Mrs. Weston added with a smile, "We'll need to make candles come October for your wedding to be brightly lit."

"You all must attend my wedding," said Lizzy.

As the afternoon waned, Lizzy's thoughts turned to Jeremiah, patrolling the Massachusetts coast. His note that said, *Keep the symbol of my heart close, as I hold you ever in my heart.* That symbol—the wooden heart he'd carved for her—rested in her apron pocket as a tangible reminder of his love. For now, she found solace in having celebrated with her friends as she prayed for Jeremiah's return.

Machias, Maine, mid-October, 1776

OUTSIDE, OCTOBER'S AIR was crisp, and the sun on the leaves, now turned vivid shades of orange, yellow, and red, made for a glorious sight. The red houses, of which there were many in Machias, added to the riot of color. Lizzy had witnessed other autumns, but she remembered none so splendid as this one. For today, she was to marry the man to whom she had given her heart, and it only seemed fitting that nature should celebrate with its brilliant colors.

The Fitzpatrick home was alive with the excitement of the day. The hope chest now held the linens and clothing she had sewn as well as a beautiful flowered quilt the women of the sewing circle had gifted her, a testament to the bond they had formed since the Fitzpatricks had moved to Machias. "We'll take the chest to Jeremiah's home later today," her father said.

Jeremiah had returned the week before with ducks for roasting and wine to drink, to which her father's hunting with Jeremiah's brothers had added venison to the menu for the wedding dinner. Isaac Taft and his fishermen friends had also provided trout.

Among the other treasures the Flying Squadron brought back to Machias were yards of a beautiful woolen fabric for Lizzy's wedding gown. "I thought of you when I first saw it," Jeremiah told her. "The blue is the same color as your eyes." The sewing circle had been working feverously ever since to help her finish the dress. Annie had leant her blue ribbon for Lizzy to wear around her neck.

Standing before the mirror they had brought from Onslow, her red hair taken up except for one long curl left to dangle to her shoulder, she admired her blue dress. The fine wool was fitted at her bosom, around her arms and to her waist. The skirt flared out as it fell to her feet. The blue ribbon was a perfect match as she tied it around her neck, finishing it in a bow.

"You are perfect," said Annie with an admiring gaze. "We'd best leave," she added, "or you'll be late for your wedding."

The meeting house, which was also the Congregational Church, awaited. Lizzy forced her racing heart to slow as she walked with her family to the church door.

As she entered on her father's arm, the congregation rose. Lizzy's eyes were drawn to the front of the large room where autumn flowers were set in a basket at the front. Jeremiah stood next to the flowers, a wide smile on his face. He wore a dark blue jacket with ivory waistcoat and breeches, so well-tailored his father must have fashioned the clothes for him. Next to him were his five brothers, their faces alight with joy.

Reverend Lyon, dressed in his finest black robe, greeted the wedding guests and urged them to take their seats.

Lizzy and her father, followed by Annie as her maid of honor, walked to the front to take their place opposite Jeremiah as the reverend directed.

As they did, young Sarah Libby came to stand next to the reverend. "I chose this hymn to sing for my friends who wed this day, because it was God who brought them together in his mysterious way." Then in a beautiful voice she began to sing,

> God moves in a mysterious way! His wonders to perform; He plants His footsteps in the sea and rides upon the storm!
>
> Deep in unfathomable mines of never-failing skill, He treasures up His bright designs and works His sov'reign will.
>
> God of mercy! God of grace! Give us eyes to see! Eyes to see Your smiling face within the mystery, within the mystery!

The song continued, its slow melodic pace and beautiful words moving Lizzy's heart. Gazing into Jeremiah's eyes, she believed that God had, indeed, brought them to this point. She had left her friends in Onslow for her father, never knowing she would find true love in Machias. And Jeremiah, still unwed at thirty when she arrived, was something of an anomaly for the colonies.

When the song finished, Sarah took her seat with the congregation, and Reverend Lyon gestured Lizzy and Jeremiah to stand before him. His voice rang clear. "Dearly beloved, we are gathered together here in the sight of God, and in the presence of this congregation, to join together Jeremiah O'Brien and Elizabeth Fitzpatrick in holy matrimony."

They exchanged the time-honored vows their parents had, simple yet binding. Jeremiah spoke his with a steady voice, his eyes never leaving hers.

When her turn came, Lizzy heard the reverend's question clearly in her mind. "Wilt thou have this man to be thy wedded husband, to live together after God's Ordinance, in the holy estate of matrimony? Wilt thou obey him, serve him, love, honor and keep him in sickness and in health, and forsaking all others, keep only unto him, so long as ye both shall live?"

Gazing into Jeremiah's eyes, she said, "I will."

As Jeremiah slid the ring onto her finger, he whispered, "Your father told me you love this ring that was your mother's, and he gave me his approval to use it."

Lizzy's eyes filled with tears to see the Celtic knots carved into the golden band she had so long admired. Lifting her eyes to his, she smiled, telling him without words how much this meant to her.

"With this ring, I thee wed," said Jeremiah, "and with my body I thee worship, and with all my worldly goods I thee endow."

Reverend Lyon smiled warmly. "I now pronounce you husband and wife. As this is a union established by God and blessed by faith and community, let no man tear it asunder." And then to Jeremiah, "You may kiss your bride."

Jeremiah's lips met hers in a kiss as soft and sweet as a whisper. "More to follow," he said with a smile before turning her to face their guests.

Applause erupted as their friends and family and the town's residents expressed their approval. Jeremiah's crew and fellow officers slapped him on the back. "Finally!" said Colonel Foster. "I never thought to see this day."

"Only a woman as wonderful as Lizzy Fitzpatrick could coax my brother from his bachelor days," said John O'Brien.

Jeremiah's mother, Mary O'Brien and his sister, Mary Burnham came to wish her happiness. "We have made some changes in Jeremiah's home to make you feel welcome," said his sister. "We hope you like them."

Lizzy, who was always the older sister, the caretaker of the family, felt suddenly as if she had become the younger one, cosseted by older women who loved her. She basked in the pleasant feeling.

The celebration that followed was a grand one. There was food in abundance, clam chowder, roast venison in wine sauce, roasted duck, potatoes, and pumpkin casserole. Spiced cider punch, made with hard cider, honey and dried apples, was served from a punchbowl by Mrs. Oakes.

A spiced bride's cake baked by Mrs. Spencer, who was well known for her talent in this area, was rich with dried fruit and nuts. Baked inside was a piece of nutmeg. The person who received the slice with the nutmeg would, according to tradition, be the next to marry. Everyone was surprised to see Lizzy's father get the nutmeg.

"Well, I never expected this!" he said, prompting warm laughter from the guests.

Mrs. Hannah Weston, her young face glowing with the pride of a new mother, giggled, "Mr. Fitzpatrick, it seems the Lord has plans for you yet. Josiah and I wish you joy!"

Mrs. Oakes nodded, "Aye, the nutmeg never lies. Spring will bring new beginnings!"

When everyone had a piece of cake, Jeremiah's father, Morris O'Brien, rose and raised his tankard in a toast. "To Jeremiah and Elizabeth, may God bless their union. May it be fruitful, and may they ever aid America's fight for liberty!"

Lizzy's father went to stand next to Morris. "I'm so pleased my Lizzy found a man of honor like Jeremiah. I join you in toasting to their happiness!"

Machias, Maine, late November 1776

DURING THE LAST weeks of October, Jeremiah was kept busy dealing with the Massachusetts General Court. The *Liberty* and the *Diligent* had been decommissioned after sixteen months of service, their officers and crews discharged as Massachusetts' naval efforts waned.

As Jeremiah thought on this, he reminded himself the state had never paid well or on time. He had often been forced to spend more than his own monthly stipend to supply provisions for his vessels, sometimes borrowing on his personal responsibility to do so. He had also used his own funds to feed and clothe his officers and crew when they were in desperate need. To make matters worse, the state had begun issuing letters of marque to private vessels that paid more and offered better provisions for the crew's comfort. So, the news of the decommissioning was not all bad.

The rise of private vessels owned by wealthy merchants looking for captains and offering liberal wages, gave Jeremiah another way of providing for Lizzy and his crews through private ventures raiding British commerce. "I'm going to set aside my Massachusetts navy uniform and find us a privateer ship," he told William.

He had learned that John Brown, a prominent merchant in Providence, Rhode Island was looking for a captain and seamen for the *Freedom*, a new ship he'd outfitted as a privateer. Jeremiah eagerly pursued the opportunity, sailing to Providence to meet the merchant in his office near the wharf. For his part, Brown was pleased when Jeremiah inquired about the new ship that he might command with an experienced crew he could provide.

"You've a reputation for success," said Brown, clapping Jeremiah on the shoulder. "Take the *Freedom*. Command her, harry British shipping, and share the profits of captured prizes."

Assured his crew would be paid generous wages and a fair share in the prizes, Jeremiah nodded, eager to continue the fight. "Aye, I'll take the commission," he said, appointing his brother, William, as his First Lieutenant and assembling a crew of seasoned Machias men, including Surgeon McDonald.

In the time between his conversation with Brown and late November, he and Lizzy had weeks together to celebrate their marriage and deepen their bond. Those were special days as they walked the paths through the woods gilded with leaves falling to the forest floor forming a golden carpet over the Machias hills.

"I shall be forever grateful for these weeks we have had," she told him. "Weeks where I have had you all to myself."

His arm around her shoulders, he drew her close and kissed her temple. "I have never been so happy," he said, "not even when we captured the *Margaretta*."

Lizzy pulled back to look at him, a frown on her beautiful face. "Best not to compare your honeymoon to the capture of a British ship, Husband."

Unable to resist a laugh, he said, "Very well, my redbird." Pulling her into his arms, he kissed her. "I shall speak of Heaven, for that is what these weeks have been."

Days later, the frost clung to the wharves of Machias, and wearing the brown coat of a privateer captain, Jeremiah stood on the riverbank with Lizzy, watching his crew in the final stage of making the *Freedom* ready to sail. She was a sleek schooner he was proud to command.

As the crew loaded the last of the ammunition and provisions, Lizzy said, "I wish you didn't have to go so soon." Her red hair framing her delicate features caught the pale sunlight, her blue eyes steady despite the ache of parting he glimpsed in them. Jeremiah took her hands in his. "I'll not be long, my love. A swift cruise along the Nova Scotia coast, and I'll return with spoils."

Lizzy smiled. "I trust you to bring yourself and your crew back safe and whole."

Jeremiah turned to his brother, John, standing nearby watching the new ship. He had recently undertaken the project of floating the *Margaretta* to refit and equip her for use as a privateer under the new name the *Hare*. "You'll look after things here?" Jeremiah asked him.

John nodded, his expression resolute. "Aye, Jere. Ben Foster, Gideon and I will keep Machias safe with the good men of the militia."

Jeremiah had also asked his servant Dick to help Lizzy, though he knew her father would look in on her. Before he climbed aboard his ship, he kissed Lizzy goodbye. With her wave and a shout of "Godspeed," he sailed.

THAT WINTER WAS a brutal one on the sea. Jeremiah often encountered storms, but staying close to the coast, they endured. By January of 1777, they were off the Massachusetts coast, when the *Freedom* intercepted the schooner *Polley*. Acting under his privateer commission, Jeremiah seized the vessel, suspecting it had enemy support. Among the cargo, they found flour, oats, sugar, butter and salt, goods Jeremiah deemed destined for British forces. In questioning the crew, he learned the schooner was owned by William Hazen of Newburyport, a merchant suspected of trading with the British in Halifax.

Hazen, furious at the loss, filed a claim for damages, dragging Jeremiah into a legal battle that tested his resolve. He had made one brief stop in Machias before traveling to Boston in March to face the admiralty court where the claim was filed. He brought with him the *Polley*'s manifest and a letter found aboard, addressed to a British officer in Halifax, which confirmed his suspicions of enemy trade. William, as First Lieutenant, testified to the ship's northward course, further supporting Jeremiah's actions.

The court proceedings were tense. Hazen, his face twisted in anger, argued his neutrality as a merchant, a common stance in Newburyport where loyalties were divided. Yet the evidence was clear, and in April, the court ruled in Jeremiah's favor, finding "sufficient reason for his suspicion". Hazen's claim was denied, and Jeremiah's reputation as a principled commander remained untarnished, the prize adjudicated as his. Elated, Jeremiah sold the *Polley* and made the voyage back to Machias on the *Freedom*. Though their travel was swift, the hours at sea gave Jeremiah time to ponder the weight of his decisions, the prize money a tangible reward for his resolve.

Jeremiah longed to see Lizzy. "She'll be telling me I'm late," he remarked to William one afternoon as they leaned on the rail staring at the blue sea.

"She'll be right," William retorted with a grin. "Months away from your new bride is not the best way to begin."

Jeremiah nodded, his brow furrowed in worry. "I did send a letter from Boston to let her know how the trial was going." He had signed it "the one whose heart is ever yours" and hoped that comforted her.

"Well, that is something," said William.

Notwithstanding his long absence, when the *Freedom* tied up in Machias that spring, Lizzy flew into Jeremiah's arms with tears in her eyes. "I've missed you, Husband."

"And I you, my redbird."

Wildflowers lined the path as if welcoming him back. As they walked home together, Lizzy took his arm. "You'll want to talk to your brother, Jere. John is very discouraged. While you were away, he sailed south on the *Hare*, only to be chased by a British man-of-war. To avoid capture, he ran the *Hare* onto the flats at Sawyer Cove, near Jonesport. Thankfully, John and his crew escaped into the surrounding country. From a distance, they watched as the British set fire to the *Hare*, burning her to the water. All his work gone in a day."

Jeremiah shook his head. "That would discourage any captain. I'll talk to him. There will be other ships for John."

Now that he was back in Machias, Jeremiah resumed his long walks with Lizzy as the hillsides erupted in a glorious spring. Trout lilies and wild strawberry flowers delighted her. In the evenings they could hear the haunting cries of loons swimming on the lakes above the falls.

When he wasn't with Lizzy or his family, Jeremiah spent time overseeing the *Freedom*'s refit, ensuring her guns were cleaned and oiled and her crew drilled for the next cruise. With William at his side, he studied coastal charts, plotting routes to evade British patrols.

The prize money from the *Polley* eased their burdens, allowing Jeremiah to repay debts and plan for the future. Yet the quiet gnawed at him—his heart yearned for action, a sentiment William shared one afternoon with a wry grin. "The sea calls us, Jere, even when Machias is enjoying a time of peace."

"Aye, but it's a peace in the midst of war. Reports say General Washington spent the first months of this year in Morristown, New Jersey where his headquarters was a tavern. His soldiers had little to eat and suffered from the cold, snow and mud. The general spent much of his time writing letters arguing for sustenance for his troops. And, as if that weren't enough trial, he developed a quinsy sore throat. Everyone feared he might die, so they sent for Mrs.

Washington, which must have been a comfort to him."

William nodded his agreement. "Aye. We must not forget the burden General Washington carries."

In May, as the trees in Machias were shooting forth new growth and wildflowers abounded, news reached Machias via a weary rider. The Continental Army had endured a grueling season, their resolve tested by sickness, snow and scarcity. Yet hope flickered with the Battle of Ridgefield, where Connecticut militia had harried British troops retreating from Danbury, their blood staining the soil. Jeremiah read the accounts aloud to Lizzy, his eyes alight with pride. "Our fight mirrors theirs, Lizzy, a spark against the storm."

Lizzy agreed. "Our young nation fights for a great cause, and I cling to the belief that with God's help, we will succeed."

Despite the war's shadow, love blossomed in Machias. As spring turned into summer, Jeremiah observed the laughter of Annie, Lizzy's sister, mingling with Surgeon McDonald's quiet counsel near the wharf, where he tended a sailor's wound. Their glances toward each other lingered, signaling an exchange of deeper emotion. William was the first to remark on the growing friendship between them, and confided his observation to Jeremiah.

That night Jeremiah told Lizzy, "It seems your sister has drawn a suitor."

Without looking up from the stew she was stirring, she said, "You mean the surgeon on your ship?"

"You knew?"

"For some time now. I like him, and I think he is good for Annie. And, should you have missed it in your absence, there is more love in the air."

"What tidings have I not heard?"

"My father has found solace with Margaret Cole, Daniel's widow. He's been chopping wood for her, and Annie tells me she often cooks for them. Her young son, James, has been seen trailing Sean about the village like a younger brother. It makes me happy to think of my father and Margaret together. Each has suffered the loss of a mate. He has been lonely, and she needs a husband and father for James."

"Young James Cole will be good company for Sean," said Jeremiah. "And Sean will do well as the older brother."

IT WAS MID-JUNE, and Lizzy and Jeremiah were in Sunday service listening to a sermon by Reverend Lyon on the goodness of God when Lizzy realized with a quiet certainty she was with child. She had been experiencing nausea in the mornings, and she had missed her monthly course for the first time. Her hand resting on her belly, she whispered to Jeremiah. "Jere, I believe we're going to have a child."

He turned to her, his face lit with joy. Putting his hand over hers, he whispered, "Another reason to thank the Almighty."

The next week, news arrived that on the fourteenth of June the Second Continental Congress had passed a resolution concerning America's new flag. Over dinner, Jeremiah read from the newspaper. "Congress has declared the flag of the thirteen United States will be thirteen red and white stripes and thirteen white stars on a blue field, representing a new constellation."

Lizzy tried to see it in her mind. "How will the stars be displayed on the blue background?"

"Well," said Jeremiah consulting the newspaper, "one report claims a flag with five-pointed stars set in a circle, said to be designed by a Philadelphia seamstress, has been seen on the battlefield."

Lizzy could imagine that and thought of her sewing circle. Perhaps they would attempt to make such a flag, though much of her time with the other women was taken up with making clothing for the child she and Jeremiah expected in January of the next year.

As she stitched, she said a prayer for their growing family and the nation's hope of victory. Annie attended the sewing circle, and it was there on one occasion that Lizzy asked her sister about Surgeon McDonald. "Might there be good news soon?"

Annie smiled, her blue eyes twinkling. "I think so. He was only waiting until I turned eighteen this year. He has made his desire to marry me known to Father."

"And does our father approve?"

Annie's face lit up in a broad grin. "He does."

Lizzy leaned in to embrace her sister. "I'm so happy for you! McDonald is a good man."

"He wants to have the wedding next month when we celebrate our independence."

"A good choice," said Lizzy. "July is a grand month for a wedding, and this one will see a great celebration."

Lizzy was not wrong. On the fourth of July, Machias celebrated the first anniversary of independence with a fervor that echoed the nation's hope. The militia fired salutes at the liberty pole, and the village gathered for a feast of roasted fish, fresh corn and pickled cucumbers. Lizzy's sewing circle had managed to create the country's new flag, as she and Jeremiah had discussed, and now it flew from a flagpole outside the meeting house.

Amid the revelry, Annie and Surgeon McDonald stood before Reverend Lyon, saying their vows to the rejoicing of the town. Though Lizzy was not yet showing her pregnancy, most in the town were aware of their good news. With her hand on her belly, she smiled as her sister was wed. Margaret Cole and her young son, James, stood with Sean, at Thomas' side, a family in the making. Apparently the nutmeg was wrong this time, for Annie wed before their father.

When the wedding celebration began, Jeremiah raised his tankard of ale in a toast. "A new couple joined in our new nation!" Following the toast, he whispered to Lizzy, "And a new family member for us come next year."

"The fate of unborn millions will now depend, under God, on the courage and conduct of this army."

– John Adams (1777)

CHAPTER 12

WITH RENEWED VIGOR, Jeremiah trained his crew through July. Pacing the riverbank, he watched the *Freedom* gleaming under the summer sun, her sails furled and the crew at work. His thoughts drifted to Lizzy and their unborn child. That he might be away for some time weighed on him, so he ordered extra provisions for their home, ensuring her comfort in his absence. His servant, Dick Earle, assured him her safety would be seen to, and Jeremiah trusted Dick.

In August, a letter from the State of Massachusetts, bearing a letter of marque, summoned him to Newburyport, where a wealthy merchant, Nathaniel Tracy, offered him command of the *Resolution*, a brig armed with ten swivel guns and provisioned for twenty-five men.

"Apparently, the state wants me to accept," Jeremiah said to William.

"It seems that way," his brother replied, "but what of the *Freedom*?"

"I'll have to give up command of her, but perhaps, if merchant Brown agrees, our brother, John, might take that commission with John Lambert as First Lieutenant."

"That would be one solution. Both are known to be experienced captains."

Jeremiah bid Lizzy farewell, the child growing inside her a reminder of his need to return as often as he could. "Should your father wed Margaret Cole while I'm away, we'll celebrate their union when I return."

"Don't worry about me, Jere," Lizzy said, her voice steady despite what he knew was concern for his departure. "My sister will be with me, and we have many friends in Machias. I am never alone."

With a promise to his brother to speak to John Brown about the *Freedom*, he and William sailed for Newburyport.

THE NEXT DAY, August thirteenth, the British finally took their revenge on Machias. Lizzy had just come from the meeting house when the alarming news arrived of British ships in Machias Bay. Her heart pounded to hear that three Royal Navy frigates, including the HMS *Blonde*, and the sloop HMS *Hope*, were in the bay, their decks full of Royal Marines and their masts flying red ensigns. A grim promise of vengeance for the *Margaretta*'s capture two years prior.

With Jeremiah at sea, Lizzy and the families of Machias looked to Colonel Ben Foster and to a man who had recently come to Machias from Nova Scotia, Colonel Jonathan Eddy, a friend of Reverend Lyon, for the town's defense. Eddy, a tall man with a determined gaze that marked him an experienced soldier, had not come alone. He had brought with him fifty Maliseet, Passamaquoddy and Penobscot warriors, who stood ready to protect the town.

Warned of the British attack, the Machias militia under Colonel Foster's direction had laid a log boom across the river and constructed earthen forts upriver armed with cannon taken from local privateer ships. Lizzy's father and Gideon O'Brien, along with Jeremiah's other brothers still in Machias—John, Dennis and Joseph—labored alongside the men of Machias to construct the defenses.

"They'll not take Machias without a fight," Foster declared, his militia standing shoulder to shoulder with the Passamaquoddy, Maliseet, and Penobscot warriors, their war paint and native dress a stark contrast to the militia's homespun coats.

"The women of Machias will do all we can to support you," Lizzy told Ben Foster, her voice steady despite her fear. With Annie, she gathered her sewing circle together. They found the women transformed into a band of Patriots.

"We'll not stand idle," said Mrs. Spencer, her hands already sorting linen for bandages. The other women nodded enthusiastically.

"We knew this day would come," said Annie, her eyes

wide but determined, her fingers shaking as she bundled musket balls for the militia.

Together, they gathered ammunition, prepared bandages and boiled water, readying the meeting house as a makeshift hospital.

Colonels Foster and Eddy rallied the men to march to the Rim, a peninsula guarding the confluence of the East Machias and Machias Rivers, to face the might of the British navy. As the men marched away, Lizzy watched her father and Jeremiah's brothers join them, muskets in hand, her prayers rising with their footsteps. Beside her, Annie's gaze followed her surgeon husband go, too. "He will be needed," said Annie, her courage on display.

Margaret Cole stood with Sean and young James, who clung to Sean's leg, his wide eyes fixed on the departing men. Lizzy went to her. Though Margaret was a few years older than Lizzy, she felt a need to reassure her. After all, she had already lost one husband. "They will be all right," she told Margaret, though her words were more a prayer than a certainty in her mind.

The other women of the sewing circle stood ready to tend any wounded. "We'll not fail them," said Mrs. Spencer.

Mrs. O'Brien had insisted her husband remain in the village. "Your musket is better needed here," she told him. Lizzy could see the worry in her eyes. Her eldest son was at sea hunting British merchantmen, while her younger sons were marching off to fight the British on land. Even her son-in-law, Job Burnham, had gone with the men.

At high tide, the town's residents braced themselves as news spread that the *Blonde* and the *Hope*, towing seven barges, had sailed upriver with hundreds of Royal Marines. The larger frigates remained in the bay, their cannon a distant threat. When the *Blonde* and the *Hope* reached the log boom near the Rim, a firefight began. From the meeting house, where she stood with the women, Lizzy heard the distant crack of muskets, a staccato rhythm that echoed over the river, followed by the deeper boom of cannon firing from the earthen works.

The sounds sent a chill through Lizzy, each shot a reminder of the danger her father and Jeremiah's brothers faced. By afternoon, a thick plume of black smoke rose in the distance, staining the sky above the tree line, and the acrid scent of charred wood drifted into the village. Lizzy later learned the British had set Fort Foster ablaze, burning its timbers along with the farms on the peninsula.

The militia fought fiercely but retreated under the onslaught. Men began to trickle into the village. A few were bloodied and weary with tales of what had happened. Annie went to help some into the meeting house. Lizzy offered to assist Surgeon Chaloner who was tending a wounded young militiaman named Thomas Avery. Barely nineteen, his arm had been torn by a musket ball. Bracing herself against nausea, Lizzy knelt beside him, helping the doctor clean, suture, and bandage the wound, her hands steady despite the blood. "You fought bravely, Thomas," she whispered, keeping her voice calm.

He smiled up at her, his voice full of pride. "We kept the British from attemptin' a landing today, Ma'am."

"You did well," she said, returning his smile, her heart swelling with admiration for his courage.

"Did you see how the O'Brien brothers fared?" she

asked him, afraid of his answer.

"All standin'…when I last saw them," he said in halting words as he fought the pain.

As darkness fell, the native warriors began chanting and shouting, their voices echoing across the river in a haunting chorus. Lizzy wondered if it was an attempt to make the British think their numbers were greater than they were. The eerie calls sent a shiver through her, but the tactic, if that's what it was, must have proven effective. She heard no answering cannon fire from the British ships. Later, a militiaman returning to the village reported that the *Blonde* and the *Hope* had begun to withdraw, but the *Hope* ran aground in the dim light while retreating downstream.

That evening, the sounds of renewed fighting reached the meeting house as Foster's and Eddy's men, including the native warriors, ambushed the stranded *Hope* from the riverbank. Lizzy heard the sharp crack of musket fire and the shouts of men, followed by a triumphant cheer. A runner soon arrived with news: Passamaquoddy Chief Neptune had felled a British officer with a long musket shot, breaking the enemy's advance. The British retreated, their barges battered as they fled downriver.

Onshore, Lizzy joined the cheers, her heart swelling with pride for Machias' defiance. Sadly, one Machias man had died and one had been severely wounded—the young militiaman she'd tended—but Ben Foster reported the British losses, estimated by the native warriors, were between forty and one hundred. "Not since Bunker Hill have the British faced such resistance from so small a force," he remarked, his voice heavy with the weight of their victory.

Jeremiah would be so proud.

The next morning, the fourteenth of August, Lizzy awoke to the distant boom of a swivel gun, its shots ringing out as the militia rained fire upon the *Hope*. A militiaman later confirmed the sloop, refloated by the rising tide, had limped back to Machias Bay, joining the frigates as they withdrew.

As Lizzy changed the bandage on Thomas Avery's arm, she thought of Jeremiah, out at sea, and murmured a prayer for his safety and the future of their unborn child. "We've held our own, my love," she whispered, her gaze lifting to the sky where the Stars and Stripes still flew over the meeting house, a testament to their unyielding spirit.

Newburyport, Massachusetts, August 1777

THE TWELFTH OF August found Jeremiah in Newburyport, the center of New England shipbuilding, accepting command of the *Resolution*, a 35-ton schooner fitted out by the Massachusetts State Navy. With ten swivel guns and a crew of two dozen men, she was a lean vessel, ready to harry British shipping. The ship's owner, Nathaniel Tracy, had petitioned the Massachusetts State Council, and the council approved Jeremiah's commission.

He had asked merchant Brown about John taking command of the *Freedom*. He was amenable, and Jeremiah dispatched a letter telling John the good news.

Days later, as he prepared to sail, word arrived of the British attack on Machias. Despite the town's success, the battle had left everyone there shaken, and another attack was expected. Jeremiah feared for Lizzy and his family and all in the town.

That evening, Jeremiah penned a letter to Lizzy, his quill scratching across the page by candlelight.

My dearest redbird,

News of the British assault on Machias has reached me here in Newburyport. The tragedy weighs heavy on my heart. All of the Resolution's crew are concerned. I pray you and those at Machias are safe. British ships swarm the coast, making our departure ill-advised. Thus, I delay, torn between duty and my longing for your safety.

Know that my thoughts and prayers are with you. I fight for you and our unborn child and pray that God keeps you both until I return.

All my love, Jeremiah.

He entrusted the letter to a rider headed north, praying it would reach her.

Days later, a report from a local fisherman heightened his caution: a British sloop had been sighted off Cape Ann, her red ensign a stark warning against venturing north. Reports as late as the sixth of September confirmed British patrols lingered near Machias and south toward New-buryport, their frigates and sloops a constant threat to American vessels.

Jeremiah, his jaw firmly set, spoke of the threat with William. "We'll not risk the *Resolution* in these waters," he said. "We'll wait for a safer passage."

"'Tis the best course," said his brother, "though like you I worry."

The crew, many from Machias, shared their unease, as their concern for their families lingered, particularly Surgeon McDonald, who had left Annie, his new bride, in Machias. Jeremiah encouraged him, "She's not alone," he told his surgeon. "Lizzy and the women of Machias are with her, and the militia are on high alert." Though his officers and crew continued to fret, they heeded Jeremiah's caution.

As they lingered in Newburyport, they caught up on news of the ongoing war. Significantly, in June, the Marquis de Lafayette, a nineteen-year-old French aristocrat, escaping the French king who forbade his departure for fear of angering the British, sailed to South Carolina intending to serve as Washington's second in command. From there, he joined Washington in Philadelphia. Lafayette fought alongside Washington at the Battle of Brandywine in Pennsylvania. Though they lost that battle, and hence Philadelphia, the capital, Lafayette had demonstrated courage, leading the army safely from the field.

Jeremiah's spirits rose to think the French were finally joining the fight, at least in some capacity. As he read the article, he remarked to William, "We need a victory to encourage the troops, and convince France we can win."

"Aye, and a thousand more like Lafayette."

In mid-September, with intelligence suggesting the British presence on the coast had eased, Jeremiah sailed, his course set for Nova Scotia. Sailing north, they passed the familiar waters off Machias Bay, the town's riverbanks a distant blur on the horizon. Jeremiah stood at the helm, his heart heavy with the urge to anchor and see Lizzy, but duty drove him onward. "We've been delayed long, so we must continue," he told William, his decision firm despite the ache of separation. "We'll return soon, with prizes to secure our future."

On the twenty-ninth of September, off the rugged coast of Cape Negro—named for its black rock formation that loomed like a sentinel in the dawn—the *Resolution*, alongside other Massachusetts privateers, spotted a vessel flying British colors. His spyglass fixed on her deck, Jeremiah told William, "She could be from Ireland, another ship laden with beef, butter and claret for the British army."

The chase was swift, and the ship surrendered under the *Resolution*'s guns. Jeremiah assigned a prize master, young Samuel Holt, and three trusted sailors to sail the prize to Machias.

Unfortunately, the victory was short-lived. The British frigate HMS *Scarborough* bore down on them, recapturing the captured vessels and taking Holt and his small prize crew as prisoners.

Jeremiah watched from a distance, his jaw tight, a pang of guilt piercing his chest. "May they find mercy in a prisoner exchange," he muttered to William, knowing the British sometimes sent captives to the wretched prison ships in New York where many died. Unlike the Americans, who treated their prisoners fairly, the British were known to starve Americans and treat them cruelly.

"We'll have another chance," he told his remaining crew, turning the *Resolution* toward safer waters.

Eleven days later, on the ninth of October, fortune smiled again. Near Cape Negro, the *Resolution* joined forces with the Massachusetts armed schooner *Blackbird*, commanded by William Groves. Together, they seized the 100-ton sloop *Annabella*, her hold brimming with goods.

With Nova Scotia under British control, Jeremiah and Groves sailed southwest to Boston, the Patriot port with a maritime court that was acceptable to Groves. There, on the ninth of October, they filed a claim to secure the prize and their share of its value.

In Boston, Jeremiah sought news of Samuel Holt and his men, hoping they'd been included in a recent prisoner exchange, but word from the court was grim. No record of their release had reached Boston. "They may be on a prison ship," a court clerk warned, "but Massachusetts pushes for swaps. There's hope yet."

As the court proceedings concluded in late October, Jeremiah received word from Nathaniel Tracy that the *Resolution* was no longer available for service, its fate unclear. Whether reassigned or retired, the schooner's time under his command had ended. With a heavy heart, he bid farewell to the vessel that had carried him through the waters off Cape Negro.

That evening, as lanterns cast a golden glow over Boston's streets, Major General William Heath, commanding the region's defenses under General Washington, invited Jeremiah and William to the Green Dragon Tavern. They were happy to go and eager to hear news from the war.

The tavern's warm air, thick with the scent of ale and

mutton, offered them respite as Heath, a stout figure in the blue coat of General Washington's officers, greeted them warmly. "Captain O'Brien," Heath said, "and your first officer," he added noting William's uniform.

"My brother, William," supplied Jeremiah.

His voice carrying the weight of command, Heath continued, "General Washington heard of your *Annabella* capture through court reports, and asked me to convey his commendation for your contribution to our efforts to choke the British supply lines."

"He is kind to think of us with all he has before him," said Jeremiah. "What news of the war?"

Over a simple meal of stew and bread, Heath shared the broader state of the war. "The campaign has been harsh this year," he began. "After our victory at Trenton last winter, we faced setbacks at Brandywine in September, and just weeks ago, on October fourth, Washington struck at Germantown. A bold move, but fog and British resolve turned it to a costly retreat."

"Since then?" Jeremiah asked, hopeful some good had followed.

General Heath smiled. "On the seventeenth, Providence granted us a great victory in New York. General John Burgoyne and six thousand of his British regulars surrendered at Saratoga after losing two battles to Generals Gates and Arnold."

Jeremiah shared a smile with William. "That is wonderful news! The victory we've been praying for. Please give our congratulations to General Gates, whom we met in Cambridge and to General Washington for his leadership. Hopefully, there will be news from France soon."

General Heath nodded. "Benjamin Franklin remains in France and continues to press for their aid. Congress receives word of his efforts. France's covert supplies have bolstered us, and Franklin writes of French enthusiasm, but no formal alliance has yet been secured. General Washington hopes the victory at Saratoga will bring the French to our side."

Jeremiah took heart with this news, and then recounted both his successes and the loss of one of his prize crews for the general.

"General Washington holds hope for an exchange in such cases," Heath assured them. "He relies on privateers like you to sustain us until France joins the fight." As they downed the last of their ale and rose to depart, Heath clasped Jeremiah's hand. "Carry on, Captain. Your commitment to the cause strengthens us all."

Jeremiah left the tavern with renewed purpose. As he returned to his lodgings, his thoughts turned to Lizzy. Taking quill to parchment, he wrote,

Dearest redbird,

We sailed to Boston, which is where I am as I write this letter. With the Resolution, we took a good prize and the claim for our share of its value was successful. However, that ship is no longer available as a privateer, so we will seek another ship. There is the possibility of a schooner, the Cyrus, that may be available. I am hopeful as she will carry a crew of forty-five, large enough to accommodate all my crew and then some.

I trust your pregnancy goes well and you are in good health as this reaches you. I left funds for you with

Reverend Lyon so you will not be in need despite my long absence.

William sends his love, and Surgeon McDonald wishes Annie to know she has his devotion. He's a good surgeon and the men are grateful he is one of our officers. My thoughts and prayers are with you.

Your loving husband,

Jeremiah

Machias, Maine, Massachusetts, January 21, 1778

OUTSIDE THE HOUSE a winter storm raged, rattling the shutters, as Lizzy slowly crossed the length of the bedchamber, her breath coming in sharp gasps as labor pains gripped her. Annie walked beside her, their arms linked. A moan escaped her lips, causing her to lean on her sister for support.

Annie's voice was steady despite the worry in her eyes. "You're nearly there, Lizzy," she said, brushing damp hair from her forehead.

Lizzy had been enduring the pains for hours. They ebbed and flowed but now were becoming stronger and more frequent.

The midwife and a few other women of Machias, Mrs. O'Brien and Mrs. Spencer among them, had come to help, and were busy readying cloths and warm water, their voices a chorus of encouragement.

Lizzy heard the storm howl, rattling the shutters, and turned to see snow piling up against the trees, but inside,

Dick Earle had stocked the hearth with wood, and the fire blazed, warming the house. Lamps and candles added a glow to all in the bedchamber.

"Time to take to your bed," said the midwife.

As a pain gripped her, Lizzy clung to her sister who helped her into the bed. In her mind Lizzy kept hearing the line from one of Jeremiah's letters, *"I fight for you and our unborn child."* Drawing strength from his resolve, she rode the pains for another hour and bore down when told to push.

With a final push, she brought their son into the world. Once he was cleaned, Mrs. O'Brien placed the babe into her arms. Lizzy looked into his sweet face. "Jeremiah...he will be called Jeremiah O'Brien Jr." Tears of joy mingled with exhaustion, as she cradled him. "Your father will be so proud, though he's far from us now."

"He's a fine son," said Jeremiah's mother, smiling at her grandson.

"Indeed he is," said Annie, leaning over the bed, her blue eyes welling with tears. "Such a beautiful boy you have given Jeremiah, Lizzy. I'll stay with you to help take care of him."

JEREMIAH CONTINUED HIS privateering into 1778, but with less fortune. He took command of the *Cyrus*, sailing from Massachusetts. It was good to be back in command with additional crew, but they had only one good capture. After this, he commanded the *Little Vincent*, a small schooner with ten guns and sixteen men. Jeremiah considered none of their captures notable, for the British navy had grown ever more vigilant along New England's coast following the Penobscot Expedition's failure.

In the spring, off New Hampshire, the *Little Vincent* narrowly escaped a British frigate, Jeremiah's quick orders to hug the shoreline saved them from capture. "We'll live to fight another day," he told William, his voice steady as the enemy's sails faded over the horizon.

Once in port, news reached them from Boston of a turning point in the war. In February, France formally allied with the American cause, signing treaties in Paris. The Franco-American alliance promised naval support, easing some pressure on privateers like Jeremiah as French ships began to challenge British dominance along the coast. Despite this, the British redoubled their patrols, making each voyage a test of nerve and skill.

On the faces of his crew, Jeremiah saw a weariness from the sea's relentless trials. They had been long at sea with their only respite brief stops in port. Desperate to see Lizzy and his new child, and knowing his crew missed their families, he decided a trip home for Christmas would do wonders for them all.

They arrived at dusk on Christmas Eve.

Though the day was cold and there was snow on the ground in Machias, Lizzy must have gotten word of the schooner's arrival, for she met him at the wharf with her sister Annie, who had come for Donald.

Jeremiah leapt down from the deck to the ice-covered planks of the wharf and rushed to Lizzy bundled up in a heavy cloak. In her arms she cradled a babe wrapped in a blanket, a knit cap on his head. "Your son, Jeremiah, named after you."

Jeremiah Jr. gazed up at him with wide, curious blue eyes, his tiny hand grasping at the air, full of life. Jeremiah swept them both into his embrace, his throat tight with emotion. "My redbird," he said, kissing her forehead, "and my boy." Little Jeremiah's small fingers brushed Jeremiah's weathered cheek, a soft laugh escaping him.

"We've missed you, Jere," Lizzy said, her blue eyes bright with love. With feigned anger, she said, "I would mention you are late," she said, her frown turning into a grin, "but we are so glad to see you, I'll dispense with that. Little Jerry, as we call him, was born in last winter's worst storm, and he's been a joy ever since."

Nearby, Surgeon McDonald embraced Annie, his voice warm with relief. "Annie, my bonnie lass, yer courage at home kept me goin' at sea."

The families of other crewmembers began to arrive, and soon a crowd had gathered to welcome them home.

Seeing Lizzy begin to shiver, Jeremiah said, "Let's get you and our son out of the cold."

"We've a meal waiting for you at our house, Jere. Annie and Donald are to join us along with your family and the Lyons. Many in Machias want to welcome you home."

"The sea is my element, and I will fight there as long as I have breath."

– Anonymous privateer captain (circa 1778)

CHAPTER 13

Machias, Maine, Massachusetts, December 1778

JEREMIAH AND LIZZY left the wharf, trudging through the snow to their home, little Jerry bundled in his wife's arms, the town's lanterns guiding them home. Their house glowed with candlelight that night, the scent of pine boughs and roasting venison filling the air.

Dick Earle tended the roast, while Lizzy served apple cider amid the chorus of happy voices. Outside, the snow fell gently, but inside a fire blazed in the hearth, warming the room and casting a glow over the families taking their seats.

The table groaned with the evening's feast—venison carved by Jeremiah's father, its rich aroma mingling with a steaming clam chowder thickened with what little milk the town could spare, and bread baked from hoarded flour. Apples, stewed with a hint of molasses, added a sweet note.

Jeremiah sat next to Lizzy, little Jerry sleeping in a cradle nearby. The O'Briens, including Jeremiah's brothers, flanked them. Annie and Donald sat across from Jeremiah with the Lyons, Lizzy's father, Margaret and Sean and young James.

Sean had grown taller while Jeremiah was at sea. Now fourteen by Jeremiah's count, he was beginning to look more like his father except for his red hair. "The boys have grown while I was at sea," he said to Lizzy.

"They have," she said, casting a glance at Sean and James. "Soon Sean will be asking to be your cabin boy."

Jeremiah nodded. "While I could use one, I think it can wait a few years."

"My father has become quite the hunter," said Lizzy with a glance at Thomas. "The venison is his contribution to our dinner."

"And our young men dig for clams in mud that's not frozen," said Reverend Lyon, "so we have chowder when we can get milk and steamed clams when we cannot."

"We brought provisions," said Jeremiah, hoping that additional food would bolster the town's winter stores. "I imagine with the British patrolling the coast, not many boats get through."

"Since the Penobscot disaster," said Jeremiah's father, "Machias is more alone than ever."

"But the town has also taken on a greater importance," said Reverend Lyon, his voice encouraging. "We're a haven for Nova Scotia refugees and a staging area for invasions of territory held by the British. Most importantly, Machias is a bastion against British invasion. As long as we hold out, the smaller settlements of Maine draw strength."

"And we can hold out as long as the Indians remain our friends," added Martha Lyon.

Jeremiah knew the Indians around Machias had long been their allies but Mrs. Lyon's word suggested doubt about their future alliance. "On what does that depend?" he asked.

"Their friendship depends largely on the provisions we can give them and the diplomacy of Colonel John Allan," said Jeremiah's father.

"Colonel Allan is from Nova Scotia where he learned the language of the native tribes. He was appointed by General Washington to be the Continental agent overseeing Indian Affairs at Machias."

Jeremiah nodded, recollecting. "A good man working with Ben Foster for our defense."

Jeremiah took a bite of the venison just as Lizzy leaned into him, her hand finding his. "I dreamed of you being back home," she whispered, her eyes glistening. "What I prayed for each night."

Jeremiah squeezed her hand, content to be home.

"Tomorrow is Christmas Day," Reverend Lyon reminded them. "Not a Sunday, so no service, but we'll gather all the same...for a wedding—Thomas and Margaret's."

That brought a smile to every face and a blush to Margaret's.

"We'll be a real family," said Sean, grinning at James.

Jeremiah quirked a smile at Thomas. "Were you waiting for William, Donald and me to return?"

Thomas chuckled. "No, but now that you're here, you can join the celebration. Lizzy and Annie were anxious you should be there."

THE NEXT AFTERNOON, Machias' meeting house buzzed with quiet anticipation, its benches filled with townsfolk braving the cold to take part in a ceremony all had anticipated. The fireplace sheltered a crackling fire that smelled of spruce. Snow dusted the windows as Reverend Lyon stood before Thomas Fitzpatrick and Margaret Cole, her dark hair and eyes a contrast to the red hair of Lizzy and her siblings. She was glad to see Margaret's features were no longer etched in grief.

Margaret wore a simple gown of rust-colored wool, a sprig of holly pinned to her green shawl—a symbol of renewal. Lizzy's father, his brown hair threaded with strands of silver catching the firelight, took his bride's hand. "Margaret, you've borne much and shown great courage. I'm honored to stand with you."

"And you, Thomas, are an honorable man who has come through much hardship, always caring for your family. It is my joy to become your wife."

The ceremony was brief but solemn, their vows the same ones Lizzy and Jeremiah had spoken at their own wedding. The reverend's words wove hope into the winter air. After Thomas had slipped a gold ring on Margaret's finger, the reverend declared, "In the sight of

God and this community, I join Thomas Fitzpatrick and Margaret Cole in marriage." The guests sighed with approval.

Lizzy, sitting beside Jeremiah with Jerry in her arms, wiped a tear from her eye, her heart swelling for her father's joy in this union. This is what she had hoped for when they came to Machias, a new life, a new beginning.

Jeremiah squeezed her hand, his gaze warm. "Truly a new beginning for both of them," he whispered, echoing her thoughts.

After a celebration of hot cider and bride's cake, the dense fruitcake with dried fruits and spices served by Mrs. Spencer, the townsfolk shared stories and laughter, their voices rising over the scrape of spoons.

Gideon offered a toast to his business partner. "To a productive and joyous union, and many happy years!"

Everyone raised their tumblers, joining the toast. "To many happy years!"

The newlyweds did not linger long. A short while later, Lizzy's father led Margaret outside to a waiting sleigh with a horse wearing bells on his harness. The crowd spilled outside, where children tossed snowballs at each other while the people waved.

Margaret waved back as she climbed into the sleigh. Sean stood near Lizzy, holding James' hand, a proud stepbrother. Lizzy shouted, "We'll look after them tonight!"

Machias, Maine, Massachusetts, January 1779

AFTER YEARS OF relentless privateering, Jeremiah had returned to Machias, his heart anchored to Lizzy and their young son. The familiar riverbanks, where the Stars and Stripes flew in front of the meeting house, welcomed him with the scent of pine and the distant murmur of the falls. He relished the quiet of home, the rhythm of village life and the Sunday services with Reverend Lyon, though the war's shadow lingered. With that in mind, he set aside his privateering for the time being and took up service in the local militia with his friend, Ben Foster where his success as a privateer captain earned him the respect of Colonel Allan and the town's defenders.

One morning, as he pored over the latest *Gazette,* his younger brother, William, joined him for breakfast. Reading news that stirred hope, Jeremiah said, "In April, Spain joined the war alongside its ally, France. Even better," he said, his voice lifting, "they have declared war on Britain."

"They've been secretly sending weapons and loans to us since '76, haven't they?"

"Aye," said Jeremiah, "but now their navy—dozens of ships—will bolster the French fleet against the British."

Lizzy paused by the table with a basket of bread, offering them more.

"Thanks, dear, but we're nearly finished," said Jeremiah.

"Why did Spain step in?" she asked.

Jeremiah scanned the paper for the answer, then looked up at her. "It seems they aim to reclaim Florida and Louisiana, lost to Britain in '63."

"With America, France, and Spain united," said William to Lizzy, "we might master the seas at last."

Jeremiah glanced at the hearth rug where Jeremiah Jr. played with a wooden spoon and pot. "This could end the war before our son bears its scars."

"I hold that hope," Lizzy replied, her expression reflecting optimism.

On that same day, duty called to Jeremiah. At a town meeting, Ben Foster told them of British efforts in Canada to incite the region's tribes against Machias. "With our long ties to neighboring Indians, it is hoped Machias will remain a bulwark against the enemy's schemes."

"The British think to stir the tribes against us," said John Lambert, "but many of them have been our friends for decades."

On the twenty-third of June, 1779, Colonel John Allan, as overseer of Indian Affairs for the General Court, summoned Jeremiah to a meeting with Ben Foster, who, by this time, was commander of the 6th Lincoln County Regiment. At the meeting, Allan appointed Jeremiah Captain of the Ranging Company, which had been approved by the Massachusetts General Court. "Your orders are to raise men immediately to guard against unfriendly tribes roused by the British to come against us."

"O'Brien's a sound choice," Foster said, his voice reflecting his years of command. With a puff on his ivory pipe, he added, "He's proven himself at sea, and I've no doubt he will hold the line here."

With a firm nod, Jeremiah accepted the position. "I'll

do my part to keep Machias safe. The British and their Indian allies will find no easy path here." He set to work immediately, recruiting men from Machias and the nearby towns, hardy souls who knew the forests well.

Among them were his younger brothers, all except John who, unaware of the threat, had gone to New-buryport to meet the family of a girl he was courting. Surgeon McDonald, who had returned to Machias with Jeremiah, was also willing to join. "Aye, I'll lend my hands to this fight, Captain," McDonald said, his Scottish lilt warm with determination. "The woods are no stranger to me, and Annie's expecting our first child, so I am glad to be near Machias."

"We are happy to have you, for a good surgeon is always needed," said Jeremiah. "And a good brother-in-law as well!"

As the summer lengthened, Jeremiah and Ben Foster drilled the men until they were a skilled fighting unit.

DURING THE WARM months, while their husbands were with the militia, Lizzy and Annie found solace in their sewing circle, gathering in the shade of a great oak near the meeting house. With Jeremiah Jr. toddling at their feet, clutching a wooden toy boat, and Annie's hands resting on her growing belly, the women stitched bandages and mended militia uniforms.

Margaret had joined the circle when she married Liz-zy's father and soon became a regular member of the group. When she was with the women, her young son, James, would either be with Sean or in the schoolhouse with the other children.

"Your little captain keeps us smiling," Mrs. Spencer said, chuckling as Jerry waved his toy from the floor.

Lizzy nodded, her eyes softening as she watched her young son. "He has his father's spirit, even now."

Annie, her fingers deft with needle and thread, added, "And soon we'll have another to join him—God willing, another safe delivery."

The circle's conversation and laughter mingled with the summer breeze, a brief respite amid the war's shadow. Each of the women had a man in the fight they knew was coming. They prepared for it yet avoided discussing the worst of their fears.

One sunny afternoon, Jeremiah's parents, Mary and Morris O'Brien, welcomed the family to their hearth where they told them of the good news that John had married Hannah Tappan in Newburyport in August. "She's a lovely girl," said Mrs. O'Brien, He'll be bringing her back to Machias, at least for a time, according to his letter."

They sat around the hearth celebrating John's marriage. "I'm so happy for him," said Lizzy.

Little Jerry toddled between the adults, giggling as Jeremiah lifted him high.

"He's got your sea legs, Jere," William teased.

Morris, now in his sixties and his hair fully gray, testifying to his status as patriarch of the family, spoke with pride. "A fine lad to carry the O'Brien name."

The gathering, filled with hope for peace, strengthened the family's bond. As they departed to their own homes, Mary O'Brien pressed a loaf of fresh bread into

Lizzy's hands. "For your table, dear, to keep your family strong."

Machias, Maine, Massachusetts, August 1779

THE LATE SUMMER sun dipped low over Machias, casting a golden hue across the river where Jeremiah stood on the rugged wharf, inspecting a sloop's rigging with a critical eye. The air carried the scent of pine and salt, a reminder of the sea not far away, the sea that had shaped much of his life. Though bound to the militia under Colonel Allan's orders, he yearned to return to the fight on the sea.

Ben Foster's heavy footsteps broke his reverie, the man's face grim as he approached, a folded newspaper tucked under his arm. Taking his pipe from his mouth, he exhaled a slow plume of smoke. "Jeremiah, you'll want to hear this." His voice was low, as if the news itself weighed on him. "Something dreadful has occurred in Penobscot Bay—worst defeat of the war, they're calling it."

Jeremiah turned, his brow furrowing. "Penobscot? That's not far—sixty miles down the coast. What happened?"

"You'll recall the British took the Bagaduce Peninsula in Penobscot Bay in June."

"Aye. I recall hearing of that. At the time, we were meeting with Colonel Allan, who ordered us to raise a company of men to fight the British threat from Canada. I suppose my attention was diverted to that."

"Well," said Ben, "while you were raising that company, the British built a fort on Castine Island in Penobscot Bay with the intention of establishing a new base to guard the Bay of Fundy and protect Nova Scotian shipping from harassment by New England privateers. To no one's surprise, they called it Fort George. What we did not know at the time was that the British, led by Captain Mowat—yes, the same man who burned Falmouth—fortified the area with eight hundred British troops from Halifax."

"Good Lord, so many of the enemy so close," Jeremiah said, his mind flashing to Mowat's attack on Falmouth.

Ben unfolded the *Boston Gazette*, its ink smudged from travel. "The Massachusetts General Court sent a fleet to drive 'em out—over forty ships, a dozen privateers among them, and over a thousand militia and colonial marines. I knew some lads who went, including my nephew Zeke, all eager for a fight." He shook his head. "They failed, Jere."

"How could they fail?" asked Jeremiah. "What's the *Gazette* say?"

"The British knew they were coming and were prepared. There was an exchange of fire with the three British sloops-of-war in the harbor and some success by Colonel Paul Revere's artillery, but the main problem seemed to be that Commodore Saltonstall, who led the fleet, failed to attack the British ships, despite his officers urging him to do so. He delayed for three weeks when six British warships arrived in a massive show of strength. Our forces fled, leaving the American fleet strewn along the Penobscot River. They burned most of the ships to prevent them falling into the enemy's hands. The unhappy soldiers and sailors had to find their way back to Boston through the wilderness."

Jeremiah couldn't believe what he was hearing. "All those ships lost?"

"Aye," said Ben, consulting the newspaper. "But the *Gazette* says the New Hampshire privateers *Hampden* and *Hunter*—one of the largest of the Massachusetts privateers—were taken by the British. The *Hampden*, commanded by Titus Salter, simultaneously engaged the British frigates HMS *Blonde* and HMS *Virginia* until she was forced to strike her colors."

Jeremiah shook his head, a pang of loss striking him. "I met Bill Douglas once, a good man who spoke of the *Hunter*'s might. And Salter's a name I've heard in Portsmouth. A terrible loss. You say there were other privateers among the American fleet?"

"Aye, a dozen."

"I could have been one of them, Ben, had not Colonel Allan had other plans for me."

"I'm glad you were not. You might have lost more than a ship."

Jeremiah's gaze drifted to the horizon. "Aye. A thousand militia and marines—how many killed?"

"Over four hundred," said Ben, reading from the article. "At its end, more than five hundred Americans were dead, wounded or taken prisoner."

"Any from Machias?"

Ben nodded, his voice heavy. "Very likely since a few lads from the local militia joined up, thinking it a quick victory. The survivors are straggling back now through the woods. Heard one of 'em at the tavern last night—said

Saltonstall froze, wouldn't fight. And the commanders couldn't agree among themselves. The Committee's already blaming Saltonstall for the whole mess. And Paul Revere, of all men, is under house arrest for disobeying an order."

"Saltonstall will be drummed out," said Jeremiah. "But Revere? The man's a Patriot through and through. If he disobeyed an order, he likely had reason." A frown crossed his brow as the weight of the defeat settled in. "This'll hit Boston hard—those privateers had investors, men who'll feel that loss in their purses. And Massachusetts won't be able to cover the loss." As the enormity of the tragedy sank in, Jeremiah said, "The state will be bankrupt. And the disgrace will sting for years."

Ben folded his paper, his expression darkening. "And have you considered, Jere, what Penobscot in British hands will mean for the Maine coast?"

Jeremiah nodded. "We'll be more in danger than before, and more isolated."

"My very thoughts. We've held our own here, thanks to you and your brothers, and our militia, but this…it's a blow that will require our vigilance. And even that may not be enough."

Jeremiah turned back to the sloop, his resolve hardening. "Then we'll fight harder. The British won't take Machias—not while I have breath. With more British ships and Loyalist privateers prowling our coast, I must sail again soon, maybe before winter."

Ben clapped his shoulder, a grim smile breaking through. "That's the spirit, Jere. The militia and I stand with you."

As Ben walked back toward town, Jeremiah lingered by the water, the distant roar of the Machias falls a steady reminder of home. Penobscot's shadow and its aftermath loomed. So many British so close and Loyalists with vengeance on their minds. What choice did they have but to fight on when their families, their friends and the town depended on them?

IT WAS AUTUMN of 1779 when Allan's scouts brought Jeremiah and his militia troubling news. The enemy had dispatched Major Robert Rogers to rally unfriendly native tribes against Machias. Rogers was a notorious figure, head of the Queen's Rangers, whose men were a motley group, famous for pillaging. A veteran of frontier warfare, Rogers, had been tasked with leading a war party from Canada, following the River St. John, to strike Machias in the spring. Jeremiah had anticipated the planned attack but Rogers' addition made the prospect all the more daunting.

Under Ben Foster's strategic oversight, Jeremiah and his men prepared for the worst, their days filled with patrols along the river and through the dense forests surrounding Machias. Scouts were sent up the river, their eyes sharp for any sign of Rogers and his war party. The tension weighed heavily, but hope emerged when intelligence revealed an unexpected reprieve.

The Indians of River St. John, loyal to the Patriot cause and influenced by their French allies, intercepted Rogers' party. They told the tribes advancing with him, "The French and we were brethren. To fight against us would be to fight against our father the French King." Persuaded, the Canadian tribes turned back, leaving Rogers' plan in tatters.

"A blessing from Providence," Jeremiah said to Ben as they stood by the Machias River, the autumn leaves a blaze of crimson and gold. "But we'll not let our guard down. I'd wager the British have other schemes."

Following the demonstration of loyalty by the tribes, on the eighteenth of November, Machias hosted a significant gathering, a conference with the St. Johns and Passamaquoddy tribes, joined by delegates from St. Francis in Canada and other tribes. The meeting, held in a longhouse near the town, warmed by a central fire, was a delicate dance of diplomacy.

Colonel Allan led the proceedings, with Colonel Foster and Jeremiah attending as militia leaders, their presence a testament to Machias' commitment to the alliance. The air was redolent with the scent of cedar and tobacco as the tribal leaders smoked the calumet pipe, their voices rising and falling in measured tones.

"We stand with you against the British," declared Chief Neptune of the Passamaquoddy, his fierce eyes resolute. "But we need powder and shot to defend our lands."

In response, Allan promised support, "You will have what you need."

Foster added, "Your strength bolsters our defenses. We'll see you supplied."

Jeremiah spoke of the shared struggle, his voice carrying the weight of his years at sea. "The British seek to divide us. Do not let them, for together, we'll hold this frontier."

The conference was successful, ending with renewed bonds between the tribes and the Patriots in Machias, bonds that would serve as a bulwark against British influence in the region.

Through the waning months of 1779, Jeremiah remained vigilant. Though the necessity for his Ranging Company no longer existed, and they were disbanded in November, he continued to work with Ben Foster on local defenses. Since the disastrous Penobscot Expedition, the British were in control of northern New England, cutting off trade and threatening the safety of the coast. Worried for Machias, Jeremiah organized informal patrols along the Machias River.

Amidst the trials, Jeremiah found solace in the laughter of his son, Jerry, now a toddling child of nearly two, who called him "Papa" in his little boy voice. And, as always, he was bolstered by Lizzy's unwavering support.

"You've kept us safe, Jere," she said one evening, her hand resting on his as they sat by the fire. "And God continues to bless, as Reverend Lyon reminds us."

Jeremiah nodded, his gaze fixed on the flames. The fight for liberty was far from over, and he sensed his own part—whether on land or sea—was not yet done.

And then came the most brutal winter anyone could recall. Snow began falling in November, and storm after storm followed—more than twenty—piling up snow so deep even hunters were kept from the woods. Large blocks of ice floated in the river and no one could dig for clams in the frozen mudflats. Food was scarce, but with

Reverend Lyon's urging, it was shared by all.

In December, as they prepared to celebrate the Savior, Annie gave birth to a daughter with tufts of red-blonde hair on her head…little Margaret McDonald.

"We should never despair, our Situation before
has been unpromising and has changed for the
better, so I trust, it will again. If new difficulties
arise, we must only put forth New Exertions and
proportion our Efforts to the exigency of
the times."

– George Washington (1777)

CHAPTER 14

Machias, Maine, Massachusetts, 1780

BY EARLY 1780, the war had stretched into its fifth year, and the British had continued to tighten their grip on the Maine coast. Royal Navy cruisers and Loyalist privateers patrolled daily, their presence in Penobscot Bay aimed at severing New England's eastern frontier. Machias, with its defiant spirit, remained a thorn in their side.

Jeremiah, no longer with his Ranging Company and no longer at sea, felt the weight of these developments, his thoughts often drifting to the safety of Lizzy, little Jerry and the rest of their family. Though he missed the sea, there were times when he felt fortunate to be in Machias. Reports from Morristown, New Jersey, where General Washington's army was encamped for the winter, described the men suffering severe cold and deprivation. Soldiers felled thousands of acres of timber to build a log house city for the twelve thousand men to protect them from the bitter cold.

Worried about a smallpox epidemic, General Washington was having his army inoculated, as well as many of the civilians living in and around Morristown. When Jeremiah heard this, he immediately went to see Surgeon Chaloner about offering inoculation to the people of Machias. "Washington's having his troops and civilians inoculated. We should have our people inoculated, too."

Educated in the colonies, Chaloner was aware of such measures. "It's not without risk," he told Jeremiah, "but with your travel to other ports and towns, it would be a good idea at least for you and your crews. They are even inoculating children in Philadelphia."

At Jeremiah's urging, the surgeon obtained the necessary fluid from infected people to see it done. "Your men will need to stay away from their families for two weeks as they will have a mild case."

"We can make provision for that," Jeremiah assured him. Then, remembering his own family, he said, "My father is immune. He had a mild case of the disease and recovered when he was still in Dublin. He will support our efforts."

Within two weeks, the inoculation was offered to all who wanted it. Though the men initially groused about it and some genuinely feared even a mild case, in the end, all of Jeremiah's former crews and his brothers accepted it, believing it was only a matter of time before they would sail again.

Soon after, Jeremiah was offered another command, this time on the schooner *Tiger* with six guns and a crew of fifteen, sailing out of Portsmouth, New Hampshire. With Machias more isolated, the opportunity to secure much-needed provisions and sail from a safe port lifted his spirits.

Weeks later, the *Tiger* returned to Portsmouth, her crew weary from chasing shadows.

They'd taken a British merchantman off Falmouth and gained spoils—barrels of salt fish, sacks of flour, and rum. "Enough to help Machias," William said.

Jeremiah leaned against the rail, his breath fogging. "Aye, not the haul we'd hoped for, but enough all the same." Aware his brothers, John and Joseph, were just south of Portsmouth in Newburyport, where they had undertaken a new venture to construct a privateer, the *Hannibal*, he asked William, "Why don't we call upon our brothers? Newburyport is not far and I'd like to see their progress on the new privateer."

"An excellent idea," said William.

Even in spring, the sky over Newburyport was gray as Jeremiah guided the *Tiger* down the sluggish Merrimack River, its waters muddy from spring rains. The shipyards buzzed with activity, hammers ringing and saws whining. They soon found the yard where the new schooner was taking shape. Tying up the *Tiger*, Jeremiah and William gave the crew the afternoon off while they stood on the dock staring up at the nearly finished schooner.

The *Hannibal* was impressive in appearance, her fully planked hull gleaming with fresh pitch, and her twenty-four gun ports yawning open like dark eyes, ready for cannon. Two masts rose proudly from the deck, their rigging half-complete with taut lines and nascent sails fluttering in the breeze, while the last of the framing still braced her sides as men swarmed the scaffolding, caulking seams and fitting ironwork.

John, his face smudged with pitch, greeted Jeremiah with a bear hug. "Jere, you old sea wolf! And William! Heard your *Tiger*'s been quiet—trouble finding prey?"

"Aye," Jeremiah chuckled, "the British are warier now. We're here to lend a hand if we can." Joseph, now in his twenties, emerged, blueprints in hand, and the four brothers settled by a brazier, steam rising from their mugs of hot cider.

Jeremiah studied the *Hannibal*'s design, his years of privateering sharpening his eye. "'Tis a good design, and she'll have a large crew."

"And room for it," said John, pride in his voice. "The *Hannibal* will rival a small frigate—250-tons built to carry a crew of 130 men."

"Ammunition?" asked Jeremiah.

John looked up at the ship. "We'll be stocking her hold with 2,500 pounds of powder and shot in proportion."

Jeremiah offered his expertise on her armament and crew needs, drawing on his years of privateering experience while John sketched notes.

Joseph grinned. "Your *Margaretta* trick with the sweeps might work here."

"Aye, might work," said Jeremiah. "Meantime, she's a beauty from what I can see."

Eventually, the talk turned to family, the war's toll, and Machias' resilience. Jeremiah felt a rare peace, the *Tiger*'s quiet cruise a small price for this moment with his brothers.

"As soon as she's finished," said John, who was heavily invested in the ship along with Jeremiah, "I will petition the Continental Congress for a letter of marque to hunt British shipping."

"You'll get it," said Jeremiah.

John got his license in April and took command of the newly finished *Hannibal*, sailing with Joseph on her maiden cruise to Santo Domingo that summer. The cruise was successful, and he returned to Newburyport with several valuable prizes with cargoes of rum, tobacco, limes, sugar and cocoa that bolstered the Patriot cause and helped to pay for the ship, a point of pride for the O'Brien family.

Jeremiah had just finished his command of the *Tiger* and was excited for his brothers' success. "I'm proud of you," he told them, meeting both again in Newburyport. "A new ship and many prizes. You could not have done better."

With a sincere expression, John said, "I have a proposition for you, Jere. You've the experience to do well by her. Take the *Hannibal* for her next cruise with William. I've a chance to command a privateer in Brunswick, and Hannah and I are thinking of residing there for a time."

Joseph nodded in agreement. "She would benefit from your steady hand, Jere."

Torn between his family in Machias and the call of the sea, Jeremiah felt the pull of duty to his brothers and the cause. After a quiet evening with Lizzy, her blue eyes filled with understanding, she said, "Go, for your brothers need you. You have longed for the sea, and the *Hannibal* is built by your own family. I will miss you dearly but worry not. Jerry and I will be waiting when you return."

Jeremiah agreed. "I'll return to you soon, my redbird," he promised, kissing her. With a final embrace and a kiss on little Jerry's forehead, he left Machias, journeying to Newburyport in late summer to see to the *Hannibal*'s final provisioning. Meantime, John petitioned the Council of the General Court of Massachusetts to formally commission Jeremiah as the *Hannibal*'s commander. It was approved in September.

With commission in hand, Jeremiah stood on the wharf at Newburyport watching his new ship riding at anchor, the sun glistening off the water, the wind whispering of distant shores. She was the largest ship he'd ever commanded, well-armed and well-provisioned. William would sail with him as First Lieutenant and Donald McDonald as surgeon. Many of the crew he'd recruited had sailed with Jeremiah before, some had sailed with John, while others were new.

Sailing in late 1780, they seized a British brig laden with grain off New York in early December, sending it back to Newburyport with a prize crew. After that, they sailed farther south, still in the waters off New York. The hunting ground teemed with British merchantmen, but they had armed escorts, which had to be avoided. "The rewards will be rich if we prevail," he told his officers.

Meantime, the harsh winter lingered, with icy winds and snow flurries testing the ship's agility and making maneuvering the waters off New York more difficult. Icy water splashed onto the deck making them treacherous sheets of ice and causing all to shiver.

One crisp morning in early 1781, as the sea churned under a winter gale, the lookout called "Sail ho!"

Jeremiah's pulse quickened as he gazed through his spyglass. A fleet of British merchant ships were vaguely visible through the storm. They were not alone, but were under convoy of several large frigates, looming on the horizon. "Rich prizes, if we can take them," he said to William, who stood at his side. "But we'd need to separate a merchantman from the frigates."

The *Hannibal* had twenty-four guns, a good number but less than those on the British frigates. Still optimistic, he ordered his crew to make sail, just as two British frigates broke from the convoy, their sails billowing as they ran out their guns, giving chase.

Recognizing the futility of engaging two vessels superior to his own, Jeremiah ordered the *Hannibal* to turn their stern and run. "We'll outmaneuver them," he told his officers, his voice steady despite the rising tension in his chest.

A shot fired from one frigate came too close to the *Hannibal* for Jeremiah's comfort. Narrowing his eyes, he barked, "Return fire with the stern guns!" The *Hannibal's* crew responded, her guns roaring as they loosed a volley, splintering one frigate's bow.

For a tense hour, the ships traded gunfire, the icy deck shuddering under each recoil. But the frigates' heavier armament and the storm's fury overwhelmed the *Hannibal*. As ice clogged their guns, Jeremiah ordered a retreat.

The crew, battling icy decks and snow-laden sails, demonstrated their skill and training as they worked with precision, but the frigates held their course and did not separate. Thinking only to save the *Hannibal* and his crew, Jeremiah lightened the ship, ordering his water casks, supplies and guns over the sides.

The chase stretched on for two days, an exhausting struggle against wind, wave and weather. Finally, William fought his way across the icy deck to Jeremiah. "The crew is spent," he said. "Several are injured and two are dead. Further resistance will doom them all."

"Aye, your right," he replied, shaking his head. "I cannot allow that." Scanning his crew, their faces gaunt with exhaustion, their hands trembling from the biting cold, and their breaths misting in the frigid air, he accepted the approaching end.

The *Hannibal*'s agility waned as ice weighed her rigging, and a sudden squall reduced visibility, sealing her fate. The British frigates overtook them off New York harbor.

As the enemy ships drew alongside, their cannon gleaming with menace, Jeremiah's heart sank. With their strength gone and the frigates' cannon looming, to prevent further destruction, Jeremiah hauled down the *Hannibal*'s colors.

The ranking British officer boarded the *Hannibal*, his blue coat a contrast to the stormy gray sea. In accordance with the rules of warfare, Jeremiah handed over his sword, his jaw tight.

The officer, with a wry smile, accepted the sword. "Well, Captain, it is your turn to surrender today, but it may be mine tomorrow," he remarked, a rare moment of camaraderie by the enemy in the midst of defeat.

Machias, Maine, Massachusetts, spring 1781

IN MACHIAS, SPRING arrived not with renewal but with a creeping dread. Word of the *Hannibal's* capture reached the town in April, carried by a merchant ship from Boston. Lizzy stood frozen as John delivered the tidings, his voice heavy with guilt. "The British took them off New York," he said, his hands clenched at his sides. "Jeremiah, William, Donald—all of them, prisoners now on the HMS *Jersey*."

Lizzy's heart sank, her thoughts spiraling to the horrors she'd heard of the British prison ship anchored in Wallabout Bay in New York Harbor. A thousand men and boys were imprisoned on the aging hulk that had been designed for four hundred sailors. Crammed below decks in inhuman conditions, the Patriot prisoners endured guards who meted out beatings for the slightest defiance. Diseases—smallpox, dysentery, typhoid and yellow fever—ravaged them in a place with no light or fresh air, and they were fed rations of spoiled food and brackish water. Families were barred from aiding them. "The *Jersey*...it's the one they call 'Hell', isn't it?"

John nodded, his face a grim reflection of the fear they all felt.

Jerry, now three, tugged at her skirts, his blue eyes wide with confusion. "Where's Papa?" he asked, his small voice piercing her heart.

She knelt, pulling him close to hide her tears. "He'll come back to us, my sweet," she whispered, though fear gnawed at her certainty, "just not today."

Annie, told of Donald's capture, held her sixteenth-month-old daughter close as tears streaked down her cheeks. "My Donald's on that horrible hulk. I can't bear to think of it."

That evening, Annie sat with Lizzy by the hearth, staring into the flames. With a voice more sure than his expression, Dick Earle added a log to the fire and said, "Captain Jeremiah, William and Surgeon McDonald are strong. We must pray they survive along with the crew."

"Yes," agreed Lizzy. "We must hold to that hope and pray. God is able to deliver them." But the rumors of the HMS *Jersey*, a floating tomb where men died by the hundreds, haunted Lizzy's nights. Each day without news brought a heavier burden. "Thank God Jeremiah had them inoculated against smallpox," she told Annie. "It may yet save them."

"And Donald is there to tend the wounded," said Annie. "We can be thankful for that."

The O'Brien family gathered at Morris and Mary's home one evening to pray, their faces etched with worry. John spoke with conviction, masking his fear. "The *Hannibal* was built to fight, not to yield," he said, his voice breaking. "Jere and the crew are fighters as well. They would not have surrendered if they'd had a choice."

Mary O'Brien, her eyes red from silent weeping,

prayed aloud. "Oh, Lord, we beseech You to bring back our men from that terrible place."

John and Joseph, who had urged Jeremiah to take command, bore the weight of their decision. "If I'd not pressed him to sail…" John murmured, his words trailing off as he stared into the crackling fire.

"You cannot blame yourself," said Lizzy. "Jeremiah sought this command and, more than most, he knew the risk. With all his captures, he was aware this day might one day come. We spoke of it…he wanted to prepare me."

Morris O'Brien, a man of great faith, prayed for his sons taken captive and for the other officers and crew, asking God to return them to Machias and their families, ending with "You are able, Lord, and we trust in You."

Reverend Lyon, sensing the town' despair, called the community to the meeting house on a gray Sunday morning. The benches were filled with anxious faces—wives, mothers, and children who feared for their own on the *Jersey*.

Standing at the pulpit, Lyon's voice rang with quiet strength. "We are tested, as Job was tested," he began, his eyes sweeping over the congregation. "Captain O'Brien, his officers and their crew suffer for our liberty, but we must not lose faith. Let us pray for their deliverance, for the Lord hears the cries of the righteous."

Lizzy bowed her head, little Jerry's small hand in hers, and prayed with a fervor she'd never known. "Grant us mercy, Lord, and bring them home," she whispered, her voice joining the chorus of murmured pleas filling the meeting house.

Annie, beside her, added her own prayer for Donald, her arms wrapped around her sleeping child, little Maggie.

IN LATE JULY, as the summer sun cast long shadows over the riverbanks, a weary William and Donald straggled into Machias with the rest of the *Hannibal*'s crew that had survived both the capture and the *Jersey*. Hearing of their arrival, Lizzy hastened to meet them. After six months on the dreaded prison ship, the crew of the *Hannibal* had been released as a part of a prisoner exchange. With them was Sam Holt and the small prize crew that had been captured by the British earlier. Their gaunt faces, their too thin bodies and their clothes hanging in filthy tatters were silent witnesses of their ordeal.

"Jeremiah?" Lizzy's voice faltered as she asked, her heart breaking when, after embracing William, she did not see Jeremiah among the other men. "Is he not with you?"

William shook his head, grief etched on his too thin face. "The British would not let him go, Lizzy. He is being taken to England, to Mill Prison."

It was all Lizzy could do to remain standing. Shaken, she swayed. Annie, who had come to meet Donald, steadied her.

William handed her a letter, its edges worn from its perilous journey from the *Jersey*'s hold. "I have carried it from the *Jersey* at Jeremiah's request."

Written in Jeremiah's hand, Lizzy read the letter as tears flowed down her cheeks. "Jeremiah. Oh, Jeremiah, my love," she sobbed.

Realizing she must share it, she asked Reverend Lyon

to read the letter aloud to the congregation, which he did the next day. To a crowded meeting house, he said, "Elizabeth O'Brien has asked me to read this letter to you. It's from her husband, Captain O'Brien."

My dearest redbird,

From the dark belly of the HMS Jersey, where I languish with my crew, I pen these words with a trembling hand. We have little to eat and nothing to warm us against the cold. Even this parchment and quill are borrowed from another prisoner.

The air is foul with sickness, and the days are marked by the groans of the dying—dozens lost daily. My one consolation is that while smallpox abounds in this barren hulk, none of us will see that disease for all are inoculated.

My heart clings to you and our young son, and my constant prayer is that God will allow me to return to you. I am told of an exchange that will soon free William, Donald and our crew, as well as the prize crew we lost to the British earlier, but I am to be held back, marked for special punishment by the British for my past defiance. That is to say, for all the good we have done America. The British have tempted the men with enlistment to serve the British navy, but none will trade their honor for ease—better death than betrayal of our cause.

Know that your love and the prayers of all at Machias sustain me. I picture Jerry's laughter, his small hands reaching for me, and your quiet strength beside him. Pray for me, as I pray for you, that God may grant me deliverance to see your face again.

Tell my family I fight to stay alive for them, too. Their faith in me and in God are my shield.

Until I return, hold fast, my love. The evils of British confinement have not yet claimed me, and I vow to find my way back to you.

Your devoted husband,

Jeremiah

Tears streamed down Lizzy's cheeks as the final words echoed again in her mind. Little Jerry leaned against her, his small face forlorn, for he knew his father remained a prisoner. Around her she could hear the crying of women who empathized with her pain. Some had lost their men in the capture. At least Lizzy still had hope.

Beside her, Annie sobbed softly, Donald's arm around her and their young daughter, who had fallen asleep in his embrace.

Reverend Lyon encouraged them. "God is master here, not the British. He has delivered those of the *Hannibal*'s crew He did not take to Heaven, for which we thank Him. Jeremiah survived six months on the prison ship that claimed the lives of many others. We must pray God will deliver him from Mill Prison, as He delivered Daniel from the lions' den." He closed the meeting with a fervent prayer, his voice lifting over the murmur of the crowd. "The Lord has heard our pleas," he said. "Captain O'Brien lives, and we will not cease to petition the Good Lord for his return."

Wallabout Bay, New York, late July 1781

ON THE HMS *Jersey*, Jeremiah continued to endure the horrors of captivity, now alone without his brother or his crew. The laughing cries of herring gulls pierced the air, a grim reminder of better days in Machias. The stench of decay and despair was a constant assault as the groans of the sick and dying reverberated through the dank hold.

For six months, he had faced deprivation, with dozens succumbing to dysentery and fever, made worse with July's stifling heat. The bodies of the dead were interred in shallow graves along the East River's banks, where bones and skulls often washed ashore, a grim testament to British cruelty. He remembered how well they had treated the British prisoners they had taken to Cambridge and Watertown, feeding them the same food they ate. Not so the British.

British officers, desperate for recruits, pressed the prisoners daily to enlist in the king's service, promising deliverance from their suffering. Many of the men had families waiting at home, their absence a heavy burden, making such offers tempting. Added to that, the near-certainty of death on the *Jersey* loomed large. Yet Jeremiah and his crew had held firm, their loyalty to the cause of freedom unyielding. "I'll not betray our fight," Jeremiah had whispered to William one night, their voices low amidst the creaking timbers. "Better death than dishonor." His men, inspired by his resolve, echoed his defiance, clinging to the hope of exchange.

In late June, after six months of torment, a cartel for a prisoner exchange freed the *Hannibal*'s crew and her officers, including William and Donald, their names called out as they shuffled toward liberty. But Jeremiah, singled out for "special punishment" by orders from England, was not among them. The British, aware of his renown since the *Margaretta*'s capture, sought to make an example of "the Irish Yankee" as they called him, their voices dripping with disdain.

Sitting alone on a splintered bench, his once-strong frame hunched under a tattered blanket, damp seeping into his bones, Jeremiah rubbed his temples, the memory of young Samuel Holt flashing before him. The lad, barely eighteen, had been part of the prize crew he'd sent with the captured brig in '80, taken by the *Scarborough*'s guns. Jeremiah had spotted Holt weeks ago, gaunt but alive, his eyes hollow from the same hell. "Captain," Holt had rasped, "we held out, but they broke us on this floating grave." The reunion had been a bitter comfort, but Jeremiah found solace when Holt and his prize crew were included in the exchange.

His parting from William, Donald and his men tore at his heart, but he kept his words encouraging. "Go with my blessing, and take this letter to Lizzy," he said to William, pressing the smudged paper into his hand. "Tell her not to lose hope. Tell John and Joseph, too. They must have no regrets."

In July, he was shackled and transported across the Atlantic to England, the stormy seas mirroring his heavy heart with the separation from his family, an ocean now between them. The uncertainty of his fate gnawed at his heart with each mile he was taken farther from his home.

Arriving at Plymouth, he was thrown into Mill Prison,

a fortress of stone and misery nearly as dreadful as the *Jersey*. More massive than he had first imagined, the prison was a huge rectangular structure with high walls and a large inner courtyard where poorly clothed men walked alone or in small groups. Buildings, including those where the prisoners were locked in at night, lined the perimeter. The air inside the prison was damp and thick with despair. Many prisoners were stricken with smallpox, some dying of the disease.

The rations they were given were so meager, the prisoners ate grass, snails, and rats to stave off hunger. Those who had money were allowed to buy food from enterprising merchants who came once a day to stand outside the prison. While some prisoners had coin and Benjamin Franklin sent money to the American prisoners from time to time, most days all experienced severe hunger. Fortunately, Jeremiah had some money when taken, though it was not enough to buy food to sustain him.

There was one positive change. During the day, they were not deprived of fresh air, for the courtyard was allowed them. There, he met other Patriot officers, men such as Captain Gustavus Conyngham, an Irish-born American naval officer whose bold raids had so nettled the British they kept him in irons, Captain Silas Talbot, commander of the nineteen-gun *General Washington*, who had many captures to his credit, and Captain John Green, another Irish-born American naval officer whose defiance had landed him in these stone walls. Knowing such valiant captains had also been taken by the British eased Jeremiah's guilt over the loss of his ship and his crew's fate.

Sharing their company lifted his spirits, although regrettably in a place as dismal as Mill Prison.

The prison also housed French and Spanish prisoners of war, but as "rebels", the Americans were treated more harshly and given smaller food rations than their European counterparts. Worse still, the guards singled out Jeremiah for special punishment. More than once, he endured half-rations and harsh solitary confinement in what the prisoners called "the Black Hole", a dark dungeon where there was nothing to sleep on but cold, hard ground, often wet from rains. When he was allowed out, one guard shoved him so hard he fell to the ground and struggled to rise in his weakened condition. His body was left emaciated from the ordeal, but his spirit remained unbroken.

There was a great deal of talk among the prisoners about France entering the war, the guards murmuring among themselves that the English vessels had received insults at sea from the French. At first, the guards resented such insults, cursing the French, but as time went on, they appeared to be afraid, giving Jeremiah and the other prisoners hope.

Though denied newspapers, the prisoners managed to receive them weekly through one means or another. As a result, they were aware the war had moved to the south and General Cornwallis had surrendered to Washington at Yorktown in October. Such developments were encouraging but they did not end the war, as British forces remained stationed in Charleston and their army still resided in New York.

One night after being returned to the cells and locked

inside, some of the prisoners broke out in songs of liberty, for none had given up hope, and news from the war encouraged them. The guards, hearing their singing, threatened the prisoners with half-rations should they persist. When silence ensued, Jeremiah rested his head against the cold stone wall, listening to the distant crash of waves against the Plymouth cliffs, a reminder of the sea he loved. His thoughts turned to Lizzy and his young son, their faces shining amidst the darkness.

The fight for liberty had brought him to this bleak shore, but he had no regrets. For love of his country, he would do it again. Instead, he looked to the future, determined to survive, to escape and to return to his family. And, before he slept, he prayed, asking God to guide him.

"The ways of Providence being inscrutable, and the justice of it not to be scanned by the shallow eye of humanity, nor to be counteracted by the utmost efforts of human power or wisdom, resignation, and as far as the strength of our reason and religion can carry us, a cheerful acquiescence to the Divine Will, is what we are to aim."
– George Washington (1773)

CHAPTER 15

Machias, Maine, Massachusetts, February 1782

THE WINTER WINDS howled through Machias, rattling the frost-crusted windows as snow piled high against the door. Inside, Lizzy sat by the hearth, its flames doing their best to warm the room. Winter had gripped the town in a vise of cold and scarcity, a cruel echo of the hardships that had plagued them in the war's early days. The mills along the Machias River stood idle—silent sentinels of a prosperity stolen by British blockades and the *Hannibal's* capture.

With trade severed and privateering halted, food had grown scarce, the town's stores of corn, oats and flour long depleted. Fruit from the O'Brien orchards had all been consumed. Families subsisted on clams when they could dig them from frozen mudflats, fish when they could catch them, and wild roots foraged from beneath the snow, a bitter reminder of better days.

Lizzy sat by the fire, mending a threadbare coat for Jerry, her fingers trembling from cold and worry. Donald's return with the crew had brought joy to Annie, her sister's laughter returning, a stark contrast to Lizzy's solitude.

Donald had assured her that when he'd last seen Jeremiah, he was well and uninjured, though much too thin. She felt the weight of his absence keenly, each creak of the house a cruel echo of his missing footsteps, her bed half-empty. His brothers tried to make up for his absence, coming often to share an evening, but it was not enough.

Winter's brutality gnawed at her, for if it was this harsh in Machias, how much worse must it be for Jeremiah, with no proper food or clothing and brutal treatment at the hands of guards who wanted revenge. She whispered a prayer for his survival, though doubt shadowed her faith. Would he ever return?

Little Jerry, now four, huddled beside her, wrapped in a patched blanket. His blue eyes, so like Jeremiah's, searched her face with a question that broke her heart anew each time he asked. "Mama, when will Papa come home?" His small voice trembled, the innocence in it a dagger to her determination to stay strong.

Lizzy pulled him onto her lap, pressing a kiss to his

forehead to hide the tears welling in her eyes. "Soon, my sweet," she whispered, her voice steady despite the turmoil within. "Papa is strong, and with God's help, he'll find his way back to us. He promised, didn't he?"

Jerry nodded, clutching his carved wooden boat. But Lizzy's heart faltered—how could she assure her son when she doubted herself?

Jerry slipped to the rug at her feet to resume his play. "Sean come tomorrow?"

"He might," said Lizzy, "if the storm stops long enough. Maybe he'll bring his game of jacks to show you."

Jerry smiled at this for he did love to watch his Uncle Sean play the game. Though her brother was now seventeen, out of kindness, Sean would entertain Jerry for hours. And often Sean came with young James Cole, the son of their father's new wife who considered Sean his older brother.

Dick Earle, Jeremiah's faithful servant, came down the stairs, his boots hitting the wooden plank steps. "I'm gonna bring in some of that firewood stacked near the door, Mistress."

"We could surely use more," she said. "It's going to be a dreadful night, I fear."

He gave her a concerned look as he took his coat and hat from a peg and passed through the front door. Lizzy knew he worried for her, and while she tried to put on a brave front, she probably failed more times than not.

When Dick returned, he stacked the wood near the fireplace and brushed the snow off his coat before hanging it up.

Lizzy managed a smile. "Thank you, Dick."

He added a log to the fire, and then glanced back at her. "Are you and the lad all right?"

"It's hard, Dick. The cold, the hunger…I think of Jeremiah. Even if he's alive, what must he be enduring?" Her voice broke, and she turned away, brushing at her tears.

Dick's voice was reassuring. "The Cap'n's a fighter, Ma'am. I've seen him face storms and cannon fire without flinching. He's out there, and he'll come back. I feel it in my bones. Don't you give up on him now, not when this town needs hope as much as bread."

"You're such an encouragement to me, Dick."

Annie and Donald came to visit the next morning when the storm had passed. Donald carried two-year-old Maggie in his arms, bundled with a blanket around her coat, her reddish-blonde curls just poking out. Raising her head, she glimpsed little Jerry and smiled wide.

"Come in, come in," said Lizzy.

Annie's eyes softened with concern as she took in Lizzy's weary frame. Donald set Maggie down and handed her a rag doll, which she promptly took to Jerry to show him.

"I'll just stir the fire," said Donald, leaving the two women alone.

Annie drew Lizzy to the chairs around the table. Her voice tender, she said, "Lizzy, I see the toll this takes on you. I fear for Jeremiah, too. He's endured so much, and this winter…well, we pray he feels our love across the sea, and that it gives him strength." Her words wavered, revealing her own fears beneath her hope. "We must believe, for Jerry's sake and yours, that Jeremiah will return."

Lizzy nodded. "You're right, of course."

"I have some good news," said Annie. "Donald and I are expecting our second child."

"That is good news, indeed," said Lizzy, happy for her sister.

From the fireplace, Donald turned to Lizzy. "With Cornwallis' surrender at Yorktown in October, the war cannae last much longer."

Before Lizzy could reply, Reverend Lyon's voice rang out from the other side of the front door. "Hello the house! We've come to visit with the last of the Christmas cider."

Lizzy's spirits rose despite her worry. Opening the door, she said, "Do come in. Annie and Donald are here with Maggie."

Reverend James and Martha Lyon, entered with smiles on their faces. "We've come with the last of Christmas cheer and to remind you that winter will pass and soon spring will be here."

The children rose from the floor at the word "Christmas" and were greeted by the Lyons.

"Bless you both," said Lizzy.

Dick Earle heated the cider and they sat around sharing it and the story of the party Jeremiah gave when he served cider he had made from his own apples. The memory and the hot cider warmed Lizzy, encouraging her not to give up.

"Tomorrow is Sunday," Reverend Lyon reminded them. "I have written a new hymn for us to sing. And, I've written a special sermon for you."

"In that case," said Donald, "we'll nae miss it."

"We wouldn't miss it anyway," Annie said with a grin.

Lizzy nodded her agreement. In truth, the church was their wider family and the Sunday services an encouragement to them all. "You are a blessing, Reverend, to everyone in Machias."

A few hours later, when their guests departed, Lizzy bundled Jerry in his cloak and took him outside to play in the snow. By afternoon, he was ready to come in. With him nestled against her in a chair, she read him the story of *The Fox and the Grapes* from Aesop's Fables, its yellowed pages a cherished O'Brien heirloom, until he drifted asleep.

Dick sat nearby tending the fire as he listened and sometimes laughed at a turn in the tale, the fox's sour grapes excuse drawing a grin. "Reminds me of the Cap'n's stubborn streak!"

Lizzy smiled. "It's that stubborn streak I'm counting on, Dick, to see him home."

The next day, with great anticipation, Lizzy bundled Jerry in his coat and trudged through the snow beneath overcast skies with Dick to join the shivering crowd in the meeting house, their breaths visible in the frigid air, for the fireplace failed to heat the large space well.

Reverend Lyon stood at the pulpit, greeting the congregation, his voice a steady beacon amidst the cold winter. "People of Machias, we gather this winter to lift our hearts in praise to the Almighty," he began, his eyes sweeping over the congregation. "No matter the hard days, we can rejoice in our Salvation. I've a new hymn to teach you, one that will encourage you."

He then shared the words and the tune to a new song.

When overwhelm'd with grief,
My heart within me dies
Helpless and far from all relief
To Heav'n I lift mine eyes
To Heav'n I lift mine eyes

The congregation caught on quickly and their voices rang out as verses were added. Lizzy was happy to join them. Focusing on God instead of her troubles lifted her spirits.

When the song ended, Reverend Lyon said, "Our mills stand still, our tables are bare, and some of our sons and husbands—like Captain O'Brien—serve the cause far from home. Yet we are not forsaken! As the Lord provided manna in the wilderness, so He sustains us now. We pray for the men of Machias who are not with us today, that God may shield them from cold and cruelty as they serve our new country, that His angels may guide them back to us. Let us hold fast to our Savior, the Lord Jesus Christ, for in our faith we find strength." The reverend's voice rose, fervent and unyielding, as he continued, sharing the story of the persecution the Lord's apostles endured at the hands of Rome. "It is not unlike what Captain O'Brien is enduring. God rescued Peter from a Roman jail and he can rescue Jeremiah. We must trust Him." Then Reverend Lyon led them in a prayer that echoed through the meeting house.

Bowing her head, Lizzy joined the prayer, her heart clinging to the reverend's words. Tucked into her side, Jerry's eyes grew heavy as he nodded off, his small hand in hers. Annie squeezed her other hand, a silent promise of shared hope, and for a moment, the weight on Lizzy's shoulders lightened—just enough to face another day.

"We have it in our power to begin the world over again."

– Thomas Paine (1776)

CHAPTER 16

Mill Prison, Plymouth, England, June 1782

NINE MONTHS OF captivity passed in a haze of hunger, harassment, filth and endurance, each day sharpening Jeremiah's observation of the guards' routines. By spring 1782, he had forged a plan of escape.

He began by neglecting his dress and appearance for months, growing his beard and hair long, allowing his clothes, some taken from dead prisoners, to be reduced to rags. He befriended a French washwoman, the dark-haired Madame Boyer, who laundered for the prison. She routinely brought clothing to the prisoners, and was friendly to Americans. She knew a bit of English and Jeremiah remembered some of the French his father had taught him and his brothers.

"The French," she said one day, as she scrubbed a shirt, "we are now allies of America. At Yorktown, your General Washington and our Comte de Rochambeau, they defeated the British."

"We thank God for that," he told her, the memory stirring a flicker of hope. Any surrender by the British was good news, and it was a joy to hear the French were fighting with America.

When Madame Boyer heard Jeremiah's plan, she agreed to help him. "Both my husband and I, we will assist your escape." In early June, the day before the one he had fixed for his escape, he paid her the last money he had, a guinea, to bring him a suit of clothing that would blend with the guards. The clever woman did better. "With these," she said, handing him the red and white uniform of a British soldier, "they will not suspect you."

With her assistance, he washed, shaved and donned the uniform she had given him, draping an old coat over it, as he mingled with the other prisoners in the courtyard. That evening, secreting himself under a platform in the yard, he escaped the notice of the guards when the prisoners were sent into the cells for the night.

As the sun set, with his heart pounding in his chest, he rose from his hiding place and shed the old coat. Checking to make sure he was not observed, he strolled at a leisurely pace across the yard and through the principal keeper's house in the dusk of the evening. Taken for a British soldier, he paused long enough in the barroom to down a tankard of ale offered him.

And then he was free.

Scarcely believing his good fortune, Jeremiah thanked

God and hastened to the rocky shore, his heart pounding with hope. Madame Boyer had promised her husband would furnish a boat. On the shore, while awaiting Monsieur Boyer, Jeremiah met two other escaping American officers, one a Captain Lyon. Though he was no relation to the Machias minister, the name was a comforting reminder of divine guidance.

"Captain O'Brien?" Lyon whispered, his voice hoarse, as he stared at the British soldier's uniform he wore. "We've been waiting for we knew a third man was coming, a privateer named O'Brien. My heart nearly stopped when I saw you approaching."

"My apologies," said Jeremiah, managing a grin. "This disguise allowed me to walk through the front door of the prison."

"You're very convincing," said the other officer, a gaunt lieutenant. "I bribed a guard with my last coins two days ago—nearly got caught."

"I tunneled out last night under the prison wall," said Lyon. "Been digging for many weeks. Another officer, half-dead from fever, whispered of Madame Boyer's helping men escape and smuggling letters to Franklin."

Before Jeremiah could respond, Monsieur Boyer appeared with a small skiff, its hull weathered but sturdy. They climbed in and rowed down the River Plym in silence that eventful evening, he and the other Americans taking turns at the oars with what strength they had. The night was so still Jeremiah could hear the tread of the English sentinels on shore and a guard's whistling as he sought to while away the hours.

From the river, where the summer breeze wafted over

the water, they boarded a fishing boat based in Brest, its nets reeking of herring from channel waters. With the promise of coin upon reaching France, the fishing boat captain agreed to ferry them across the English Channel.

Apparently the fisherman was a friend of Monsieur Boyer and had helped Americans before. He beamed with pride in telling them he and his crew were from Brest where Comte de Rochambeau had sailed from the year before with five hundred officers and five thousand soldiers. "To give the Americans victory, *oui?*"

Landing near the bustling French port of Brest, Jeremiah immediately shed the red jacket. Thin from more than a year of captivity, the clothes Jeremiah wore hung loosely on his tall frame.

The locals greeted the Americans warmly, welcoming them to friendly shores. Word of their arrival reached the local authorities, and a French naval officer, Capitaine Pierre Dubois, welcomed them with open arms and money for the fishing captain. "Americans, *bienvenue!*" he said, his blue uniform with red trim stark against the harbor's gray dawn.

Jeremiah was relieved and elated at the same time. *"Merci, mon ami,"* he replied, a weary smile breaking through.

"You are allies of France, *oui?*" Dubois said in accented English. "Dr. Franklin, he has tasked us to aid Americans in your plight. The enemy's surrender last year was a great victory—our armies together broke the British will. Now, peace talks begin in Paris." And then with a shrug, he added, "Though the sea remains a battleground, so you must be cautious."

Dubois arranged for their care, providing water to bathe, food, clothing, and a small sum of livres to ease their recovery. The hospitality shown Jeremiah and the other Americans brought him nearly to tears. He could hardly remember the last time he had been clean or had a good meal. Nor could he recall a time since his capture when such kindness was shown to him. And, because of it, he was tempted to linger on the pleasant shores. But Lizzy's beautiful face never left his thoughts. Home was merely an ocean away.

Within days, Jeremiah secured passage on a French merchant ship, the *Espoir*, bound for Boston with supplies for the Continental Army. Her captain, Monsieur Fortin, eager to defy the British as one of America's allies, welcomed him aboard.

"You may tell General Washington that the French, we stand with you, *toujours*," Dubois said as Jeremiah embarked, a faint smile on his face.

"And tell all in France we are grateful," replied Jeremiah.

As the ship set sail, Jeremiah stood at the rail, the French coast fading into the horizon. The kindness of Madame Boyer and the French had given him a lifeline. Turning his eyes toward America, he vowed he would not squander the freedom he'd been given. He would return to Machias with a renewed commitment to see the war to its end.

THE ATLANTIC STRETCHED endlessly before the French merchant ship *l'Espoir*, her sails billowing in the wind alongside her French frigate escort, *Surveillante*. Jeremiah stood in the bow, the salt wind stinging his cheeks, each swell bringing him closer to home. A tempest of memories swirled in his mind, memories of the *Jersey*'s horrors, Mill Prison's stone walls, and the daring escape that had led him to France's shores and here. Nightmares still haunted him, but memories of home and America grew stronger with each day.

Monsieur Fortin, the ship's captain, had proven a steadfast ally, his crew sharing their provisions with the escaped Patriot captain. "We sail for Boston," Fortin had said in halting English, "and from there, you can catch a vessel north, *oui?*"

"*Oui,*" Jeremiah said with a smile, then hesitated. "And what of our escort?" They had become separated from *Surveillante* in a storm. "The British still prowl these waters."

Fortin chuckled, gesturing to the ship's deck where six small cannon gleamed. "*Oui,* we began with *Surveillante,* and it is true a storm parted us a week ago, but we are sufficiently armed, and the risk of attack, though real, has diminished. The British prioritize defensive operations now, awaiting peace from Paris. We rely on speed and the French flag to see us through."

The *Espoir* carried supplies for the Continental Army—barrels of powder, bolts of cloth, and crates of muskets—but to Jeremiah, she bore something far more precious: freedom. His hand on the rail, his eyes on the sea, his thoughts were on Lizzy and little Jerry, and on his brother, John. He must stop in Brunswick on his way north from Boston to explain all that had transpired. And to ask for his brother's forgiveness in losing the *Hannibal*. The French alliance, sealed by men like Benjamin Franklin and Capitaine Dubois, had given him this chance, and he would honor it.

Six weeks later, the *Espoir* docked in Boston Harbor. The ship had sailed unescorted for the last part of their trip, her crew tense but relieved after evading a distant British sail with naught but speed and prayer.

Jeremiah stood at the rail, the sun beaming down on the bustling American port alive with wartime activity. American and French ships unloaded supplies side by side, French flags fluttering near the Stars and Stripes. The sight stirred his senses.

Jeremiah disembarked at the first opportunity, eager to be on his way. Capitaine Fortin waved to him from the deck. *"Bon voyage, mon ami!"*

"Godspeed!" Jeremiah shouted back.

The next day, he secured passage on a fishing boat headed north.

Brunswick, Maine, Massachusetts, late August 1782

TWO WEEKS LATER, Jeremiah arrived in Brunswick, a modest shipbuilding port as well as a hub for privateers. The late August sun hung low, casting golden streaks across the Kennebec River, where schooners and sloops bobbed at anchor, the cries of gulls drifting over the water. After weeks aboard the *Espoir*, and then more travel by fishing boat, the sight of solid ground—and the promise of family—stirred a deep relief in Jeremiah.

Making inquiries in the harbor, he was directed to the modest home near the waterfront where he could find his brother.

John met him at the door, his frame filling the threshold, his face breaking into a grin that belied the worry etched in his eyes. "Jere, by all that's holy, you're alive!" He pulled Jeremiah into a fierce embrace, the strength of it a balm to his months of solitude. Behind him, Hannah emerged, her apron dusted with flour, two small children, a boy of about two clinging to her skirts, and a girl barely a year Hannah set on the floor, the child's blue eyes wide with curiosity.

"Hannah," said Jeremiah, "you have little ones now!" His voice was rough with emotion as he knelt to ruffle the boy's hair.

"Aye," said John. "Born here in Brunswick."

"What are their names?"

"This is Jeremiah," Hannah replied, smiling softly, "named after his famous uncle, and little Mary, named after your mother and sister. Our blessings in the midst of war." She ushered the men inside, where the scent of fish stew mingled with the breeze off the river.

John led Jeremiah to a rough-hewn table by the hearth, pouring two tankards of ale. "Sit, Brother. I want to hear how you did it, and then I've news for you."

Jeremiah took his namesake up on his lap and, smiling at the boy, recounted the tale of his escape from Mill

Prison. "It was May, the nights still cold at the prison. It wasn't as dreadful a place as the *Jersey*, but the guards were worse and they singled me out for 'special' treatment, starving me when they weren't throwing me in a black pit. I knew to escape I must make the guards think of me as someone else. There were over six hundred prisoners so I thought I had a good chance to lose myself in the crowd. I'd been watching the guards and planning for months. I disguised myself, letting my hair and beard grow and wearing rags until I looked like someone time forgot. In the end, with France coming into the war, a French laundress helped me, an angel sent from God. She spoke of the British surrender at Yorktown and the role of the French. That gave me hope. I walked out of the prison disguised as a British soldier."

John's eyes narrowed, a mix of pride and disbelief. "God's hand was on you, Jere."

From behind him, Hannah, her brown curls loose under her white lace cap, said, "We prayed for you every day."

"Thank you," said Jeremiah, humbled by Hannah's words. "Your faithful prayers surely kept me going." Meeting his brother's sympathetic gaze, Jeremiah said, "I'm sorry about the *Hannibal*, John. She was a beautiful ship. It hurt me to take down her colors, but I could see with the two British frigates closing in and the crew failing after days in chase and battle, there was no choice."

"William has explained all to me. It was always a possibility that one day we would be captured. I'm just sorry it was you."

"I'll make it up to you, John."

"No need. I've been busy while you were away, commanding several privateers with good success. In May, I was commissioned to command the *Cyrus*, a fine schooner out of Portsmouth. Sixteen guns, forty men— she's mine to harry the British 'til the war is officially over."

"That's good news," said Jeremiah, his spirits lifting. "Capitaine Dubois in Brest said the British surrender at Yorktown hailed the end, with peace talks in Paris now. Yet the captain who brought me to Boston said the British are holding back, awaiting outcomes. Are we not at the war's end?"

"We are at the beginning of the end," said John. "The fighting on land is done. Parliament called for peace in March. Now they talk peace in Paris. But we're free to plunder British shipping 'til it's settled. Owners will line up to give you ships, Jere."

Jeremiah set his namesake on the floor and took a long draw on his ale. "So, America will have her independence at last." Tears came to his eyes. "There were times I doubted this day would come."

Hannah set bowls of stew on the table with a loaf of bread, her voice gentle. "Rest here today and tomorrow, Jeremiah. John will want to show you his ship, and the children will love a tale from their famous uncle. Since he was born, little Jeremiah has heard about you and your son, his cousin of the same name."

"Thank you, Hannah" said Jeremiah. "You must visit us in Machias. Father and Mother will be wanting to see their grandchildren."

John leaned over to clap him on the shoulder, and for

a moment, the war's shadow receded, replaced by the warmth of his brother's family in Brunswick's quiet harbor.

Two days later, Jeremiah boarded a sloop bound for Machias, his blood racing with each mile they sailed north. He watched the coast as the days passed, until the rugged coast of Machias came into view, the Machias River glinting beyond like a sparkling silver ribbon. Jeremiah stepped down from the fishing vessel. Thanking the captain, he waved goodbye as he strode off toward town.

Machias, Maine, Massachusetts, September 1782

SEPTEMBER'S WIND CARRIED the scent of pine and salt to where Lizzy stood on the Machias riverbank, her hair whipping behind her. The trees along the river still wore summer's green for autumn had not yet arrived. She and Dick had just harvested the plums in Jeremiah's orchard. At the water's edge, her young son played with a new toy boat his Uncle Gideon had carved for him. Would Jerry one day command ships like his father? Even at his young age, she could see he had his father's courage and his quick mind. Surely one day, Jerry could command a vessel if he wanted to.

The seven years since she came to Machias had carved lines into her face—years of tending Annie and Sean, years of waiting for Jeremiah when he was at sea, years of deprivation from the war, and finally years of praying for news. The *Margaretta* victory, Jeremiah's privateer triumphs, his captures—all faded into a silence broken only by the falls' distant roar.

As she watched her son with his toy boat, she caught sight of a figure approaching from the side. Turning, her breath caught, her heart a tangle of relief and disbelief as her throat tightened. He was leaner, his face gaunt, but she did not fail to recognize her love, his blue eyes bright despite the ill treatment he had received at the hands of the British. Jeremiah, somehow escaped from Mill Prison, was home at last.

"Papa!" yelled little Jerry, rising to run to his father, the toy boat forgotten.

Jeremiah dropped his worn satchel, and swept his son into his arms, his gaze locking with hers.

"You are late, Captain O'Brien." Her voice trembled as the tears began to fall. "Very late."

"Indeed, I am, Mrs. O'Brien," he said, setting down his son, his voice rough but warm. "I promised I'd return, and I have. The British could not hold me, but you and Machias hold me still." He stepped closer, offering a hand scarred by chains. "Will you have me now, with my battles behind me?"

Tears stung her eyes as she took his hand, the long nights of waiting, hoping and praying over. "Aye," she said, her voice faltering, "if you'll have a woman who's fought her own wars in your absence."

He took her into his arms. "My redbird, my love, I'm home," he said, burying his face in her hair, the scent of her assuring him he spoke truth.

Behind them, the falls kept up a steady sound, as if welcoming the captain home.

NEWS OF JEREMIAH'S return spread like a wind rushing through the pines, and the next day the townsfolk gathered at the meeting house to welcome him, their cheers a balm to the hardships of the past years. His parents and his brothers, who were still in Machias, were there with joyful faces. His sister, Mary, and her husband Job Burnham had come as well. Annie and Donald arrived with their daughter, little Maggie, while Thomas Fitzpatrick and his new family, along with Sean, now a young man, also came. Added to these were the men of his crew who had survived the *Jersey*.

Amid the celebration, Ben Foster and his wife Martha burst in with their brood of children, their smiles radiant. "We never gave up hope," said Ben. "It was only a question of time."

All the men shook Jeremiah's hand, and the women embraced him in turns, as Lizzy stood beside him with little Jerry, who beamed his pride at having his father home, the privateer captain all hailed as a returning hero.

Reverend Lyon raised his hands, his voice carrying over the crowd. "Good people of Machias, the Lord has answered our prayers and delivered Captain O'Brien, as we asked. We must thank God for this. Our men survived the *Jersey* and Captain O'Brien the dreaded Mill Prison."

Jeremiah held his family tight amid the celebration, the warmth of their welcome banishing the cold of his captivity. The peace was yet to be secured, but in this moment, he had reclaimed what mattered most—and he would fight on for them, for Machias, and for liberty until the peace was certain.

Burnham Tavern, Machias, Maine, Massachusetts, autumn 1782

THE WARM GLOW of candlelight shone from the windows of Burnham Tavern, its sturdy oak beams a welcome respite since the war's early days. The tavern, where the O'Brien brothers had first planned to raise the liberty pole, now hosted a quieter but no less resolute gathering.

Jeremiah sat at the large table in front of the hearth, his brothers—Gideon, John, William, Dennis and Joseph—around him, their faces weathered by years of conflict but alight with purpose. They were stronger men now than they were when the fight for America's independence began, their bond forged anew with Jeremiah's return from Mill Prison. Tonight was a reunion of sorts, a pause before they scattered to new horizons.

Their older sister, Mary, passed out tankards of ale, then stood back with her arms crossed, a smile of admiration on her face. "It's good to see you all together again."

Jeremiah traced the grain of the table with his finger, his thoughts drifting to the ships they'd commanded—the *Liberty*, *Diligent*, *Resolution*, *Cyrus*, *Tiger*, and the *Hannibal*—and the home front where Gideon's strength had been so needed.

John, ever the steady voice, broke the silence, his tankard of ale untouched. "We've lost much, brothers— the *Hannibal*, our men, years we'll not get back—but we've gained much, too. Our families grow and, if peace holds, America's future—and ours—lies ahead. An independent country, blessed by God. It is what we fought for, what we prayed for. Meantime, for those of us who sail, there's still plunder to be had from the British."

William nodded, his eyes sharp. "Privateering's our trade now. With the *Hannibal* gone, we'll captain for others. I've an offer to sail to Spain on a merchantman. None of us have yet seen the Continent, at least not willingly—eh, Jere?"

Jeremiah chuckled. "Aye, my trip to England was hardly by choice, and while I'd not mind Spain's sunny shores, I've been offered command of the privateer brig *Hibernia*."

"It cheers me to know you'll soon be again at sea," said John, "for I know you love it."

Joseph, the youngest, spoke up, his voice firm. "We've proven ourselves and our efforts are recognized. A Newburyport owner has offered me command of the *Swift*—a sloop with eight guns and a crew of twenty. After that, John and I want to start a business in Newburyport serving merchantmen."

"Aye," said John, "an enterprise to carry us beyond privateering at the war's end."

Jeremiah's gaze met John's, a silent understanding passing between them. "We'll sail again," he said, his voice carrying the weight of his vow. With a glance at Gideon, he added, "And the mills will rise again, stronger than before."

Gideon nodded, his hands rough from years at the saw. "The mills have decayed during the war, but Thomas Fitzpatrick and I are eager to refurbish them for our families and all those at Machias who will be building. My

Abigail's been asking when the lumber will flow steady again."

Jeremiah raised his tankard, his brothers joining him. "A toast to our future and the future of America!"

They raised their tankards in unison. "To our future and America's!"

Outside the river flowed, its waters reflecting the last rays of the sun as the autumn wind sent leaves shuddering to the ground where they joined others in a carpet of gold.

AFTERWORD

I hope you enjoyed my story of Jeremiah and Lizzy. If you did, please post a review on Amazon. It only takes a line or two or even a rating by stars alone.

The next in the Dawn of America will be another privateer story, *The Salamander*. For notices of future releases, follow me on Amazon (amazon.com/Regan-Walker/e/B008OUWC5Y). You can also sign up for my infrequent newsletters on my website (www.reganwalker author.com). I give away a free book each quarter to one of my new subscribers.

Should you be on Facebook (facebook.com/groups/ ReganWalkersReaders), do join the Regan Walker's Readers group. I post special opportunities and giveaways there.

For pictures of the historical places, sources and main characters in *The Irish Yankee*, see the Pinterest Storyboard (pinterest.com/reganwalker123/the-irish-yankee-by-regan-walker). It's my research in pictures.

AUTHOR'S NOTE

On July 3, 1775, the Continental Congress gave General George Washington command of the Continental Army with broad powers to take action as he saw fit. But Congress said nothing about operations at sea. Convinced that his army could be aided by privateers, men from his army who could supply them from the sea, without asking permission, Washington ordered Colonel John Glover's Marblehead schooner *Hannah* to be fitted out as an armed vessel. On September 7, 1775, the *Hannah* set sail, launching America's militia at sea and the beginnings of her first navy.

Months before the *Hannah* set sail, however, Jeremiah O'Brien, a lumberman living on the coast of Maine (then a part of Massachusetts), seized the opportunity to capture a British schooner, the *Margaretta*, with little more than a few swords and pitchforks. His courage inspired seamen from Maine to the Carolinas to join America's privateers. He was afterwards hailed as the hero of the "Concord and Lexington of the Sea". His successful capture of the British ship was celebrated as the first naval battle of the American Revolution, and he was the first to take down a British flag. In the words of his biographer, Andrew Sherman, O'Brien was "one of the most ardent patriots and most notable heroes of the Seven Years' Struggle for National Independence."

My goal in writing this story was to bring the American Revolution to life for my readers, beginning with the role of the American privateers such as Jeremiah O'Brien. The history is as much a character as are Jeremiah and Lizzy, whose love story was a real one. Though we know much about Jeremiah and his life, his wife, Elizabeth Fitzpatrick, remains a mystery. The only reference I found to her in all my research was of her making a pine tree flag for his ship, which helped me understand her a little. A wife who loved her husband and was proud of his privateering for America would do that. This pride echoed in the women who kept the home fires burning, tended the wounded and raised children in their men's absence—contributions that inspire women today.

I have portrayed Jeremiah as his biographer described him: "...of light complexion, having blue eyes, and hair of a light brown hue. A prominent nose added character to an otherwise strong face; which, in the latter part, and presumptively in the early part, of his life, was beardless. He was large-hearted and kindly-natured, and generous to a fault." Sherman also noted Jeremiah was "from a bold and energetic Protestant family."

Jeremiah O'Brien's father had endued his six sons with a sense of their Irish warrior heritage, a love of freedom and a disdain for the English and their treatment of the Irish. He also taught them to read, write and sail from their youth. Given the opportunity to fight for their country, Jeremiah and his brothers bravely stepped forward. Morris O'Brien would live to see his sons prosper, dying in 1799, the same year President Washington passed.

Jeremiah dined more than once with George Washington, likely in 1775–1776, a testament to his growing stature and his affection and admiration for America's commander in chief.

Jeremiah's five brothers married and each fathered children. Several of his brothers outlived him, including Gideon, John, Dennis and Joseph. His brother, William, became a merchantman and died of fever in Spain in 1787. His death must have hit Jeremiah hard as they were close. When William's wife died a few years later, Jeremiah and Lizzy stepped in to raise their young niece, Lydia.

Later, in his life, in 1811, President James Madison made Jeremiah the federal collector of customs for Machias. By then he was a widower, Lizzy having died in 1810. He held the position until his death in 1818. Before he died, Jeremiah asked that the hymn, "Our Sin the Cause of Christ's Death" by Isaac Watts be sung at his funeral. Its words tell us much about Jeremiah's faith.

> *And now the scales have left mine eyes,*
> *Now I begin to see:*
> *O the cursed deeds my sins have done!*
> *What murderous things they be!*
> *Were these the traitors, dearest Lord,*
> *That thy fair body tore?*
> *Monsters, that stain'd those heavenly limbs*
> *With floods of purple gore!*
> *Was it for crimes that I have done.*
> *My dearest Lord was slain,*
> *When justice seized God's only Son,*

And put his soul to pain?
Forgive my guilt, O Prince of peace!
I'll wound my God no more;
Hence, from my heart, ye sins, be gone.
For Jesus I adore.
Furnish me, Lord, with heavenly arms
From grace's magazine,
And I'll proclaim eternal war
With every darling sin.

Jeremiah and Lizzy had one son, Jeremiah Jr., born in the fires of the Revolution, who became a U.S. Senator from Maine's 6th district for the period March 4, 1823 to March 3, 1829. He fathered eleven children and died on May 30, 1858 in Boston, Massachusetts, at the age of eighty. Like his parents, he was buried in the O'Brien Cemetery in Machias, Maine. He lived to see his father's name etched on the hull of at least one of the six US Navy ships named after him, a legacy of freedom for his descendants. These vessels were the first instance of an American ship being given an Irish name.

The English considered "Yankee" a derogatory term for a New Englander, and they generally regarded the Irish with the same contempt they had for the Scots. So, it made me smile to think an "Irish Yankee" became a celebrated hero of the Revolutionary War in America.

During the course of the war, 55,000 American sailors served as privateers, hunting for British merchant ships. Some sailed private vessels (schooners, sloops and brigs) under letters of marque that gave them permission to seize enemy vessels and their cargoes as prizes of war; others sailed with privateer commissions focused on disrupting enemy shipping.

At the opening of the war, Britain's navy consisted of 7,000 vessels. Before the end of 1782, American privateers had captured nearly one-third of these, causing $18,000,000 in damages to British shipping. This had a significant impact on Britain's ability to resupply its troops and allowed them to supplement the limited resources of Washington's Continental forces. So successful were the American privateers that they caused the British mercantile classes to protest against continuing "the American war".

While the privateers were not initially commissioned by the Continental Congress and thus were essentially pirates, Americans embraced the idea and called Washington's little fleet of pirates "Washington's Navy". Individual colonies (states after 1776), like Massachusetts, also commissioned privateers, like Jeremiah. But it wasn't until March 1776 that the Continental Congress legalized privateers and began issuing commissions. America's fledgling navy never had enough ships to do all they did without the help of the Patriot privateers.

In speaking of the New England privateers, Thomas Jefferson wrote, "The enterprising genius and intrepidity of these people are amazing." Indeed, they were.

The American Revolution officially ended on September 3, 1783, with the signing of the Treaty of Paris. On

December 23, 1783, General George Washington addressed the Continental Congress in Annapolis in order to resign his military commission. His resignation signified the end of his tenure as commander in chief, the position to which he was appointed on May 9, 1775. It was his desire to return to his Mount Vernon estate as a private citizen, which he did. Americans ever since have viewed this event as a testament to Washington's republican values, as he willingly surrendered power of the army back to the governmental body that first appointed him.

You may ask why there is so much of the Patriots' faith on display in this story. It is because these people, to include General Washington and those who served under him, like the citizens of Machias, were people who worshiped God and trusted their Creator to give them victory. A significant portion of Colonial Americans, particularly those in New England, were descended from the Puritans.

During the war, Washington regularly attended church services held by military chaplains and local civilian congregations. As the war's tide turned toward the Americans, despite all the hardships and errors of the Continental Army, Washington became more convinced that God had chosen him as the man to lead America to freedom. In his resignation before Congress at the end of the war, his voice breaking with emotion, he commended "our dearest country to the protection of Almighty God."

Reverend James Lyon was a real historical figure, a minister who spent most of his life in Machias, caring for his flock. He was, as I have portrayed him, a writer of hymns, recognized as America's first hymnodist. He was one of the "Black Robed Regiment", the American clergy who rose to argue for independence, some picking up weapons to fight as Patriots. The British gave them that name, blaming them for American Independence, and rightfully so, for there is not a right asserted in the Declaration of Independence that was not discussed by the New England clergy before 1763. And prior to that time, the series of revivals called the Great Awakening that swept through the colonies led by the famous evangelist George Whitefield had a profound effect on the faith of the people and the unification of the colonies.

Reverend Lyon's black slave, London Atus, who came to Machias from Nova Scotia in 1771 with Lyon, was also a Patriot. He was about fifteen in 1775 when my story begins. London enlisted in Colonel John Allen's company of artillery in the Revolutionary War (not the same man as Colonel John Allan of the Indian Department in eastern Maine), served under Lt. William Albee of Massachusetts, and served under Captain George Little for three months on the sloop *Winthrop* in 1781 for extra pay when things were dire in Machias. He was able to purchase his freedom from Lyon to become a free citizen of Machias. He became a lumberman and began shipping lumber to the ports of Portland (the historic port of Falmouth) and Boston and the east coast of America. He married a white woman, Eunice Foss, of English ancestry. They had eleven children. Their marriage was one of the very few such marriages in Maine at the time.

As promised in the Author's Note for book four in The Clan Donald Saga, I was pleased to include a McDonald in this story, and I didn't have to imagine him. Per Henry James Lee's *History of The Clan Donald*, the surgeon serving onboard the *Machias Liberty* was, indeed, named Donald McDonald. There were one hundred and twenty-eight soldiers and sailors by the name McDonald (or variations thereof) serving the Colony of Massachusetts alone. In each of the colonies the men of Clan Donald joined the fight for freedom to share in the ultimate victory. Surprising to me, having done much research into England's cruelty to the Scots, there were also Scots who fought on the side of the British.

You first witnessed privateers in my story *To Tame the Wind*, book one in the Donet Trilogy, where Benjamin Franklin issued a letter of marque in Paris to the fictional Jean Donet and his ship *La Reine Noire*. Like that ship, the ones Franklin actually commissioned were French-owned, but they had American captains and Irish and American crews.

AUTHOR'S BIO

Regan Walker is an award-winning author of more than twenty historical novels set in the Regency, Georgian and Medieval periods. A lawyer turned writer, her years of serving clients in private practice and several stints in high levels of government have given her a feel for the demands of the "Crown". Hence, many of her novels feature a demanding sovereign who taps his subjects for special assignments.

The Dawn of America series is her newest venture. Set in the Revolutionary War, these stories tell of American Patriots who brought our country into being, whether on land or on the sea.

Regan lives in San Diego with her dog "Cody", a Wirehaired Pointing Griffon, who is dearly loved.

BOOKS BY REGAN WALKER

The Agents of the Crown series (Regency):

Racing with the Wind
Against the Wind
Wind Raven
A Secret Scottish Christmas
Rogue's Holiday

The Donet Trilogy (Georgian):

To Tame the Wind
Echo in the Wind
A Fierce Wind

Holiday Novellas (related to The Agents of the Crown):

The Shamrock & The Rose
The Holly & The Thistle
The Twelfth Night Wager

Medieval Warriors (England and Scotland 11th century):

The Red Wolf's Prize
Rogue Knight
Rebel Warrior
King's Knight

The Clan Donald Saga (Scotland 12th-15th centuries):

Summer Warrior
Bound by Honor
The Strongest Heart
Born to Trouble

Inspirational

The Refuge: An Inspirational Novel of Scotland

The Dawn of America series (Revolutionary War)

The Irish Yankee
The Salamander (Coming soon)